"I'VE BEEN TRYING TO TELL YOU ALL DAY.

"I had no right to say the things I did last night," Mac murmured roughly.

"No, you didn't." But Tey's body was yielding him every right that he asked for tonight. Standing on tiptoe, she touched her nose to his and widened her wet lashes, as if she could stare through his beautiful blue eyes straight into his heart.

Then the almost solemn line of his mouth quirked in a smile, her own lips echoed it, and they kissed. Tongue slow-dancing with tongue, heart calling to heart, there was only one way left to come closer. Tearing their mouths apart, they stared at each other, breathing hard, savoring the silent question and the answer. "So if I can't make apologies, can I make amends?" he drawled at last.

ABOUT THE AUTHOR

The easiest way to write adventures is to live adventurously. Visiting the Caribbean "the slow, hard and best way," by small yacht, Peggy Nicholson gathered the background material for this book through hands-on experience. "Mongooses' eyes do turn red when they're riled!" she reports.

Books by Peggy Nicholson

HARLEQUIN SUPERROMANCE
193–SOFT LIES, SUMMER LIGHT

HARLEQUIN PRESENTS
732–THE DARLING JADE
741–RUN SO FAR
764–DOLPHINS FOR LUCK

These books may be available at your local bookseller.

Don't miss any of our special offers. Write to us at the following address for information on our newest releases.

Harlequin Reader Service
901 Fuhrmann Blvd., P.O. Box 1397, Buffalo, NY 14240
Canadian address: P.O. Box 603,
Fort Erie, Ont. L2A 5X3

Peggy Nicholson

CHILD'S PLAY

Harlequin Books

TORONTO • NEW YORK • LONDON
AMSTERDAM • PARIS • SYDNEY • HAMBURG
STOCKHOLM • ATHENS • TOKYO • MILAN

Published November 1986

First printing September 1986

ISBN 0-373-70237-X

Printed in Canada

To Mom and Dad

I'd like to thank Professor G. Roy Horst, a real-life mongoose biologist and raconteur, for showing me how to trap *Herpestes auropunctatus*. I won't forget his stories or his generosity.

PROLOGUE

Up until the moment Josh screamed, it had been a very good morning.

They'd biked into town, Josh behind him on the caretaker's old three-speed, hanging on to his belt and nearly upsetting them every time he pointed out another black-and-white cow, another farmhouse bright with flowers, a pond full of ducks. As always, Bo marveled at the change in the kid when he was away from his father. Watchful, big-eyed silence gave way to gleeful commentary and nonstop questions.

"Bogie, up there! Let's go up there!" A small, open hand patted his back.

"Where's there, partner?" He stole a glance over his shoulder, catching a glimpse of silver-blond hair, then quickly turned his eyes back to the winding little road ahead. It was a Saturday, and more than a few cars, all as bright and well-tended as the Swiss countryside, were zooming past them on the same route into town.

"Up there!" The child flapped a hand toward the white-capped mountains across the green valley, and the bike wobbled again.

Grinning at the image of them pedaling this clunker all the way to the jagged tops of the Swiss Alps, Bo shook his head. "Not today, Josh. We've got some shopping to do. We've got to get you some shoes."

"Don't need shoes. I got shoes. See?" He stuck a small sneaker forward and prodded Bo in the thigh.

"Those are great shoes, but aren't they a little tight?" Another week and he'd have to cut their ends off, if Josh didn't want to end up with toes like a mandarin's lady. This would be the second time he'd bought shoes for the boy; he was growing like the proverbial weed. And his father still hadn't noticed the last pair Bo had bought him, the week after he was hired, back in Miami. *Or maybe he just never mentioned them to you,* he corrected himself. Aston didn't mention much, but he didn't miss much, either.

"A puppy! Bogie, there's a puppy!"

The smiling, older woman in the shop they found spoke no more English than Bo could speak German, but growing children are understood in any language. Bo had only to pinch the ends of Josh's sneakers, make a few expansive gestures and a pleading grimace, and with much nodding and clucking, she did the rest.

Afterward, they strolled through the narrow stone streets, Bo letting himself be towed along by eager yanks of Josh's hand when the sidewalks weren't crowded, and Josh riding aloft on his shoulders when they were.

Later that day he would remember when he'd first noticed the man, but at the time, there was nothing very remarkable about him.

In the bookshop, where they were searching for children's books and adventure novels—in English, of course—the overweight, middle-aged man with the mirror sunglasses looked out of place, and seemed a bit shabby to be Swiss, with his wrinkled khakis belted under his gut and the shirttail of his chamois shirt working its way out of his trousers. And a bit rude.

When the clerk approached him with a question, obviously offering help, he merely grunted, put down the detective novel he was holding and left the shop. And whether that was a Swiss grunt or an American one, Bo didn't even think to notice. Nothing out of the ordinary there.

The bookshop yielded a spy novel for himself and an English edition of Hans Christian Andersen's fairy tales—that was a find! Josh knew the *Cat in the Hat* by heart now, though that only seemed to increase his pleasure in having Bo read it to him each night at bedtime. Come to think of it, these command performances were more duet than solo nowadays. But little mermaids would be a welcome relief from cats in hats as far as Bo was concerned. And he strongly suspected that, as long as Josh had all Bo's attention and an arm around his shoulder, the child would be content to have one of Bo's texts on the theory of phonics read aloud.

As they ambled back to the little park where they had left the bicycle, with their arms full of packages and each holding a sticky stub of an ice cream cone, Bo wondered for the hundredth time if he should be reading to the kid at all. The question was, did it interfere with Josh's learning to write his own stories? Might it be inhibiting for a child to compare his own stumbling words with those of a Dr. Seuss or a Hans Christian Andersen? On the other hand, to show a child what a treasure house books could be—how printed words stored memories, experiences and adventures—how could that possibly do anything but good? Anyway, that was an academic question, he reminded himself. They both enjoyed the readings too much to quit now.

And that story he'd written yesterday, about Fritz, the glowering Great Dane who patroled Aston's estate at night, had shown no inhibiting influences; it had been downright precocious for a four-year-old. *But don't be too sure you and your revolutionary teaching methods get the credit,* he admonished himself dryly. Josh was hardly a standard subject for study; if Jon Aston's son had a third of his father's brains, that only made him a genius twice over.

After their shopping, he'd intended to head straight back to the estate. Aston was less than thrilled whenever they roamed off the grounds, and he was the boss, after all, even if he was a touch...well...paranoid was too strong a word. But after eight months of guarding Josh, Bo had yet to see even a hint of interest in the boy. If Josh was in any danger, the threat would come from a different quarter than the one Aston was watching. Isolation from other children seemed more of a menace to his small charge than any imaginary child snatcher.

Pausing at the gate to the small park, watching the well-mannered Swiss children skipping between the slide and the swing sets while their mothers and older sisters chatted on the sun-warmed benches, Bo had to admit that Josh wasn't the only one who could use some social interaction. Back at the walled estate, Aston communed almost exclusively with his computers and his telex. The caretaker spoke no English and probably wouldn't have given Bo the time of day if he did. Even the damned dog wasn't friendly. That left Josh, who was more than good company, but not the same sort of company as the young blonde who was inspecting them from a bench not far away.

As if Josh could read his mind, the kid tugged his hand and led him down the brick walk toward the

blonde. Halting just before her, he surveyed her unblinkingly.

He couldn't be *that* precocious, Bo told himself,
wondering what to say now that Josh had got him in
this fix. Or if he was, he sure had good taste. She had
wonderful hair, not a yellow blond, but sort of silvery
gold. Women would have some precise name for the
shade; to Bo it was just nice. Awfully nice.

The girl leaned forward, smiling, all her attention
seemingly focused on Josh. "Hello!" she exclaimed in
a charming accent, obviously guessing they were
American.

Josh scowled and turned away.

Not his type? *Buddy, you don't know what you're
missing!* Bo shrugged and gave her a compensating
grin. "Hi!" With a sudden decision, he sat down beside her. His shoulders were so tense that he fumbled
the bag in which the books were wrapped. Feeling the
fool, he pulled out his spy novel and studied it as if he
couldn't wait a minute longer to start it.

"Such a pretty boy," she murmured, still watching
Josh, who had turned his attention to the giggling line
of children at the slide.

That's the boy! Bo cheered him on silently, over his
open book. *If I can stick my neck out, then so can you.*

"He is your son?"

Oh, cripes, of course she'd think he was married!
"No! I mean, no, I'm just his—just his . . . uh, tutor."

"Please?"

While they got that straightened out, then pro-
gressed straight on into what he was reading, Josh
edged closer and closer to the children. But apparently
it was too great a step to get in line for the slide; he

pulled himself into a nearby swing and pretended not to watch them from there.

Bo knew exactly how he felt, but at the same time was busy wondering if it was too soon to ask her name. And how old was she? With that complexion she looked too young, but she seemed oh, so sure of herself. Or maybe—more likely—she was just being friendly to a stranger. The Swiss were a friendly people.

At a break in the conversation, he looked up in time to see Josh take his place in line at the slide behind two little girls, and his heart warmed with pride. *Good for you, sport!* He scanned the park beyond him. Nothing to worry about. An older woman walked a white toy poodle, a thickset man in wrinkled khakis wandered across the grass from the direction of a gate that gave on to the far street.

It was time he asked her name. The resolution sent his hands to his glasses; he had them off and was squinting critically at the lenses before he even realized he'd performed that old nervous trick again. He caught himself just as he reached to pull a shirttail free.

"Would you like this?" She held out a white folded handkerchief with a smile that was so mischievous, so entrancingly sympathetic, that his heart turned right over.

And a child screamed.

Swinging around, Bo squinted, looking for the white-topped head that would be Josh. At the bottom of the slide, an adult—the shabby man he'd noticed a minute before—was leaning over a child, blocking all but his kicking feet from Bo's view. The child shrieked again, and this time he was almost sure it was Josh. Jamming his wire rims onto his nose, Bo was already reviewing the possibilities. A skinned knee, most likely. He dropped the glasses as he stepped forward, nearly trod on them, and stooped to collect them. Possibly a chipped tooth. At the worst, a broken wrist if he'd somehow managed to fall over the side of the slide. The girl would know where to find a doctor...

Josh yelled again, and this time Bo looked up sharply as he pushed the glasses into place. *That wasn't pain, that was*— The man was moving, leaving, was already ten yards beyond the slide, heading for the far gate and the street. A white-blond head tossed at his shoulder.

"Josh!" The yell was knocked out of him, as if someone had punched his stomach. Breathless, lurching forward, he seemed to be running through quicksand while those wide frightened eyes stared back at him over that broad, bouncing shoulder. "Josh!" Lord, Aston had been right all along. If they got to the street, there'd be a car. He'd never—

Behind him a woman screamed. Children were darting around his knees like chickens. Something white flitted into his path, stopped short and squealed as he loomed above her. Catching the child's tiny shoulders, he somehow kept her upright, swung her aside, let her go and lunged on. *Josh!* This time he had the sense not to yell it. No breath left to yell with, but the bastard up ahead seemed to be laboring, too. Josh wasn't a featherweight, and his wriggling couldn't be helping.

Twenty yards to the street, about the same to his target. Josh's eyes were enormous. *You can do it!* The sprint came from somewhere deep inside and he caught them just before the gate.

My glasses, he realized, as he grabbed the man's sleeve, heard it rip, changed grips to his shoulder and jerked him around. But there was no time for fear now. No time to wonder what to do. Panting, sobbing, the man held Josh out from his side like a prize in a game of keep-away and that gave Bo his opening. Swinging from the waist, he saw at the last second that the guy was wearing glasses—shades—as well. The punch landed clumsily as he tried to turn it. It hit the guy's jaw just below his ear and the red face disappeared in a blinding flare of pain.

Gasping with that pain, gulping for air, Bo staggered, held his hand, and watched the man do a slow knee bend, then sit. Gently, he set Josh off to one side and touched his jaw with one big, meaty fingertip.

That's how he'd look if I'd shot him, Bo thought. Then Josh hit him at knee level like a small, desperate octopus.

The guy was still sitting there, holding his jaw. Somehow there was nothing to say, and Bo was breathing too hard to say it—was maybe going to be sick any minute. And any second now his fear was going to turn to rage, and then what would he do? Peeling Josh off his legs, Bo somehow hoisted him one-handed; then he was clinging so tightly that there was no need to hold him. "It's okay, fella, 's okay." But the rage was starting and he couldn't trust his voice anymore.

They retreated across the park, and when Bo looked back as they reached the slide, the guy was only just pushing himself off the ground.

The thought of cops, questions, slowed his steps for a moment, but it made him sick again. What they both needed was quiet, no more fuss...home. A breathing space. If Aston wanted to pursue the matter, he could. Bo's first concern was Josh. *And you nearly blew that, didn't you?* he taunted himself savagely.

He didn't remember the girl until he'd lifted Josh awkwardly to the back of the bicycle. Looking around, he found all the women in the park standing, staring at them. But there was no slender blonde. *What did you expect?* Holding the handlebars carefully with his injured hand, he settled down in front of Josh and felt small fingers clamp onto his belt. ''So let's go home, partner.''

He didn't think of the shoes or the books till they were far beyond the town.

CHAPTER ONE

BLACK, SKIP THE WHITE, black, skip the white, black, skip, black... Tey Kenyon's feet hit the black linoleum squares precisely as she paced the checkerboard floor of the hospital waiting room. Five strides from the door to the battered, black Naugahyde couch and she didn't step on one crack. *Step on a crack and you'll break your*— Pivoting on the black square by the couch, she measured off the width of the room. *Black, skip the white, black, white, black, Lori, you're going to be all right,* she vowed silently. *All right!* Turning again, Tey stopped in midstride as she caught the authoritative approach of a woman's heels.

Looking even angrier—if that were possible—than when she'd departed for Lori's apartment two hours ago, Margie Taylor wheeled around the door frame and into the room. "How is she?" she demanded, advancing on the younger woman.

"No change yet. They still won't let me see her." Tey's gray-green eyes followed the swing of the overnight bag as Margie deposited it on a chair. So Lori still had that... Tey had given it to her older sister for her seventeenth—no—her eighteenth birthday. To take off to college, that was it. "California, here I come!" she'd lettered on one side of it in masking tape. She glanced around the waiting room in sudden loathing. *California, yes!*

"I know why she did it now." Pushing the bag aside, Margie dropped into the chair and pulled her purse onto her lap. As she fumbled with its clasp, the early morning sunlight from the window beyond lit her hair—turned it to red, chin-length silk shot with copper. But what the sunshine gave to her hair it took from her face. In this light, from this angle, Lori's lawyer and friend looked all her thirty-five years and more; with her creamy complexion, the blue-green shadows beneath her eyes were all too apparent. It had been a brutal night. "Here it is." Margie squinted up at her, offering her a folded square of lined, yellow paper, dense with writing. "I found this on the counter in her kitchen."

"Mmm..." The handwriting was unbelievable; cramped, slanted—no—collapsing to the left rather than the right...not Lori's, she realized after a long moment; her mind was running on one cylinder this morning. Not a suicide note, then. Who?

"Tey, sit down before you fall down."

She nodded at the note, drifted backward until her calves touched the couch and sat. "Dear Mrs. Aston"—she could make that much out, anyway. *Aston*. If Lori had stayed a Kenyon this would never have happened. Squeezing dry eyes shut, Tey opened them wide again and reached to push her thick, curly dark hair behind her ears; she'd lost her barrette on the plane last night somehow. "Dear Mrs. Aston..."

"A drunk with hiccups or is it just that it's hieroglyphics?" she asked finally.

"No, that's Herbert Kopesky." As Tey looked up blankly, Margie elaborated. "The detective who's been working for Lori these past five months."

"Oh, the Black Hole!" Tey glanced down at the letter again.

"The what?"

"The Black Hole…" Tey mumbled, wondering what this phenomenon had to say for himself. "I used to have a savings account before Lori hired this guy." With nearly enough for a down payment on a house— a small house—in it. And yet last night, she'd had to pay her Boston to L.A. ticket with a charge card; there hadn't been enough left in her checking account to cover it. It was another week till payday, and who said she'd be there to collect it now?

"He's a good detective," Margie was saying with cool precision. "I recommended him myself."

"Oh."

"He's not exactly polished, but he's streetwise, very capable, and he's been taking nothing but his expense money from Lori for the past six weeks now, Tey."

"I'm sorry, Marge, I'm just tired. I—she's out of money again?" It had gone that fast?

"Close to it, since she lost the job at Datatronics." The lawyer's eyebrows lifted at the look on Tey's face. "She didn't tell you that?"

"No, she— When?" Fired, on top of everything else. Lori, who wanted—needed—to please everyone, who had never lost a job in her life. That rejection could well have been the final straw.

"Almost a month ago. I'm surprised she…" But Margie didn't finish that thought. Her voice trailed off as her eyes slid away from her companion's frozen face.

Margie was right, though. They should have been close enough that Lori could share that latest blow with her; she'd thought they *were* that close. Judging from

the phone bills they'd run up this past year, and the
money she'd sent... Tey shook her head bitterly.
Somehow she should have found a way to come out
here before this; all the long-distance support in the
world didn't equal one hug in person. And then she
could have used her own eyes to judge how Lori was
coping, rather than taking Lori's word for it...but
then, she hadn't. What with her new job as a technical
writer, and the need to earn money for Lori as well as
herself, and Brian, and then last month— "Oh..."
That was why. It didn't excuse a thing, but at least it
explained.

"What?"

"Last month, I was...ending a—" *what to call it?*
"—relationship," she decided with a rueful grimace.
Lori had called and caught her in the middle of packing, caught her for once in her life when she couldn't
be practical, cheerful, tough little Tey, the managing
one of the family. Sitting on one of the cardboard
boxes full of her books, she was the one who had broken down, and Lori who had listened, when all the time
Lori must have been desperately in need of some comforting herself. For the breakup of one very imperfect
love affair didn't compare with the hell Lori had gone
through this past year...these past *five* years... She
should have—

"Tey, stop it!" Landing on the couch beside her,
Margie gave her shoulder a shake.

"Hm?" Tey glanced at her and then down at the
note again. Should have—

"Just cut it out!"

Tey looked up unwillingly. This must be how Margie sounded in the courtroom.

"First of all, we're not even sure that this was a suicide attempt," Margie reminded her crisply.

An empty gallon jug of wine, an empty bottle of Valium. How much more evidence did it take, Tey wondered.

"Second, even if it was a genuine attempt, it is *not* your fault."

"But I—"

"It's not *my* fault, though God knows if anyone should have seen it coming—" But Margie shook her head as if shaking that thought aside. "And it's certainly not Lori's fault. There is just one person who should blame himself, and that's that jerk Jon Aston, and you know it! Now read this." She flicked the note that Tey still held.

"I don't think I can." Tey managed a shaky little smile and lowered her head over it.

"I know, his handwriting's dreadful. But I'm used to it. Would you like me to read it to you?"

"No, I..." Somehow, she'd manage to decipher the writer's lurching originality.

Dear Mrs. Aston,
I hate to have to say this, but I'm off the case. I just got back from Switzerland last night with my jaw in pieces, and I don't mean to be a bad sport, but enuf's enuf. If I was getting paid, I'd say—well, it's all in the line of duty, but you gotta admit it's a bit much for a freebie case. And it's gonna be hell for business, you know. Investigators with their traps wired shut don't exactly inspire confidence, know what I mean?

But I did see your little boy—hell, I picked him up—I was that close—and I want you to know he looks fine. (Yells fine, too.) Unfortunitely, he's got himself a bodyguard now that is tougher than he looks, and the joker landed a lucky one.

By the time I got out of the hospital they were gone—your husband, your kid and the body-guard. I spent a day with an aching head and a pair of binoculars making sure of that. There was nobody left on Aston's estate but the caretaker and the Great Dane. So I checked the airport on my way out and they've split the country all right—I found out that much, but my informant didn't know the destanation.

So, I don't know what to tell you. I think maybe it's time to give up and see if you can't negosiate. In the long run it might be cheaper. If he'll deal at all. With the money he's got, and that jet, the slippery bastard can stay ahead of anybody you hire on a shoe string for a long time if not for-ever, and now he knows we're after him, it's gonna be even tougher.

I'd say call me and we'd talk it over, but firstly, I won't be there. My brothers loaned me his camper and I'm going fishing till I don't have to drink my beers with a straw. Secondly, I couldn't do more than grunt if you did call me, so save your change, honey.

I did find out one thing, case you want to keep hunting. I buddied up to Aston's pilot last week. By the amount of talking that one does, you'd think it was *his* jaw was busted—I've met clams with more to say—but I did pry a couple of things out of him. There's 2 places outside the U.S. be-sides Switzerland they fly to pretty regular. The first is the Caribean—St. Matthew. (U.S. Virgin Islands.)

The other is Rio.

My best guess is the kid's been taken to one of those 2 places. If it was me, I'd check St. Matthew first. It's a whole lot closer and cheaper.

So, good luck to you, honey, I'm sorry I didn't get your boy back for you. I sure as hell tried.

Respectfully and Sincerely yours,
Herbert Kopesky
Private Investigator

P.S. About the bills—if you ever strike it rich, well, I'm not proud. I could use what you owe me. Otherwise, forget it. It's been a real learning experience.

Tey folded the letter along its crease lines and sat, slapping it slowly against her blue-jean-covered kneecap. *So close*. He'd actually touched Josh—picked him up! And Lori hadn't held Josh for nearly a year now. No wonder she'd— Tey shivered, her shoulders tensing with the effort to contain the rage that was sweeping up her spine. *So close*. "So Lori got this yesterday?" she asked bleakly.

"Yes. The envelope was still there beside it, along with the rest of her mail."

And so there Lori had been, slammed back to square one after months of hoping and waiting and scrounging to finance the ever-mounting expenses of a detective who'd tracked her husband and small son from New York, to Montreal, to Miami, to God knows where else and finally to Switzerland, only to touch him and lose him again. Back to square one, minus her de-

tective, minus all her own money and all that she'd
borrowed from Tey, minus even a job to earn more to
continue the search. Hell, yes, it was enough to drive
one to suicide!

Or to murder. Tey's mind ran more to murder at the
moment. Jon Aston... How could he treat a woman
he'd once loved enough to marry this way? It wasn't as
if he loved or wanted Josh himself; Tey had noticed
that two years ago, the last time she'd visited. Aston
could hardly bear to stay in the same room with his
two-year-old son. That was part of the reason Lori had
decided to divorce—

"Miss Kenyon?" A nurse stood in the doorway,
looking as if she too had been pacing floors all night—
as no doubt she had. "Doctor says only one at a time,
for now," she added quickly as both women leaped to
their feet.

PULLING THE DOOR SHUT behind her, Tey stood waiting, but its soft click brought no response. Across the
shadowy room, face buried in her pillow, Lori lay mo-
tionless, her outflung, tousled hair dimmed and life-
less against the white of the pillowcase.

Easing around the foot of the bed, Tey could see just
her right eye, closed, the wide, smooth lid pale above
the thick lashes and the bruise-dark shadow beneath
them. Her fist was jammed to her mouth, as if, even in
sleep, her pain had to be contained. *Lori*. Except for
that shadow she could have been eighteen again instead of twenty-eight, stubbornly sleeping on in their
tiny bedroom long after her younger sister was up and
tiptoeing about on any Saturday morning.

The too-pale face before her blurred for a moment,
and fearful of bumping the chairs ahead, Tey stopped

until she could see again. *Oh, Lori* ... She wiped her eyes almost angrily. Light, that's what they needed. Much better to wake up to sunshine than this gloom... The venetian blinds ticked up smoothly as she pulled, and the waiting sunlight shouldered past her like an anxious visitor, then stopped just short of the bed.

Much better. Careful not to bounce, Tey perched on the edge of the mattress, and Lori's lashes fluttered, then stilled again. Good. Let her wake slowly. There was no rush to drag her back to a less-than-wonderful present—a present that had nearly overwhelmed her.

Her eyes filled again, but even through the tears she could admire Lori's hair and, gently, Tey lifted a strand of it. Ash blond like their mother's had been—dull silver, pale gold, streaks of tawny and threads of light. How she'd wanted to have hair like Lori's, to look like Lori, when she was in high school, back when it had seemed tall, golden Lori had all the luck. For it was she who had gotten the scholarship to Stanford, and Tey who had had to live at home during college as their mother began to fail. And it was Lori who'd been hired straight out of Stanford to be a systems analyst at the tiny but already respected firm of Haley-Astech. And then it was Lori who'd married brilliant, good-looking, aloof Jon Aston, the man who, a year after their marriage, would invent the Astech microchip, which was now revolutionizing the computer industry.... That had seemed Lori's luck all over—to marry for love and then have fabulous, ridiculous, unbelievable wealth dropped in her lap, as well.

But she hadn't seemed all that lucky when Aston had finally permitted Tey a visit, not long after Josh was born. It had been hard to put a finger on, but to her younger sister's eyes, Lori had seemed less certain of herself, shyer and more fragile than ever she'd been back in Boston.

And the next time Tey had insisted on coming out to L.A., since Lori wouldn't, or couldn't, come to Boston—the year Josh was two—the changes had been even more apparent. Lori still smiled—when her husband was out of the room—but she didn't laugh aloud. She apologized too often, for incidents that were not her fault...

Lori's eyelid quivered, then lifted slowly. One large gray-green eye, its pupil too wide and black, stared sightlessly toward the window, then vanished beneath a sweep of lashes.

"Lor?" Tey moved the lock she'd been holding behind Lori's shoulder. Hooking a forefinger beneath another curl of dusty gold, she smoothed it back from Lori's eyebrows, eyebrows that had somehow always reminded Tey of a butterfly's antennae—delicate, crinkly and mobile. Her own were darker and more direct....

Lori's eye opened again, and this time it seemed to focus. Beneath the drooping lid, it slid deliberately up to the corner to find Tey, then surveyed her unblinkingly.

"Lor?"

Her eye flared wide in recognition and then she was rolling over, revealing a green-white face crisscrossed with pink pillow marks and smudged with shadows below the eyes. "Tey?"

"Uh-huh."

"I got you?" Her normally clear voice had a scratchy, fuzzy timbre to it, like a child just waking with a cold.

"Got me?" Tey brushed another wisp back from her eyes. "You're stuck with me, kiddo!"

"No..." Like a sick child, she looked befuddled and a little peevish. "I...phoned you? I...kept trying and I remember I got a woman in Ohio...and I dialed again and I got another wrong number, and then I...I don't... Did I...?" Her lids drooped again.

"Get me? No, Margie called me. They found her number in your purse." But was she taking this in? The nurse had said she'd be groggy, but... "Lor?" Taking her hand, Tey squeezed it and smiled at the contrast between Lori's long, slender, seemingly boneless fingers and her own—smaller, sinewy, the nails clipped close and buffed, but not polished. "Lori?"

"Hear...you..." Her fingers returned the pressure for a moment, then went limp again. "Who... found me?"

"Your landlady. She had a couple who wanted to rent your apartment." But would they want it now, after finding Lori half dead on the living room floor? "You didn't tell me you were planning to move." To someplace cheaper, Margie had explained.

"Mmm..."

"Lori, let's prop you up." Maybe that would keep her awake.

It was easier than it should have been. With an arm around her shoulders, Tey realized how thin her sister had become—too fragile to hug as fiercely as she suddenly wanted to as a wave of tenderness and rage washed over her. But of course Lori felt like a starved cat—she'd been starving ever since she married Aston, with that cold bastard withholding first his own love and now Josh's, when it was all in the world she wanted or needed! Blast him!

Easing her back against the pillows, she found Lori's eyes were as full as her own.

But not for the same reason. "They—"

"What, Lor?"

"They think . . . the doctor thinks . . . I did it on purpose, Tey, doesn't he?" Her huge eyes were wells of grief and indignation, overflowing even as Tey watched. "*Doesn't* he?"

Careful. But she couldn't guard against the sudden hope leaping within. "What *did* happen, Lor?" she asked casually, and pulled enough tissues out of the box on the nightstand for both of them.

"I . . ." But the memory brought the tears again, and her lids squeezed tight against them.

Too late—they trickled out from under the long lashes, and Tey blotted them gently. "Hmm?"

"I got a letter . . ." Lori murmured, relaxing beneath her touch.

"I know, Lor. Margie found it, and we both read it." Dropping the tissue, she collected Lori's hands again and frowned. Ice cold. "So what did you do?"

"I . . . went a little crazy, I guess." Eyes shut, she made an apologetic grimace. "Don't really remember . . . after a while I was in the bedroom . . . on the floor . . . holding Bogie."

"He was always good for that." Loosing one hand, Tey found the tissues and applied them again, gritting her teeth at the picture of Lori clutching the matted teddy bear who'd been first her childhood treasure and then her son's. Bogart the bear... It was just one more bit of the overwhelming evidence of Jon Aston's heartlessness, or his incredible, self-centered ignorance, that he'd snatched Josh and not even bothered to take Bogie along. Well, she'd lay odds that Josh had made him regret *that* mistake. "So what did you do then?"

"I . . . think I took some Valium. . . ."

"Think?"

"I started to and then I went to call Mr. Kopesky . . . but he wasn't there . . . and then I went back to the kitchen and the pill bottle was still out . . . and the glass of water looked almost full . . . and I couldn't remember if I'd really taken them or just meant to . . ."

"So you took some more?" Poor darling nitwit!

"I just took one . . . just in case," she murmured humbly.

"Uh-huh." Tey didn't try to disguise the dryness of that response. "And then?"

"I tried to call you, but they said you were in some meeting . . . and I tried to call Margie, but she was out taking a deposition . . ."

"So then what?"

"I don't . . . I was walking around and around the living room, trying to think what to do now that . . . and I was shaking so hard I had to put my hand in my mouth to stop my teeth from clicking . . . and the Valium wasn't helping at all . . . so I had a glass of wine. . . ." Again that guilty, apologetic little face.

You're not supposed to do that! But Lori knew that already, had learned it the hard way, and the nurse had said absolutely no blame or accusations, so Tey swallowed that protest. And, most likely, Lori would have gotten no more than groggy if she hadn't mistaken the initial dosage.

"Then the phone rang," Lori's voice had dropped to a scratchy half whisper. "I thought it would be you. . . ."

"Me?"

"I just thought . . . I guess because I needed . . ."

"It should have been, Lor—I wish to God it had been. I've been meaning to call you all week, but—" Tey gave her own rueful smile.

"It was Jon," Lori whispered flatly.

Oh, damn! Rats! He hadn't called Lori once since he'd taken Josh last January, and then to call yesterday, of all days. "Where was he calling from?"

"He wouldn't tell me. It was long distance; there was a sort of echo, and the words seemed to be delayed— there were all these gaps and pauses . . ." Shuddering, Lori pulled her hand away and crossed her arms, hugging herself. "He sounded . . . so—so cold, Tey . . . like a . . . a zombie . . ."

To Tey's mind that was always how Aston had sounded—that cool, precise, inflectionless voice—a computer talking. "That pause means it was a satellite transmission, Lor. I suppose he's still overseas someplace. But what did he say?"

"He said I'd been a bad girl, sending Mr. Kopesky after him," Lori recited dully.

"That's our Jon," Tey agreed. *The patronizing, domineering, insufferable—*

"He asked me if I'd forgotten what would happen to Josh if I disobeyed. . . ." Lori hugged herself spasmodically, her face pinched like Josh's when he was fighting back the tears.

"Oh, Lor, it's just a threat!" Tey gripped her outermost forearm with both hands and shook her gently. "He wouldn't do it!" Would he? But he might, and that was what had paralyzed Lori for so many months, the threat Aston had made by phone the day after Josh was snatched from an intimidated baby-sitter, while Lori was discussing divorce proceedings with Margie.

Tey could remember the precise words as Lori had related them, could hear them in Aston's emotionless voice almost as if it was she who had taken that call:

"If you file for custody, Lori, or if you file for divorce, this is what I'll do—or if not precisely this, something just as effective.... I'll write you a letter, Lori, from someplace far away—Kenya, perhaps, or India...someplace like that. The letter will say that I've changed my mind, that I've decided Josh belongs with his mother, after all, that I'm sorry for all the anguish I've caused you, and that Josh will be flying home as soon as I can find someone trustworthy to take him. And naturally, I'll keep a copy of that letter.

"A few days later I'll find that person, someone I've apparently never met before, a clean-cut young student or tourist who's heading to the States, someone who's not an American, and I'll send Josh off with this person, making sure I have several witnesses.

"He or she will take Josh on a route with as many connections as I can arrange—say, Kenya to Cairo, to Rome, to London, to New York and then L.A., Lori, and somewhere en route, Josh will disappear. He'll just toddle off in some crowded airport and never be seen again...

"The student will panic, Lori. He'll call my hotel, but I won't be in, so he'll leave a message as to what happened with the front desk—another witness, Lori. Perhaps he'll even neglect to mention which airport he lost Josh in. After that, the student will vanish, which should hardly surprise the authorities. And I'll help you search, Lori—if we can figure out where to search, and I'll be just as frantic as you. Many witnesses will notice that.

"And so who'll be to blame, Lori? It'll just be one of those unfortunate things.... And if you feel rich enough, and angry enough, you can hire a lawyer and try to convict me of negligence; if you can figure which country to bring the charges in. But I expect by the time the case comes to trial I'll have moved on... Do you think Kenya or Egypt would extradite me from Canada on grounds of negligence? Just think about it, and keep on thinking, Lori. And, Lori, in case you're thinking of telling anyone about this conversation, just remember that I can change all the details, and the outcome will remain the same—Josh will disappear, and I'll appear innocent. And now just picture yourself trying to make some judge in Kenya believe a story like this—you'll sound like a raving lunatic. Just one more crazy American...."

"He wouldn't do it!" Tey repeated, but she didn't believe that.

And neither did Lori, for her blind, tear-streaked face didn't change. "I told him he didn't have to do that, that I'd sign anything, anything at all! I didn't want any money, he wouldn't even have to pay child support, just *please*, p-please let me have J—Josh...." Her son's name ended in a stuttering, shaking whisper, and as she drew a ragged breath, her shoulders starting to shake with the silent sobs, Tey wrapped her arms around her and held her tight.

"Lor, it's just a threat, a threat, just a crummy threat, Lori, he won't do it!" she crooned, rocking her slowly, but Lori was shaking her head, not believing a word of it, the fragile body trembling as if it would shake itself apart in her arms. "*Lori...*" And the nurse had said not to upset her! If she walked in now, Tey would be out on her ear in the corridor before she knew it—and deserved to be. "Lori..."

"B-b-but all he'd say, no matter how I begged, Tey, was 'we'll see...w-we'll see....' And he said he was too busy to think about it right n-now."

Damn Jon Aston to a computerless, nonelectronic hell for all eternity and a lifetime of Sundays! "Lori..."

"He s-said we'd discuss it next summer!"

Summer! And here it was November. Lori *would* be a babbling lunatic by summer, at this rate.

"And he said that if I bothered him before then, if I sent anyone else after him, I could forget it, and then he s-said 'remember what I told you. It's...it's...it's very...easy...to lose a child.' And then he...hung up...." Still shaking, she was beyond grief now; the story ended in a tiny whisper of purest wonder and bewilderment. That all her love, all her hopes should have finally come to this....

"Lori, oh, Lori..."

"And so I...after a while...I tried to call you," Lori continued in that serene, detached little whisper, "but I got some woman in Ohio instead...and the Valium still wasn't working at all, so I took a couple more—that's all I had left—and then I tried to call you, and I got another wrong number...."

So the Valium had been working all too well by then. "Did you drink any more, Lori?"

"I..." She hesitated, remembering, then nodded against Tey's shoulder. "There was 'bout half a glass left in the bottle, and I decided, what the hell, if I couldn't get you, I'd drink that and just go to sleep, just wipe it all out, and start again tomorrow, so I had that ... and then I ... think I decided to call Margie again ... then ..."

"Then?"

"Then ... nothing," Lori murmured apologetically.

Nothing ... God, yes! But for her blessed landlady, nothing ever, ever again! But Lori was squeaking—she was hugging her too tightly, and Tey let her go. "Crazy nit!" she growled, and reached for more tissue.

"I'm sorry...."

Now was not the time to deliver a lecture on her abuse of that phrase, and Tey mentally bit her tongue. "So do me a favor?"

"Mmph?" Lori's pink-and-green eyes looked the question over a tissue as she blew her nose.

"Lie down and look calm, if not happy. If the nurse looks in and sees you like this, she'll bounce me out of here!" Tey pulled the extra pillow out from behind Lori's shoulders as she spoke and helped her to settle back. That was better. She looked calmer, sleepier, almost immediately, and Tey smoothed a skein of soft gold off those delicate, vulnerable eyebrows. Poor butterfly... If anyone had been born to be happy... Of all the men in the world she could have chosen...

"What am I going to do, Tey?" she whispered drowsily, eyes tragic and drooping.

"You are going to concentrate on getting well again, and you're going to trust me." Tey leaned forward, not sure if Lori could still see her face.

"T'do what?" Lori mumbled.

"To find Josh." There, she'd said it. Now she'd have to deliver. Somehow.

But Lori wasn't as reassured as she might have been, as her eyes snapped wide. "But Jon said—"

"I know, I know, and I won't do anything to alert him. I promise, Lori," Tey said quickly. "I'm going to be careful, I'm going to be discreet, I'm going to be as persistent as a wad of stepped-on chewing gum, and I'm going to get Josh back." Somehow.

"But if Mr. Kopesky—"

Tey stuck her chin out. "Do I look like a Kopesky?"

That got a smile. "No..."

"Who's 'the stubbornest, meanest, most mule-headed brat in the whole wide world'?" she quoted, standing and then nearly spoiling her effect as she staggered, light-headed.

"You are." Lori returned her grin, both of them remembering the fight as one of their best. Though after fourteen years they could never remember what it had been about.

"So trust me." Giving a lock of Lori's hair a farewell tug, Tey backed away toward the door.

"Tey..."

Looking as self-confident and stubborn as she could manage, she aimed a theatrical forefinger at her sister's anxious face. "Trust me!" She made her exit.

Leaning back against the closed door Tey took a deep breath. *What have I done?*

"ARE YOU SURE this is a good idea?" Margie flicked a frown at Tey, then turned back to the traffic, watching for a gap in that glittering stream, her hand tensed on the stick shift of the sleek little Mustang.

"No, I'm not... but have you got a better idea?"

Stomping on the gas, Margie made no reply as the red sports car squealed out of the hospital parking lot and across two lanes of oncoming grilles to merge with the stampede heading the other way. "Not really," she answered finally, checking the rearview mirror and wincing. "What about playing it Aston's way—waiting till summer?"

Slouching down in her seat, Tey braced her feet, checked her seat belt again and pulled Margie's straw sun hat down over her eyes, blocking out the too-bright sun, and the too-bright teeth of the leering young men in the pickup next to them. "Well, first of all, Margie, he made no promise to return Josh next summer. He only said, 'We'll see.' Second, do you think Lori could last that long?"

"Uhmm..."

Taking that as a negative, Tey pushed on, blindly counting the reasons out on her fingers. "Third, by next summer, Josh will have been away from his mother for a year and a half—more than a quarter of his life. I don't know if he'll even remember her by then."

"True..."

"And fourth, I'm worried—and Lori has to be worried sick—about the kind of care, or lack of it, that Josh may be receiving." She swayed forward against her breast strap as the car braked, tires yelping. Then she rocked back against the seat.

"Sorry. You mean you think Aston might...abuse him?"

"If withholding all love, all attention and all approval from a four-year-old is a form of abuse—and I think it is—then, yes, Marge. But more than that, I doubt—I *know*—that Aston isn't caring for Josh himself. He'll have put somebody else in charge of him, probably this bodyguard Kopesky mentioned—I bet he's more baby-sitter than guard. But we don't know who this fellow is, whether he's competent, or kind, or caring, or even trustworthy.''

"True," Margie murmured thoughtfully as the car accelerated up a ramp. From the sounds around them, that put them on the freeway now, Tey decided. "What do you think, Tey?" the lawyer continued after a moment. "Is Aston operating on an emotional level or a rational one?"

"Meaning?"

"Well, if snatching Josh was an emotional response to Lori's leaving him, we may never get Josh back. Aston could keep Josh forever—or lose him—out of spite."

"Uh-huh." That was a cheerful thought.

"On the other hand, if this is a relatively rational response in which Josh is simply a trading card in whatever game Aston is playing, we've got a chance. All we have to do is figure out what Aston wants, and if we can afford to let him have it."

"But Lori offered to sign away everything in exchange for custody," Tey reminded her.

"And I wish he'd go for that! Once we get our hands on Josh, I think I could break a contract like that— signed under duress. I could make a damned good attempt at it, anyway." Just behind them, a car horn blared in derision.

"And he knows it," Tey mumbled wearily.

"Yes, I suspect he does. So what exactly is Aston up to? Why wait till summer?" The car skittered sideways, changing lanes, and whatever had been breathing down their necks rumbled past.

Summer...summer... "Wait a minute!" Tey sat upright and pushed her hat back. "Margie! I heard a rumor just yesterday, in a meeting at the software firm where I work—it completely slipped my mind, what with—"

"Yes?" Margie spared her a glance, then turned back to her rat race.

"The word's out that Haley-Astech might finally go public next spring—offer its stock for public purchase, that is. Christmas Eve in Filene's Bargain Basement will be nothing compared to the stampede you'll see for that stock! Could that affect Aston's plans?"

A long, boyish whistle was her answer as Margie nodded rapidly. "That's it, Tey! That's what he's up to!"

"What?"

"Liquidity! Right now most of Aston's assets are tied up in his half of Haley-Astech. If Lori would only give me the word, I could go in there and freeze 'em solid until we negotiate this mess."

"But of course she won't give you that word while Aston has Josh. It was all you could do to persuade her to hire a detective to try and sneak him back." Tey retreated under her hat again; the mosaic of straw-gold and sunlight shining through its brim was more soothing than the hot shimmer of the cars streaming away beneath a yellow sky.

"Right," Margie agreed. "So we're in a Mexican standoff. Aston can't protect his company from Lori, so he takes Josh, who's much more portable."

"Uh-huh..."

"But now suppose, when they go public, instead of retaining his shares of the company as you'd expect,

Aston were to put them on the market along with the rest of the offering?''

"Then he'd be a multimillionaire instead of just a millionaire," Tey concluded. So?

"And those millions could be in a Swiss bank account before you could say boo! And Lori would never see a nickel of it!" Margie sounded almost triumphant.

"But then she'd get Josh back." Maybe.

"Maybe...providing there's no emotional component to this mess."

Sighing, Tey nodded and pulled the hat off. In the sky ahead, something flashed—a jet slicing down through the dirty air. "Josh came between Lori and him," she remembered quietly. "Till Josh came along, if Jon said 'frog,' Lori hopped."

"So Aston might be vengeful...or spiteful." The Mustang side-slipped one lane, then dived down an exit ramp.

Would he? That emotionless machine man? "I don't think he would be, Margie. Depriving Lori of all the money would probably satisfy any thirst for vengeance he has."

"But we aren't sure," the redhead insisted softly.

"No...so I guess I'm going to St. Matthew." Just ahead, perhaps a mile away, another jet kissed the ground.

CHAPTER TWO

"HEADS UP, JOSH, here it comes!" *And one of these days, he'll even catch it,* Bo told himself as he tossed the Frisbee.

In spite of the splint on his little finger, he hadn't lost his knack; the orange disk spun in slow and low, precisely where he had wanted it. Josh had only to open his hands and it would practically catch itself.

But he didn't wait for it. Giggling, he ran to meet it and it floated right by him. With a bat shriek, he wheeled and chased after it across the clipped green hillside.

If golden retrievers could catch Frisbees, why couldn't four-year-olds? But then, he had Josh trained to bring it directly back to him; a dog would probably tease. Waiting for the Frisbee, Bo glanced around.

They were a long, long way from Switzerland, and not just in terms of miles. Half a horizon of blue ocean stretched away from the foot of the hill on which Aston's St. Matthew estate was spread. The smooth trunks of palm trees arched up here and there from the green thickets that edged the beach and the coast road below. Bushes dotted with huge, star-shaped red flowers bordered the driveway sweeping down to that road; they'd watched a hummingbird dipping into those blossoms this morning. Yeah, this hard-edged tropical brilliance was visually about as far as you could get from the soft, cool...civilized greens of Switzerland.

What must it be like, he wondered, not for the first time, to be Jon Aston? To have the money to simply snap your fingers and change your surroundings, like a stage director commanding another set change? And why had they had to change the set at all? Wouldn't it have been easier to set the Swiss police on the snatcher's trail and simply stay put?

"Eeee-yow!" Josh arrived with the Frisbee, and he took it absently, then focused when the boy pranced expectantly before him.

"That was great, Josh. You just about had it. But this time, I want you to stand still, okay? I'll throw it right to you." With an encouraging grin, he waved the boy away again.

But Aston hadn't wanted to handle it that way. He'd insisted on leaving immediately. Odd how he hadn't even notified the police. But then, the guy *was* odd...or eccentric—that was the word, not odd. Weren't all geniuses supposed to be eccentric? Maybe it went with the territory. "Okay, Josh, now stand still." He aimed another long, slow floater.

Pity a little more patience didn't come with the territory too. It had been rugged, coming across on Aston's jet. With his father nearby, Josh had kept silent, but he couldn't keep still. That was too much to ask of any child that age for the duration of a transatlantic flight. Aston hadn't said much, but he'd looked cold daggers every time Josh squirmed or whispered.

The Frisbee was drifting in right on target. "Stay still, Josh. Wait right there." But maybe that was too much to ask a four-year-old, also. He was doing his best, bouncing up and down on his tiptoes, waving his hands, but as the toy descended, he lunged forward with a yelp. Frisbee and child collided, there was a fumble, and they both hit the lawn. "All *right*, partner! You nearly had it that time!"

Another year and he would have it, if there was anyone around to throw it to him. Ignoring the leaden feeling that accompanied that thought, he watched Josh scramble to his feet. Aston sure wouldn't take the time to throw Frisbees. Too busy, and he just wasn't a man for children. He was probably counting the days till his son reached an age where he could talk to him, man to man. But in the meantime...

"Eee-yow!" Catching his leg, Josh swung right around him and collapsed at his feet with the Frisbee.

No, in the meantime, Josh was a bit...rambunctious for a cerebral type like Aston. Maybe that's why he'd parked them here on St. Matthew and gone on. Or maybe he just thought Josh would be safer here. He prodded the child's ribs with his toe. "Getting tired yet?"

"Uh-uh!" Josh covered his face with the Frisbee, then peeked out to make sure Bo was watching.

That was a dumb question, wasn't it? "Okay." Snatching the Frisbee, he bopped Josh once on the head with it, once on the tummy and skimmed it across the hill. *We'll tire you out yet, sport!* But it was good to see him back to his old rowdy self, he admitted as he watched Josh scramble after it. He'd been pretty subdued for a day or two after the park incident.

How the hell did you explain something like that to a kid? There was no way he could tell him that the snatching had come courtesy of Josh's mother; a four-year-old couldn't—shouldn't—have to contemplate the ugliness of adult maneuverings. So after much thought, he'd decided to approach it indirectly.

That night he had told Josh a bedtime story, about a man who wanted a son. The man didn't have one of his own, and he couldn't find the right kind of son to buy, so finally he'd stolen one. When the real father finally found his son, after searching high and low through the town and the valley and the mountains, the boy was living in a circus with the thief-father, learning to ride elephants. The true father traded his faithful puppy for his son—so the thief-father wouldn't grieve—and took the boy home again.

And I'm still wondering if that was a good idea, he admitted as Josh caught up with the Frisbee. *The next time, he'll probably go quietly and then demand to see the elephants!* But at least it gave Josh some sort of reason—and an unthreatening, rather flattering reason—for the nastiness at the park.

If he applied the story to himself at all. He'd still had one of his "Mommy-Bogie-Mommy" nightmares that night . . . but then he'd been having those, off and on, ever since Bo had known him. However, that was a week ago, and he hadn't had one since.

"Yeee-ow-ow-ow-yow!"

No, no major aftereffects there, Bo decided thankfully as he accepted the Frisbee. The aftereffects seemed to be limited to a drastic change of scenery, and a drastic curtailment of their liberty. Josh was not to go off estate grounds from now on. And that was a pity.

At least the grounds included a fenced beach just across the road from the front gates. That group staying in the cabins uphill had access to it, as well. Maybe they'd be some company.

Beyond the chain-link boundary fence, an orange Jeep crawled along the coast road, and his eyes followed it wistfully. It was the type the tourists rented in Julianasted, to explore the island. This would have been a great island to explore with Josh...

Well, some other time, then. He flipped the Frisbee and Josh, yelping, tore after it. *And how many more times do you think there will be?*

THERE ARE NO SNAKES on St. Matthew, Tey thought for the third time as she forced a leg uphill through the waist-high grass. The mongooses—mongeese?—ate them all. Or so the too-cheery tourist brochure she'd picked up at the St. Matthew airport yesterday had assured her. So—what if she stepped on a mongoose? But then, whether these mythic mongooses could see any better than she could on this moonless night, they would certainly hear her coming and get out of her way. Heaving herself up another foot or so, she stopped, panting in the heavy air, and turned back to check her progress. She was high enough to see the sea now; beyond the black, ragged line of the trees that edged the coast road below, gleaming darkly, it stretched away to a midnight blue horizon, but she hadn't escaped its sound yet. A low, shuddering thud— wave meeting coral—drowned out the high, sweet, cleek-cleek of the tree frogs for a moment, then retreated into a murmurous hush once more.

To her right, as she looked downhill, the fence she'd been following—six feet of chain-link steel topped with three strands of barbed wire—marched away to meet the road. Forming a corner, it swung to the right to enclose the front of Aston's estate. There was a gate down there, of course, where his winding, hibiscus-lined driveway met the road—she'd seen it from her slow-crawling rented Jeep this afternoon. Had seen also that it sported a substantial—new—padlock, and that the coral block bungalow just inside the gates appeared to house a guard.

So there'd be no entrance for her that way. Turning uphill, Tey leaned into the waist-high grass and waded on. But there was a chance, just a chance, that someplace uphill, at the back of the estate, there would be a second, smaller, less well-guarded gate.

Beneath her descending foot, something exploded into grass-rattling flight and Tey froze, the thump of her heart in her ears overwhelming the scuttling retreat. *No snakes—the mongooses ate every last one of them! No snakes*... Taking deep gulps of air, she waited until the cleek-cleek of the frogs rang louder than the blood in her ears again, and then slowly moved on, thanking those impossible tropical stars above that she'd seen Josh this afternoon. Without that stroke of luck, she'd probably have beaten her own retreat by now, back to the Jeep hidden half a mile back down the road, perhaps even back to safe, predictable, November-crisp Boston.

The grass was getting higher now, and her hands, moving in slow breaststrokes before her, were soon wet with the dew. But she *had* seen Josh, on her return pass down the coast road; even at that distance, halfway up the hill on that wide green lawn, that tiny, white-topped figure chasing after a slow-floating Frisbee must have been Josh. When she was his age, Lori's hair had been just as fair.

The man at the other end of the Frisbee she had not recognized, however. Distant as he was, he'd still looked too short and square to be Jon Aston, and besides, she'd bet her last nickel that Aston had never thrown a Frisbee in his life, poor jerk. Pain, a line of it drawn across the palm of her left hand, brought Tey back to the present. Grass cut. Palm to her mouth, she stopped to check the fence again. Not a gap, not a crack, no sign of anything like a gate yet. It would be so much harder if she had to climb it, so much, much harder if she had to boost Josh out of there; she'd need something to cover the wire, perhaps a bathmat or— no—wire cutters.... But she could decide that later, if she found no gate by the time she'd circled the premises. Tonight was only a scouting foray, after all; this mission was too important to rush.

Remembering the one-week emergency leave her irritated supervisor had granted over the phone, Tey smiled grimly and pushed on. It was the best job she'd ever had; it would be a shame to lose it, but— Laughter, distant, not one person's but several, jerked her head around. It had come from the right, she decided, ears straining to catch it again, from farther uphill, beyond those trees, away from Aston's estate. That driveway that cut off from the coast road just before Aston's property led to a house, apparently.

That was good to know.... There were so many things she'd have to know, before pulling this off. The bushwhacking came to an abrupt end as Tey reached the edge of the high grass. Except for the taller brush bordering the fence, the hillside above seemed to be tended lawn until it vanished beneath a crowning line of jungly blackness. Laughter reached her ears again, and then a voice, a man's, his words gone before she could catch them.

They've obviously got better things to do up there than stare at a lawn, she told herself, eyes wide as she studied that open stretch. Even if there were a watcher up there in the trees, he'd not be likely to see her, dressed as she was in dark jeans and a T-shirt. Still... Too swift to be a bird, something black flickered across the sky—like the night itself blinking. There—another, unnervingly close overhead this time. Bats. Did St. Matthew have vampire bats? But the tourist brochure would hardly brag about that attraction, would it?

No vampire bats, she told herself firmly, turning to scan the fence, *but what about a gate?* Beyond the line of brush, though, the fence stretched up and away, as remorseless and symmetrical as a spider's web. Spiders... That was really what she'd been trying not to think about all along, Tey realized, the skin between her shoulder blades prickling...as if something with eight light-footed legs were high-stepping across her— *Stop!*

She had to stop moving as well, Tey discovered; with that last thought she had bounced out onto the lawn, away from the sheltering, tickling high grass, grass tall enough and strong enough to support spiderwebs the size of fences. *Just cut it out!* Ever since Bobby Turk and that daddy longlegs in third grade, she and spiders hadn't seen eye to eye...or was that eyes? The thought of hundreds, thousands, of shining, multiple eyes peering out at her from beneath every blade of wet grass set her skin crawling again. *Stop it! There are no spiders on St. Matthew; the bats ate them all.* But everything in this lush world came so big: the stars, the thirty-foot philodendron she'd seen on her drive across from Julianasted this morning, the cockroach, if that's what it was, that she'd seen in the café in Thisted this evening. An environment that could produce monsters like that could grow spiders big enough to munch bats— *Now cut it out!* This was ridiculous; she wasn't usually such a coward. It had to be the nonstop tension of the past three days—that and now this blundering through a nighttime world where she didn't begin to know the dangers, where she couldn't, wouldn't see them if they did exist....

Stop. Tey took a deep breath and held it. *There are no spiders—none. Right....* Letting that breath out, she took another. *There is only one thing you do know for sure in this place, and that is that Josh is behind that fence. And there is only one thing that you need to find out tonight, and that is if there's a gate up here. So let's get the hell on with it!* Squaring her shoulders, and disregarding another peal of laughter from the unseen house above, she started across the lawn.

But halfway across, turning back from another futile inspection of the fence, Tey saw the light. *The house,* she thought for a moment, standing very still. *But house lights don't move.* This one was bobbing gently up and down, silhouetting a clump of leaves...a palm frond like a giant, grotesquely clawed hand...a tree trunk...was coming toward her....

Like a rabbit in the headlights of an oncoming car, she froze for a moment. The light was moving downhill from her right, perhaps would pass her by—no, it was coming.... She spun around. Into the high brush along the fence, or on up the hill to her left, following the fence line up into the trees? She looked over her shoulder. Closer now, bobbing, it seemed too high off the ground to be a flashlight. *Move!* Angling away uphill at a gliding half run, she stayed in the clear without conscious decision. Still coming? Without stopping, she stole a glance behind. Still coming, the light swept down for a moment, throwing a long, black *spidery* shadow before it. *Move!* A small tree—no—a pole loomed up out of the darkness and she ducked around it.

The first touch was soft as silk upon her lips and nose, but even as she skidded to a halt, her momentum carried her forward. She could feel each separate, filmy strand winding around her, tightening across her forehead and cheeks, and something bit into her ear as she threw up her hands and tried to run. *Web! Spiders the size of*— Pain had her by the other ear now and that sucking sound came from herself, making those endless indrawn, hiccupping gasps for air—the sound you make in a nightmare when the scream won't come out. Flailing as the web trapped her hands, soundlessly sobbing, she had to—

"Hey!"

Had to get out, she had to—

"Hey, stand still! You!"

Light all around, dazzling after the darkness, blinded her, showing her only the black threads drawing tight across her face. Something was biting her ears. She had to—

"Hey!" Arms wrapped around her ribs, pulling her forward against something—someone—warm and immovable. "Hey! Whoa! Hey, it's okay, you're okay now. Be still now."

With the light smack in her face, she couldn't see, didn't want to, and she shut her eyes, shivering uncontrollably, panting for breath.

"It's okay now, you're okay, I'm here now...." Stroking words, weaving around her, soothed her as the warmth and strength of his body seemed to flow down his arms, around and into her. "'S'okay now, darlin'. Just be still now...."

Shivering, she crowded closer, pressing against him, and his arms tightened automatically. "'S'okay now, it's okay... Scared the livin' daylights out of you, didn't it, hmm?"

Nodding rapidly against his chest, she found that, in spite of the web, her hands gripped his shirt in a stranglehold. "Where is it?" she managed in a husky half whisper.

"It?"

"The spider, it bit my—" But he was laughing, silently—the vibrations were unmistakable, locked together as they were, and his amusement was like a bucket of cold water in the face; it sluiced away all her unquestioning acceptance of the past few seconds. Who the hell was he to—who the hell *was* he? Opening her eyes, she stared up through the web into light, and glimpsed his face just below it before she had to shut her eyes again. A miner... Only miners wore hats like that, with a light like a third eye. What the hell was a miner doing in the back hills of St. Matthew, holding her, or was this all a—

"God, no wonder you freaked!" The sympathy in that observation was utterly negated by the laughter shimmering beneath the words. "We're talking spiders the size of basketballs to weave a web like this! The size of tumbleweeds! I'd have yelled, too!"

"I *didn't* yell." Somehow it was important to get that point across. And it was even more important to pull back a step and get her breasts off his chest; she could feel someone's heart beating, but she couldn't tell whose.

"No, you didn't," he agreed instantly. His arms eased just so much and no more; they still held her firmly. "It sounded more like a wounded compressor." As she stiffened, he added hastily, "Now let's get you out of my net."

"Your *net*?" That's what this was? "*Your* net?" What kind of a jackass hung a net at face level in the middle of a lawn where people might walk?

"'Fraid so." But he didn't sound at all contrite. Gently loosening her death grip on his shirt with one hand, he left the other around her waist. "Hope you haven't torn it; this's my lucky net."

That snapped her eyes wide with outrage; she caught one glimpse of a straight nose bent over her hand, then squinched her eyes shut again.

"That's right—keep 'em closed," he murmured abstractedly, "and just stand still now." Slowly he let her go. A large, warm hand encircled her wrist, steadying it while he teased the threadlike strands from around her fingers one by one and untangled her wristwatch. "There. Now pull it straight back and keep it behind you." He started on the other hand.

"It's my ears . . ."

"I know, it's all around your earrings, but I've got to get this first."

"Mac?" A girl's voice came from somewhere uphill. "Got anything interesting?"

Oh, please, no gawking spectators. She was humiliated enough already!

The light swung off her face as he gave a little hiss. Exasperation? "Nope," he called back. "Just an *Artibeus jamaicensis*. But I'd like to see Gerry out here, if you could find him, Lucy?"

"Sure, I'll do that." She sounded as if she were on her way.

"I don't want—"

"Neither do I. Gerry snuck off to town an hour ago. But she's the conscientious sort; she won't give up till she finds him," he assured her easily. "There you are. Now put that behind your back," he continued, freeing her other hand.

The light came closer, turning her darkness to soft scarlet. Big hands cupped her face, lifting it gently, and then he was still for a long moment, studying where to begin, no doubt. "What's your name?" he asked abruptly.

"Tey." But she could have bitten her tongue as soon as she'd said it. It was hardly a common name.

His thumb brushed her nose, smoothed slowly across her cheek. "Funny name." The light shifted slightly and he touched her ear.

"Family name." Would he just get on with it?

He did, removing her stud earring with steady, un-fumbling fingers, as if he had a long acquaintance with women's jewelry. "So what are you doing up here in the middle of the night, Tey?" he asked casually, rubbing her aching earlobe between thumb and forefinger.

She shivered, though she wasn't cold. "It's not even ten yet!"

"Mmm," he agreed, turning to the other ear. "So what were you doin', romping through the bushes at nine forty-five at night?"

He wasn't going to quit, was he? In spite of that studied disinterest, he meant to have an answer. In fact, his hands had stopped on her earring, as if an answer were the price of her freedom. "I wanted to see a mongoose." There, let him make something of that!

He gave a little snort, just above her, conveying what she couldn't tell, and his hands moved again. "Mongooses aren't nocturnal, darlin'." He slid the other stud gently out of her ear.

"Oh? I didn't know that." So she was a dumb tourist; that was no crime. Her breath caught as his hands found her barrette and let her hair down as if he'd done it a thousand times before. *Don't shiver,* she warned herself, tensing her shoulders, but that only started a slow line of liquid fire trickling down her spine; it reached her hips, curled around to her navel and she shivered, anyway.

"There," he said quietly, slipping the last strand over her ear. "Now don't move."

The light swung away, and then he was behind her. Must have ducked under the net. She jumped as his hands closed around her waist, and his hands tightened. "Hey, be still!"

"Sorry..." She was suddenly, acutely aware of her body; her waist felt dwarfed by his hands. Shoving that thought aside, she realized she could see, with the light behind her.

"Now step straight back," he cautioned, pulling her back against him.

Opening her eyes, Tey could see the net just ahead, its gossamer mesh forming big sagging diamonds. But to her left, only a foot or so, was a darker knot. As she looked, it...wriggled and her stomach lurched. So he'd lied—there *was* a spider. And then the light caught it as he turned his head that way. A tiny, perfect face stared back at them, eyes black and alive with intelligence, nose wrinkled in a razor-edged snarl, delicate pricked ears swivelling even as she watched in drop-mouthed horror—a bat, its leathery, fragile wings entangled in the net. It had been there all along, *not a foot from her face*. "Uh!" That thought slammed the wind from her lungs, knocking her backward against her companion.

Hands spun her around, arms enfolded her and pulled her close. "Don't yell!" he commanded, his lips in her hair as she drew a gulping breath. "You never yell, right?"

"Ahhh...right," she agreed finally, weakly, her voice muffled in his shirt. And the funny thing was he *was* right. She had never screamed aloud in her whole life. Well, tonight, without his comforting presence, she would have made up for lost time! Taking a deep breath, Tey found herself inhaling an essence of warm, clean male—a whiff of soap and a whiff of sweat—and swung quickly around again.

He didn't let go. Crossing his arms comfortably over the front of her waist, just below her breasts, he directed his light on the bat. "Pretty little thing, isn't she?" he murmured, his lips at her ear.

He wasn't kidding, was he? And Tey could see—almost—what he meant, as she stared fascinated. Cunning—that was the word. "She's so tiny...and yet everything *works*...."

That amused him—she could feel it—but he understood. "Like a baby's hand," he agreed quietly. "It's the fingernails that always stun me."

She wondered suddenly, sharply, what he looked like. Mac, the girl had called him.

"You all right now?"

She nodded wordlessly. Letting her go, he went to the bat and started untangling it with patient hands.

Bare hands. "You aren't worried about rabies?"

"Nope, there's none on the island," he murmured without looking up. "And I'm vaccinated, anyway."

Who *was* this guy? Her eyes were adjusting now. Below his headlight she could just make out his profile—a series of straight, clean lines formed forehead and nose and upper lip. Then they softened subtly; the lower lip looked fuller, gentler, as did the hollow just beneath it, then the chin and jawline went straight and hard again. A clean, economical kind of face—enough flesh and bone to do the job, not an ounce more. The shock of hair hanging in his eyes right now—she stifled a sudden, absurd impulse to brush it aside for him since his hands were full—appeared to be bright, pale blond, but perhaps that was just the light.

Mac rotated his hand and pulled the bat free. "There you are, darlin'," he crooned, to which of them, Tey couldn't tell. He turned the bat to face her. "See, she was more frightened than you were."

From his hand the bat glared up at her as if searching for a sufficient insult. Her ears swiveled toward Mac, then pricked forward again, and Tey laughed. "So I see," she said dryly.

"Come up for a drink?" He nodded uphill, his light sweeping across the treetops.

Not on her life! She could still feel where his hands had touched her waist, knew somehow that he could still feel it, too. "Not tonight, thanks." She still had the fence to walk, though her skin quivered at the thought of more bushwhacking now.

"You owe me," Mac observed pleasantly.

"Owe you? For scaring a year off my life? If you hadn't set that silly net up—"

"If you hadn't trespassed—" he reminded her gently. And smiled.

Impasse. She couldn't even glare at him properly with that ridiculous light in her eyes.

"There's Gerry," he said suddenly, pointing past her shoulder with the bat.

Away off and down, two headlights were winding up the road from Thisted. Beside her, the lights switched off and suddenly, in the darkness, the frogs' piping seemed louder. "Well, what do you want to do, then?" Mac asked. Dimly, she could see him fumbling with some sort of sack that hung at his belt. He pulled a drawstring, then looked up at her, his hands empty now.

"Go back to my car, I guess," she lied.

"Where is it?"

"Just down the hill." And back toward town half a mile or so. Hidden in a pull-off above the beach.

"That was dry work, getting you out of that net. You're going to make me walk all the way down the hill and back without even a beer?"

"No, I'm not!"

"Not all spiders have eight legs, Tey. I plan to sleep tonight, and that means I have to see you to your car."

Deadlock. Obviously, he wasn't going to back down on this.

"Just one nice, ice-cold greenie?" Mac wheedled.

A cold Heinekin... A drop of sweat trickled down between her breasts. And the night was wrecked anyway, so... She shrugged. "Okay."

It was so dark under the trees that she might have been blindfolded, and Mac didn't use his light. After a moment his hand found hers and tugged her gently along through the velvety, singing blackness. Beneath their feet, grass turned to gravel and then the hollow-sounding wood of some sort of catwalk. They came around what seemed to be a hedge and she could see a light now—several. Cabins, dimly lit, scattered up the hillside among the trees. From one of them came a cheerful medley of voices—a game in progress, it sounded like. "I don't want to—"

"I know. You don't want to meet a pack of people." He urged her to the left, up a narrow boardwalk winding through the head-high overgrowth. "The boss gets his own cabin." He led her out onto a small wooden deck; it formed the porch to the tiny cabin just beyond.

"You're the boss?" Tey asked, though she'd known it already. Something in his voice, in spite of its casualness. Looking around, she saw two deck chairs facing a gap in the jungle; in the daytime you could see the water from here, she'd bet. Built along the deck's railing was a wooden bench, and under the overhanging eaves of the cabin, a hammock curved invitingly.

"'Fraid so." He sounded as if that were a mixed blessing. Turning, she found herself under the same sort of scrutiny she'd been giving her surroundings. Arms crossed, he was leaning against the screen door of his cabin, his eyes on her. A light from an interior room edged his hair with silver, and beside him, a lizard scuttled across the screen. "Kenneth McAllister," he said quietly, holding out a hand as if they'd never touched. "Mac to my friends."

"Uh—Hargrove." Brian's name. Ironic that she wouldn't take it from him and yet now she'd stolen it. Returning to the moment, she found Mac still holding her hand.

"Uhhargrove," he repeated solemnly. "How do you spell that?"

"Hargrove!" She snatched her hand away. He was teasing her, wasn't he?

"Have a seat, Tey Hargrove, and I'll get you that beer." He was gone before she'd decided.

Through the screen and beyond a dark outer room, she could see him moving around his pocket-sized kitchen. His hair *was* light blond—thick, straight, and a bit long compared with the high-tech types she knew back in Boston. Parted over the right eye, probably that morning, and since left to its own devices. He brushed it back with an unconscious gesture even as she watched, then removed the sack that hung at his waist and set it gently on the counter.

"What'll you do with the bat?" she asked as he returned.

"Scrambled with onions and eggs, she'll taste so good you wouldn't believe it." Gravely, he put a beer in her hand.

"No pimientos?" How could he smile like that, without smiling? Was it all in the voice and eyes?

"Oh, absolutely, if you've got 'em. I was talking about bush cooking, not haute cuisine." He took a long, savoring swallow of beer, his strong throat framed in the open neck of his workshirt and gleaming damply in the faint light.

"No, seriously, Mac!"

"Seriously?" He echoed the word, as if he'd not heard it before. "I'll measure her, figure her age, write her down in my life book and then let her go." He took another sip of beer. "Bats are only a sideline this trip. I'm just playing."

And that wasn't a joke. "So what's the main line?" she asked, wondering what color his eyes were.

Those night-muted eyes met her own. "Mongooses." Watching her face, he grinned.

Ooof! Of all the lies she had to choose! "Oh..." Did he know she'd been lying or was his gaze always that penetrating? "What are you doing with mongooses?"

"Studying 'em. We're collecting data on the population and taking some gene samples."

"Oh. Who's we?"

"Me, a couple of grad students and a pack of volunteers." Finishing his beer, he balanced it on the railing beside him. "It's an ongoing study, started by a good friend of mine several years ago. He got a chance to go to India this semester, to study the primary source, so I'm filling in here for him, since I'm on sabbatical."

"How long have you been down here?" she asked quickly. Better to ask questions than try to answer them.

Mac fingered his chin, and she heard the soft rasp of new bristles. "Five days," he said finally, as if the calculation were based on the length of his beard.

"And how long do you stay?"

"Another twelve days—and how long are *you* here for?" he intercepted her next question neatly.

Again Tey had the feeling that he was smiling—though he wasn't. Something in the voice... How long? Just long enough to snatch a child.... Or kidnap him. That's how the local authorities would probably see it. Aunts had no rights, compared with fathers....

"Ahh ... I haven't quite decided."

"And why are you here?" Gently, his fingers closed on the empty beer bottle she'd been resting on her knee.

So glass could conduct electricity. She'd never known that before. Where the bottle supported the weight of Mac's hand, her thigh tingled—some current passing from him to her, molecules rousing to a warm quivering dance. He lifted the bottle, lined it up with his own on the railing. Ah, why was she here... Shouldn't be here...

"Hmm?"

A caressing sound, that... "Ah...I'm hoping to break into travel writing." In spite of her rehearsal on the way up the hill, it sounded a bit hesitant, and much too husky. "I thought a story about St. Matthew— lesser-known parts, not Julianasted—might interest some editor." It was a variation of the story she'd given the youngest agent in Julianasted's most prosperous-looking real estate office yesterday. Only there she'd introduced herself as a writer hoping to do a feature on recent American émigrés—the millionaire sort. The girl hadn't believed her, Tey suspected—had pegged her as a fortune hunter, most likely. But they'd liked each other all the same and, after their third round of after-hours planter's punches—financed by Tey—she'd come across with the information: three new money men in the past six months. Two buyers and one less-or, and that one only leasing on the condition that he could add a fence—"one mean-looking fence"—to the property.

She jumped as a finger found her knee. "One more?" Mac suggested, neither retreating nor advancing.

"Ah . . . no. No, I better—I have to go." She stood and his hand fell away, but his eyes did not. *He sees too much,* she thought suddenly, looking down at him. *Even in this light.* Eyes like a cat's. . . .

"Okay." He rose with a cat's supple grace.

"You don't have to—"

"No, but I want to." That silenced her. He followed her down the wooden walk, then took her hand when the darkness closed in.

Sweet cleeking cry of the frogs, damp fragrant air, soft creak of gravel underfoot—a rutted road leading down through the trees. Tey stumbled and his hand took her weight, then loosened again. How much could you judge someone by his handclasp, she wondered. Warm, dry, steady, somehow knowing when it was needed and when it was not? They stepped out from under the trees—the stars seemed to leap at them—and he let her go.

"So how long will you be here?"

Not long. Not long enough to— "Till I come up with a story. I'm on vacation right now."

He received that answer in silence and didn't speak again until they reached the paved road when, touching his shoulder, she nodded to the left. "Could you use some local color?" he asked finally.

"Such as?"

"Oh . . . mongooses. How to trap 'em. And we're going to one of my favorite sites on the island tomorrow—you can see all the way to St. John from there."

It was tempting. So surprisingly, fiercely tempting that she automatically shook her head. Distractions she didn't need.

"Hmm?" So he hadn't seen that.

The road curved before them, and she turned back for one last look. "I don't think..." From here, high up above the darkness that must be Aston's estate she could see a light—one of Mac's cabins. To have an excuse—a legitimate excuse—to be up on that hillside tomorrow...

"Ever seen a mongoose before?"

"Not other than the illustrations of Rikki-tikki-tavi in *The Jungle Book*." She could see the dark loom of the bushes that hid her Jeep now.

"Then your life is incomplete," Mac insisted. "It's one of those itches that have to be scratched at least once, like planting a tree, or hiking the Grand Canyon, or having someone you love scrub your back..."

For just a second she could see his brown, hard-muscled back gleaming with bath water, the blond hair curling wet and dark, his head rolling luxuriously forward as her hand and the washcloth touched his neck... *Stop!* Digging the keys out of her jeans, she jingled them loudly, driving that image away. She unlocked the door, scrambled inside and rolled down the window.

"Well?" Crossing his arms, Mac leaned in at the window, as if he might stand there chatting all night.

"I'd really get to see one?" And more important, she'd get a good daylight survey of the back of Aston's estate? Maybe even see Josh again?

"That's a promise," Mac said softly.

"Okay. When should I be there?"

"Seven, at my cabin. Wear jeans, a hat, and bring a bathing suit." Moving as slowly as if she were a wild mongoose herself, he reached out, found her jaw with a gentle fingertip, traced a questing line toward her lips.

No. This she didn't need. Not here. Not now. Not so soon after Brian . . . She shook her head slowly.

His hand retreated, unhurried, unhurt, apparently. "Where are you staying?"

"In Thisted—the Dolphin." An image of her cool green, high-ceilinged room, the fan above the bed ghosting through its flickering circles, flooded her tired mind like the first mouthful of cold water on a sweltering day. She turned the key and the Jeep roared awake.

Mac straightened. "Sleep well, Tey Hargrove."

"I will, thanks." She glanced behind her, preparing to back up.

"That's one out of two, then," he said—she thought he said—as the Jeep rolled toward the road.

When the Jeep swung around, its headlights swept across him. Standing with the easy, frozen grace of a wild animal, Mac returned her stare blindly, his chin slightly raised. The red-gold bristles on his face, his silvery, tousled hair leaped vividly to life but, as the lights hit them, his eyes did not shine. Somehow she'd thought they would.

She stepped on the gas and returned him to darkness.

CHAPTER THREE

BYPASSING THE TURNOFF to Mac's camp, Tey slowed the Jeep. But at this hour, no one was stirring on the lawns of Aston's estate, and if anyone sat up on that deep porch that ran the length of the house, she couldn't see him; beyond the white columns that supported the overhanging hipped roof, all was cool darkness.

Half a mile past the far boundaries, she turned and crawled back again. No gaps on this side of the fence, as far as she could see. Her only remaining hope was the back portion, below Mac's cluster of cabins. Tey glanced at her watch; early yet. She'd left time for breakfast, then found no place open in Thisted.

As the Jeep reached the little whitewashed guard-house—as she'd begun to think of it—a man stepped out of its shadowed doorway. An islander, by the look of him, and not a friendly one; he didn't return her wave. *But he'll remember me.* She was too conspicuous like this—a lone woman, a stranger, prowling this road in a Jeep. Couldn't risk this again. He was still staring after her as she turned up the rutted drive to the camp.

"Anybody home?" Tey rapped on the screen door.

"Tey? C'mon in." There was just a hint of the west in that pleasant baritone issuing from an inner room. She hadn't caught that last night.

Texas? she wondered, stopping in the doorway that gave on his bedroom. He hadn't made the bed yet, hadn't slept as well as she had by the state of the bed clothes.

"Catch the worm?" Face half white with lather, half pink from the razor, Mac peered around the doorway just beyond the bed and smiled at her.

Blue eyes, of course. And no shirt. His chest hair—just the right amount—shone palest gold against his reddish tan. Did he have pants on, she wondered belatedly. "Ahh . . . worm? Oh, no . . . no, he got away." Had to be dressed. He wouldn't be so at ease otherwise—or would he?

"How 'bout a cup of coffee, in that case?"

"I'd love one!" Tey backed away toward his kitchen, bumped into a chair and caught it as it tottered. "Could I make you one, too?" Blue jeans hanging over the back of it. She cast a stricken glance over her shoulder, found his smile had widened a notch and beat a retreat.

"You bet!" he called after her, his voice sunny with laughter.

On his small stove, a kettle was just coming to a boil. The first cabinet she tried held a rack of test tubes, small plastic jars, a bottle of formaldehyde, a small appliance she couldn't identify; the coffee makings were in the second. "How do you take it?"

"Lots of milk, one sugar," he yelled back.

A hedonist; she was not surprised. Brian had taken his black. . . . "Are you decent?" She paused outside the bedroom.

"Last time I looked."

And technically she supposed he was, halting as she saw him. Facing away from her, he was in the jeans now and nothing else. Nice back she noticed automatically as he zipped himself, did the button and turned. "Thanks," he said matter-of-factly, coming to meet her.

His eyes were pale blue and vividly alert, their rims a much deeper hue, navy almost. "Something the matter?" he asked, stopping close enough that she had to look up.

"You've cut yourself." Not too tall. Perhaps six feet. It was always hard to judge; everyone was taller than she.

"Mmm?" He touched his jaw and it made a rakish little smear—instant dueling scar. Now if he'd just stop staring at her and take his coffee. She waggled a mug enticingly.

But he didn't take the bait. "Close your eyes."

"Huh?" A belated spasm of modesty? He was going to put on a shirt, maybe?

"C'mon, shut." His fingers brushed gently down across her lids, then lingered in her lashes for a moment.

"I'm going to spill these!" she announced, smiling in spite of herself.

But Mac ignored the threat. "Keep 'em shut," he commanded, his voice farther away now. A drawer squeaked open and closed again. "That's good," he drawled beside her, and warm fingers closed on her earlobe.

"Hey!" Coffee sloshed over her hand, but she stayed obediently blind, trying not to shiver, as he fastened the first stud in place.

One finger traced the rim of her ear, followed it down until it met her jaw, then followed that line around her chin toward her other ear. "You're a strange woman, Tey uh-Hargrove."

Under this lazy caress, her skin was awakening; tiny, prickling lines of pleasure radiating from his fingertip. "How do you mean?" she murmured unwillingly. Didn't want to talk at all, at the moment.

"Every woman I've ever known takes a dozen pairs of shoes along when she travels—at least. And here you are in the wilds of St. Matt, with only one set of earrings to your name?" He attached the second bit of silver with steady fingers.

Keep it light, keep it easy. "I travel light," she countered casually, just as his lips brushed her mouth.

Eyes flaring wide, her mouth dropped. A mistake; his tongue took immediate, gentle advantage, moving silken and sure along the quivering dampness just inside her lips while coffee dripped down her wrists. At this range there was too much to take in at once—the reddish gold of his skin, his silvery lashes, the lemony scent of his after-shave mixed with the smell of warm man, the unexpected softness of his lips—but for an instant she stood still and tried. Overload! Twisting her head away, she pulled a shuddering breath, shut her eyes as the tip of his tongue smoothed her eyebrow. "Hey!"

But Mac stepped back even as she made the protest. "Sorry." He lifted his coffee—half empty—out of her sticky fingers. "It's just that you reminded me of my mother." His grin vanished behind the tilt of the mug.

That was his idea of an apology? There had to be some scathing reply to that, something with a good Freudian slant, but her lips weren't in speaking mode at the moment and she had to fight the urge to touch them. Buzzing.

The screen door banged open. "Mac? Shake a leg! The troops are getting restless!" The bedroom doorway was suddenly filled as six feet and a good deal more of redhead stopped short, catching the door frame with both hands as he saw her. He whipped a glance at Mac, then turned back to Tey. "You sly dog!" he murmured admiringly.

"Tey, this is Gerry," Mac said without embarrassment. "My research assistant." Crossing to the bureau, he pulled out a shirt. "Tey's a writer," he drawled over his shoulder. "We're going to show her how to catch a mongoose."

"You're going to write about us? Super!" His freckled, bony face turned back to Mac. "We're just about out of fish, you know."

"I've got a pound or two." Mac put a hand to Tey's back and Gerry retreated before them. Outside, a car horn hooted *shave and a haircut.*

Two bits Tey completed it as Mac leaned into his rust-spotted refrigerator and came out with a damp brown parcel.

"Here." He clapped it into Gerry's hands. "Oh, and take this." He thrust an unbleached cotton sack, bumpy with its clinking contents, at him. "And tell Team Two we'll take the blue van." He swung to Tey. "Had breakfast yet?"

"Well..."

But he'd read the answer to that already and was setting butter and a loaf of bread on the counter. "Fix a couple of slices for me, too, will you?"

Things were moving a bit too fast for her; it was easiest to simply obey and hope to sort it all out later. Mac clapped hunks of cheddar onto the slices as she buttered them, folded them over into rough sandwiches, handed her two and a banana. He touched her hair. "Bring a hat?"

"In the Jeep."

"Good. Don't forget it." Those smiling blue eyes swept down the length of her. "Jeans, socks, sensible shoes—you'll do nicely, Ms Hargrove. Let's go."

Outside, some dozen similarly clad people were scrambling into two vans parked farther up the hill while just as many seemed to be climbing back out again with cries of "Don't leave without me!"

"George, you forgot the water!"

"Who's collecting the mail?"

A chubby older woman leaned out one window of the red van, her binoculars trained on something in the tree overhead, her lips pursing in excitement, while a tall, dark-haired woman and a small man in a snowy pith helmet stacked wire mesh, rectangular boxes—live traps, Tey realized—into the rear of the blue van.

With a grinning Gerry at the wheel, the red van revved its engine and bumped slowly down the road, its sliding door still open. The cheers of those already inside mingled with the yelps of the abandoned as they chased after it. He relented after a few yards, the waifs clambered aboard, and it rolled away again.

Peeling a banana, Mac slipped into the driver's seat of the other van and the stragglers began to find their places. Aware of the interested glances coming her way, and feeling the outsider, Tey hung back at the doors. The seat beside the driver was still vacant; perhaps there was a pecking order? But Mac caught her eye just then and pointed his banana at the front seat.

"Mac!" A woman ducked around Tey and slid in beside him. "What happened to that gorgeous beard you were growing?"

Oh, well. If there was a pecking order, busty blondes in tight T-shirts came somewhere near the top of it. Tey slanted him an ironic glance and found a place at the window just behind him. Was it her imagination, or were his ears somewhat pinker now?

Finishing his banana with deliberation, Mac gave the blonde an enigmatic smile. "Cut it." He swung around to inspect the rest of his passengers as he started the motor. "The gang's all here?"

"Yo!"

"We've been here for hours! Where were you?"

"Down in my cabin, thinkin' profound, biological thoughts," Mac retorted, starting them down the hill. "You ought to try it sometime."

"That's all George ever does!" The blonde giggled, peeking over her shoulder. "Thinks about it!"

"Come back here, Marty, and I'll show you what else I do!" offered the sandy-haired, broad-shouldered man at the back of the bus in a Deep South drawl.

Under the cover of the hoots that followed this, Tey smiled at the small, graying man who sat beside her, his hands crossed neatly on the pith helmet in his lap. "Dr. Livingstone, I presume? I'm Tey."

He had a nice smile. "Tey? I'm David. Are you joining the expedition?"

"Not exactly. I'm a writer." And she went through her story again, then repeated the spiel once more as the trio in the back seat leaned forward to catch it. In the meantime, the van had turned north on the coast road. Because she was sitting on the water side, all she'd seen of Aston's estate was the long, fenced-in strip of beach that lay across the road from the house. Snatching glimpses of tawny sand and turquoise water beyond the roadside thickets, she saw no one out there.

When she turned back to her companions, she met a pair of blue eyes in the rearview mirror for a moment, then looked away with an odd mixture of pleasure and guilt.

A real writer wouldn't be answering the questions, would she? Ought to be asking them, interviewing the whole lot of them. "Now are you a volunteer, David, and how does that work?"

Apparently they all were, except Professor McAllister—he shot her another mocking glance via the mirror—Gerry and Anne, who had stayed in camp to do paperwork today. "We're paying volunteers. We get a chance to participate in a real scientific endeavor, and the expedition benefits by our work as well as our money."

"Couldn't do this sort of study without 'em," Mac agreed. "This is a labor-intensive project, and no university can field a paid team big enough to do that sort of job nowadays."

"So you actually pay to work for Mac?"

"I'm worth every penny," he assured her modestly, ignoring the catcalls from the back seat.

The blonde—Marty—patted his arm. "He's not such a slave driver—we spend most every afternoon cultivating our tans."

To the right the land was rising, the yellow-green of the waist-high guinea grass shading to a darker, rougher scrub on the summits of the low rounded mountains. A massive tree overshadowed the road, its fat-bottomed base as gray and furrowed as a melted elephant. "What's that, Mac?" The tall brunette beyond David spoke for the first time.

"That's a baobab, Jean. The Mateans call it the dead rat tree."

Tey hunched her shoulders. You could see why, with its oblong green fruits hanging down by their long rat-tail stems. It was a tree that might walk on moonless nights, the dead rats swaying with each lumbering step.

The van slowed, then swung off the paved road and up a rutted track into the trees. "Hands inside!" Mac warned as brush clawed the flanks of the van.

"Yow!" the back three chorused as the van dipped into a pothole and heaved itself out the far side. The Southerner—George—was bracing himself against the overhead, while the shorter women did a fair imitation of dribbled basketballs. Tey clutched the seat behind Mac's shoulders and nearly smashed her nose against the back of his head as they hit the next hole.

"That's the worst of it," Mac assured her, leaning back against her fingers. The trees were giving way to scrub as they climbed, green shadows retreating as the tropic sun found them. The van roared around a hairpin turn, and they were looking down on the treetops; across the valley a green mountain shrugged rough shoulders against a sky laced with trade wind cumulus, and beyond that one, more mountains butted the blue.

Their tail feathers scalloped with white, two rosy-brown birds shot up before the oncoming wheels. "Oh! What were those?"

The corners of Mac's mouth curved, but mercifully he kept his eyes on the track ahead. "Zenaida doves. Pretty, aren't they?" He swung the van up around another turn, hugging the bushes on the uphill side, and wood shrieked across metal again, drowning out Marty's squeals as she leaned out her window to look over the drop-off. "Nearly there," Mac said comfortably.

The trail humped over a rise and they were no longer skirting empty space; a meadow with one wind-crabbed tree turned its face to the sky. Mountaintop. Tey breathed a sigh of relief, and Mac laughed softly as he pulled off the road to park in the grass. "End of the line, folks."

"You think mongooses'll be up here?" George scoffed. "It's too far from the liquor stores."

"Are you kidding?" Mac opened the rear door of the van and began pulling traps out. "This is mongoose paradise. They come up here to buy condos and get away from it all. I hear they're plannin' to build a nine-hole golf course and an Olympic-size pool next year."

By turning the traps on end and spreading her fingers wide, Tey found she could manage four in each hand as the others were doing. Fingertips hooked in the mesh, cages bouncing against her calves, she fell into step with Jean. "What's the bait?" She nodded at the hunks of meat, one per trap, which swung from hooks set in the ceiling sides.

Jean gave her a startled, hesitant smile. "Fish."

So she was shy—because of her height? "I thought they ate snakes?"

"They're opportunistic feeders," Mac declared, catching up with them.

"Meaning?"

"Meaning if they can't get a snake—which they can't on St. Matthew—they'll settle for a cheeseburger, or a kitten, or whatever else is handy."

Not joking this time, in spite of the sparkle in those blue-on-blue eyes. "They polished off all the snakes?"

"Never were any, to speak of." Ahead of them, where the meadow sloped up to a crest, then tilted out of sight, the rest of the team had dropped their traps, stood silhouetted against the sky, pointing. "They were brought in to control the rats that were devastatin' the sugar cane industry."

"And did they?" She could hear the wind now, humming as if it had traveled far, had tales to tell. A gust of it cooled her damp face as it lifted Mac's hair out of his eyebrows.

"Slowed 'em down some. But *rattus rattus* took to the treetops, and all rats are nocturnal while mongooses hunt in the daytime, so it wasn't the rousing success the planters had hoped for."

"Mac!" Marty ran to meet them. "That's St. Thomas, isn't it?"

It was the end of the earth, Tey decided, stopping beside him. On three sides below them a sea of glittering, Prussian blue stretched out to embrace a horizon softened by endless miles of sea spray.

"That?" Mac squinted toward a misty mountain at the edge of the world. Tey had taken it for a distance-blued cloud, one of the fleet of levitating clipper ships scudding westward before the wind. "That's St. John. Look to your left."

More lilac peaks nudged the sky, now that she knew what to look for. "St. Thomas." Mac made it sound like a benediction. "And Columbus sailed by down there . . . must have stared up at this cape on his second voyage. San Mateo, he called this island."

Almost five hundred years ago. And it had probably looked just as it did today. There wasn't a house along these cliffs, not one sail splitting the blue.

"Cold?" Mac must have seen her shiver.

Tey shook her head slowly. "Awed."

"Good." He started down the slope toward the sea. "Time to earn our keep, troops."

Halfway down the hill, Mac stopped beside a head-high, scrawny tree. A streamer of red plastic, tied to one branch, whipped in the breeze. Tey cocked her head, trying to read the figures in black that were printed on the marker. *A-1?*

"George, Carol . . . Marty, you take E and F rows." Marty opened her mouth as if to protest, then shut it and shrugged. She started downhill ahead of the other two. Mac studied her retreating back for a moment. "David, Jean, uh, Angie, you've got rows D and C. Look out for Christmas bush; it's mostly down in the ravine to the left."

Watching them trudge away, Tey could make out other bits of red waving above the waist-high grass. A silvery shadow rippled across the hill as a gust of wind bent the grass.

"We call this a grid," Mac explained, following her gaze. "Team One laid it out yesterday. Each marker designates a trap site."

"I see." It took an effort of will to turn and meet his eyes, now that they were alone. Reminded him of his mother, did she? Surely he'd been kidding; surely he didn't look at his mother this way?

"So . . . let's set a trap." Releasing her from that level gaze, Mac collected one and turned to study the brush growing around the tree. "This'll do." Dropping onto his heels, he caught her hand, tugged her down beside him, then slowly worked the trap backward into a clump of grass, concealing all of it but the doorway. "You've got to make sure it sits level." He rocked the trap appraisingly, then nodded, satisfied. "And it's got to be out of the sun, so Mr. Mongoose doesn't get heatstroke." The look he gave her was almost severe; perversely, she felt a sudden surge of warmth. He really cared, didn't he?

"Then, once it's in place, you swing up the door...like so, and hold it up with this little hook." His hands were rather square and capable looking—like a mechanic's, but without the grime; they completed this operation with surprising delicacy. "When our friend drops in for a sample of fish, he steps on that plate in the floor, down comes the door, and one more mongoose learns there's no such thing as a free lunch."

Tey laughed aloud. Then, as his eyes returned to her face, she bounced to her feet. Down in the grass they might have been the only two people in a very small world; she returned to sunlit reality like a swimmer breaching for air. "So your friend gets a fish and a philosophy lesson. What do *you* get?"

"Just the facts, ma'am, just the facts." Mac rose with his easy grace.

"You don't hurt them, do you?"

"Not most of 'em." His eyes didn't falter. "A few of 'em, yes."

No apology there, and no smoothing over of an uncomfortable truth. "What's the purpose of this project, Mac?" How could a mouth be that sensitive, and yet so masculine? His upper lip had no pinkness—that was it; so the first thing you noticed was the line of the mouth itself. It was changing again as she watched, the ends regaining their humor.

"That depends on who you ask. Gerry would tell you we're investigating the sex-determining chromosome in mongooses—that's his dissertation project. Anne is taking a natural history approach. Me, I'm conducting a population survey—how many mon-

gooses are there on St. Matt, ratio of males to fe-
males, distribution of ages, general level of health of
the population. Have they reached peak population
density yet, or are they still multiplying?'' Gathering
his traps, he squinted across the hillside and must have
found the next marker, for he slogged off, traps extended before him.

With Mac breaking trail, it wasn't too bad, though
the grass was up to her chin now. "But why does it
matter?" she panted, "except to another mongoose?"

"Could matter a lot," he called over his shoulder.
"For instance: mongooses were introduced on Hawaii
about the same time as here—the 1880s. They have
definitely not reached peak population out there yet.
What are the implications for native fauna when they
do? Perhaps we can help predict that.'' He stopped
beside the second marker, nearly hidden in the leaves
of a bush. "You set this one. Then you'll have one less
to carry.''

She selected a site with care, then glanced up for his
approval. His smile acknowledged her question and
refused her an answer all at once; it was up to her.
Okay, then. It took some fiddling to hold the door in
position, and then she got it; she glanced up again and
his grin reflected her triumph.

"Perfect! You're a born trapper.''

"Huh! You say that to all the women, I bet.'' Hot.
She was suddenly hot; the wind couldn't reach her,
down in the grass. She stood, nearly under his chin.

Mac shook his head slowly.

Couldn't just stand here like this; this was idiotic.
Wasn't what she'd come here for, at all. *Think of Lori.
Think of Josh. Think of mongooses, if all else fails.*

Sliding around him, she stood on tiptoe. Where was A-3? A flicker of orange caught her eye. She shoved on into the grass, beginning to sweat now, and after a moment, she could hear his rustling progress at her heels.

She set the next site, as well, clumsy under his silent contemplation. Mac took the lead again as they pushed on. The grass was over her head.

"'Nother for instance." He spoke suddenly, as if the heat and the silence were oppressing him, too. "Mongooses are a vector for rabies; they found that out on Puerto Rico in 1950. What would be the impact on St. Matthew, if rabies ever gets a foothold here?"

"Ugh," she agreed, too hot to say more. She watched as he placed the next trap; his blue work shirt was nearly drenched now, was sticking to the hard, clean angles of his shoulder blades, the curve of ribs and chest. He wiped his brow with a forearm bright with curling hair and waded on.

But this time they couldn't find the marker. "Maybe we've come too far?" she suggested after they'd circled for a while.

"Maybe." Mac put down his traps, took hers and set them aside. "You tell me." Catching her smoothly around the waist, he lifted her above the grass.

"Hey!"

"See it?" Ignoring her protest, he shifted her onto his shoulder.

Under her thighs, he felt warmly, damply alive. His hands were clasped around her shins, but it still looked a long way down to the ground. Gingerly, she rested one hand on his head, found his hair to be as silky as it looked. With her other hand she steadied herself on his far shoulder. Bone and muscle—something very pleasing in the feel of that. Her palms were tingling. So was the rest of her, for that matter. *Think of mongooses.*

"No sign of it?" Mac turned slowly.

"Ahh...no..." *So let me down, let me down.*

His hand slid gently up and down her legs a few inches. Then he looked up at her, throwing her off balance again as his head tilted. "You aren't married, are you?"

"Why do you care?" Dumb question, oh, *dumb* question. *Can I take that back?*

That expressive mouth rippled, then sobered again. "If there's one thing my dad taught me, it was never let a married lady sit on your...ah...shoulder. Sooner or later, there's always hell to pay. Are you?"

"No," she said briskly. "What else did your father teach you?" Help! What was the matter with her mouth today? It was two steps ahead of her brain.

His eyes glinted wickedly, but he let that one lie. "Mmm, all the basic dad things... How to knot my tie. How to cook chili, how to win at stud poker..."

Flash those baby blues and you'll take every hand, partner! Besides the deeper blue around the rims, there were a few rakish flecks of the same color radiating out from his pupils. Reminded her of pansies, her favorite flower, but he'd drop her on her head if she told him that. She grinned at the thought, and his hands tightened pleasurably. "Where are you from? Texas?"

"Texas!" He was scandalized. "I'm a Colorado boy—Denver." One hand smoothed down to her ankle, and his fingers encircled it. "What about you?"

"Boston." There was no harm in telling him that.

"Where the Cabots speak only to the Lowells, and the Lowells speak only to God?"

"Uh-huh. And where women are taught to stand on their own two feet." She kicked her heels gently against his ribs.

"I never doubted it," he assured her. "But what about that marker?"

As if it was she who couldn't keep her mind on business! Tey scanned the green shifting hillside again. "Don't see it behind us, but I do see Jean and—she may not know it—but she's being stalked by a flying saucer. No; it's a pith helmet. And she's all out of traps."

"Hmm . . . guess we'd better start hustlin'." Mac rotated again. "What about in that direction?"

"Umm . . . oh! There it is. About ten yards thataway."

They found the rest of the markers without incident, were wading up the hill, hands blessedly empty at last, the wind fingering their wet clothes before she thought to ask, "So when do I see a mongoose?" On the hilltop, David stared inland, a pair of binoculars screwed to his face. The rest of the crew must have gone on to the van.

"We'll run the line tomorrow."

"Tomorrow! But you promised I'd see one today." The pang of disappointment was as sharp as any a thwarted journalist would have felt.

"I know it," he said without remorse, "but I got to thinkin' . . . You ought to see the process, not just the end result, if you want to do it justice when you write about it. This way you're learning the rhythm of trapping, feeling the anticipation."

Thank you, Professor McAllister. Just what she needed right now, a lecture on writing. "But I might not be able to make it tomorrow." Couldn't get side-tracked; there must be something more to the point she should be doing. Just what, she had no idea.

"No?" He'd stopped and turned to face her. "What are you up to tomorrow?"

"I don't know yet." The truth, but it sounded evasive.

The line of his lips straightened subtly. "I see." He moved on again.

Saw what? He looked almost angry, or was that her imagination? Tey felt a sudden flicker of irritation. Brian had always sulked when she didn't follow his plans. Surely Mac wasn't going to prove that sort, was he? The Kenyon women seemed to have a genius for attracting selfish, domineering types; it had shaken her to her core when she realized at last how precisely Brian fitted the same profile as her father, as Jon Aston. She had moved out a few days after that revelation.

"Hey, dreamer." Mac's hand closed warmly on the top of her shoulder. "Look at that." He nodded in the direction that David was still aiming his binoculars. "Red-tail hawk."

Spiraling skyward on tawny square-cut wings, the bird took her spirits with him; Mac's forefinger traced the edge of her collarbone for an inch or so, then dropped away. "Nice," she murmured huskily. The bird crossed a cloud, grew darker in contrast against its peaks of sunlit snow. "So nice."

CHAPTER FOUR

"SO EVERYBODY AGREES?" Mac asked as the van hummed south past the baobab tree a short while later. "Lunch at Mary's Fancy?"

That seemed to be the consensus, and Tey bit back a sigh. Just when was she going to get a look at the back fence? They rounded the final curve, and she leaned forward eagerly; at least this time she was on the side with a view of the estate.

And at last, patience was rewarded. Outside the gates, their backs turned to the road, a fair-haired child rode the shoulders of a heavyset man; the boy's hands beat a gleeful tom-tom rhythm on the top of his mount's head. The drummed-upon one snapped the padlock, captured his tormentor's hands and, holding them in place atop his head, turned, smiling to himself. Seeing the approaching van, he lifted Josh's small paws and his own in a four-armed victory salute.

"Howdy, guys." Halting the van beside them, Mac leaned out his window. "Where you off to?"

"What d'you think, Josh?" Loosing the boy's hands, the man clasped his rider's knees instead. "Should we tell 'em?" Behind the wire-rimmed glasses his brown eyes regarded Mac with comical suspicion.

But happy no longer, Josh didn't recognize the joke. Solemnly, he shook his head, then fixed Mac with Lori's—with his aunt's—gray-green eyes, huge in that triangular little face. He was going to have Jon Aston's high forehead and pointed chin; Tey could see it for the first time in spite of the childish roundness. He shook his head again and buried his fingers in the grizzly-brown hair of his steed.

The man seemed to have sensed that negative. "Could we give Mac a hint?" he suggested. "What will we do when we get there?"

But Josh was no longer interested in Mac. Marty, who'd claimed the front seat again, was leaning out Mac's window as well, brushing against his chest as she did so, and the boy's attention was suddenly riveted on her, reminding Tey of the instinctive "point" of a bird dog. "Hello-o, you darlin', you!" she crooned.

The effect of her words—or was it her voice?—was instantaneous. That soft golden poker face contracted in a scowl and Josh looked away. Not the voice he'd been hoping for? Tey spared a glance for the blonde. Almost the same shade of hair as Lori's, yes; she hadn't noticed before.

"Are you going to get wet?" Mac guessed.

Josh nodded absently, his eyes swinging to the rear windows, and Tey brought a hand to her mouth, as if to shield a cough. Surely he wouldn't recognize her, would he? He'd been two, the last time they'd met. Watching those pensive eyes, she had to fight down an overwhelming urge to leap from the van and yank him off this stranger's wide shoulders. *Josh. Just hang on a few days, kid!* For just a moment, their eyes met, met and locked. *My God, he does know me!* But no, he was frowning again, looking not that far from tears as his eyes searched beyond her to David, then to George behind her, and did not find what he sought. Turning away from them all, he rested a cheek against the top of his bodyguard's head.

"If you're going swimming, why not come with us?" Mac was suggesting.

"Guess we better not." Josh's keeper reached up to scratch that moon-silver hair with lazy, knowing fingers. "My partner just had his siesta, but he seems a little pooped today. Guess we'll stay near the house."

"Some other time, then," Mac agreed, easing the van into motion. "Take it easy, guys."

As Tey watched over her shoulder, the pair reached the smaller gate on the beach side of the road. The bodyguard seemed to be unlocking it when the trees intervened. "That looks like a nice beach back there," she observed to David. "Pity it's fenced off." Did they swim there every day? And where was Aston?

"Fortunately we have beach rights. Each cabin has a key to the gate, and most days, that's where we swim. I spent a fascinating hour there yesterday morning, trying to get a picture of a brown pelican in the act of diving."

CLOSING THE PADLOCK, Bo turned to find Josh halfway to the water. "Josh, wait a minute! We've got to set up camp first." He waved him downshore toward the little grove of palms where they always spread the blanket. It had the best shade on the beach, and shade was something to remember, with a cotton-top like Josh.

Nice of McAllister to invite them along; the gesture still warmed him. But the zoologist was that type of guy; he'd given Josh a hermit crab the first time they met, here on the beach. Reminded him of his old Peace Corps pals—caring types, their idealism carefully—and unsuccessfully—hidden behind a pose of laid-back, smiling irreverence.

Of course Mac had plenty to smile about. That blonde... Not *his* type, of course—a bit too much of a good thing. He preferred them a little understated, but still... Stepping into the cool shadows under the trees, Bo put down the tote that held their chess set and shook out the blanket.

Now that little dark one at the window behind Mac... he hadn't seen her before. She had more shape to her face... The bones gave a sense of purpose... And he'd liked the beads of sweat along her hairline, the way the wisps of damp hair curled at her ears.

For a second there, he'd even tried to meet her eyes, but no luck; she'd been more interested in Josh than himself. But that was hardly surprising. His looks had never bowled them over. Flash, he wasn't.

"Bogie, let's go!" Josh danced before him. "Come on, let's go!"

"Wait a minute, bud. You just had a sandwich, remember? Chess first and swimming later."

"Awwwww."

"Whining will get you nowhere. Now... you're gonna like this guy." Bo pulled a chess piece out of the bag. "He's called a rook."

MARY'S FANCY was a roadside restaurant with a roof and three walls. Seated at a table with Mac, Jean and David, Tey stared out from its cool shadows through a rustling palm tree to the beach for which the others had made a beeline. Bands of color—that was how it hit you, as if a child with a five-inch paintbrush had slapped down a stripe of cool gray—the sand under the palms, then a strip of pure cream—where the sun pounced down, white for the waves lapping that cream, aquamarine for the shallows gliding deliciously on into turquoise, teal, Prussian blue, and then, finally, that sun-bleached sky. Bliss—unadulterated, absolute bliss. She sighed, looked up to find intense eyes the same shade as that sky and looked quickly away again. She'd reached a conclusion after Brian, or actually, returned to one that she'd held for a long time before him.

It was a conclusion forged through years of watching her mother pine for the selfish, domineering man who'd finally left her for another woman and never once looked back. Then later, the cold reality of Lori's marriage to Jon Aston had gradually revealed itself, and tempered Tey's theory: Kenyon women loved too well and not wisely at all. And deep love cut deeply.

But then Brian—Dr. Brian Hargrove—had come into her life last year, and she'd cheerfully tossed all her theories aside....

A sparrow-sized bird sailed over the bar at the other end of the room and skimmed toward them, its wings nearly brushing the tin roof above. Swooping down past Mac's shoulder, it perched in the palm.

"Bananaquit," David nodded at the bird, then stiffened, gazing through the tree. "Pelicans, and me without my camera!" Collecting his beer and binoculars, he pushed away from the table. "I'll be back."

"Perhaps I'll..." Jean eased her chair out, then looked at Mac.

"We'll call you when the food comes." He gave her an encouraging smile, watched her stoop-shouldered retreat in silence for a moment, then glanced over his shoulder; the yellow-breasted bananaquit was still there. "Let me see your hand."

"You tell fortunes, Professor?" Tey gave it reluctantly.

"Sometimes." Steadying her open hand on his own, he measured a teaspoon of sugar onto her palm. "I see a great sweetness coming into your life."

"That's quite a talent!" Contrasting oddly with the warmth of his fingers, the cool tickling weight of the sugar made her want to shiver.

Mac's hand moved away. "Now be very still." He nodded at the bird, which seemed to be leaning toward her, its black, brilliant eyes fixed on the offering.

"Oh!" So that's what he was up to. But the bananaquit was in no hurry. It hopped a few inches down its waving palm frond and then back up again. "Who was your friend back there?" she asked casually, watching the bird.

"My friend?"

"The man with that beautiful child."

"Oh—that's Bo."

Come on, McAllister, elaborate! But he didn't; she was going to have to drag the information out bit by bit, apparently. "He lives around here?" she tried after a moment, her eyes still on the bird.

"At the big house, just below us."

The bananaquit made up its mind at last; it was going for the gusto. Flitting to the edge of the table, it cocked its dark head at her. "That's his son?" she asked softly.

"No...I believe he's tutoring the boy." To her attentive ears, Mac's drawl had acquired a certain precision.

Bouncing stiff-legged across the tablecloth, the quit stopped again, neck outstretched. "Have you known him long?'' Perhaps Mac could provide an introduction, perhaps intercede on her behalf in some way.

''A few days. Why?''

Oops! She'd pushed too far. ''Don't know,'' she murmured indifferently, not meeting his eyes. ''He just looked interesting.'' The bird hopped the rest of the way, jabbed its beak into the sugar and broad-jumped away again.

''Another beer, sir?'' The waitress loomed between them, and the quit, its suspicions confirmed, shot away through the palm.

''And one for the lady. Please.'' Mac watched silently as Tey dumped the sugar in the ashtray, then caught her wrist as she reached for her napkin. ''Don't give up so easily. If you can't feed the birds, there's this large, omnivorous mammal with a sweet tooth...''

''Oh?'' A dog, did he mean? Glancing across the floor, Tey didn't see one. Could Mac feel the pulse tapping in her wrist?

''Waste not, want...'' Bringing her hand to his mouth, he stroked his tongue slowly across her palm.

Disbelief mingled with the sensations of supple, wet warmth, the grittiness of sugar scraping across her skin; his hand tightened as she trembled. ''Mac!'' She looked around—no one had noticed yet. His breath hot on her skin, heating the rest of her, as well, he was searching out the last few grains between her fingers. ''Hey...'' Ignoring that plea, and apparently done with the sugar, he started to nibble. *Enough*. Too much— she could feel those gentle teeth not just on her palm, but down her spine, across her breasts... Twisting her hand, she closed thumb and forefinger on the tip of his nose.

"No?" His grin was unabashed as he looked up at her, his teeth still engaged.

"Not in public, no," she said sternly, then winced as the corollary came clear. Ouch!

He didn't make the obvious rejoinder, but he hadn't missed it, either; his eyes gleamed with laughter as they let each other go.

"Here come our drinks." Thank heavens. And behind the waitress, David and Jean were knocking the sand off their shoes. The shorter man offered his hand as the brunette stepped up onto the restaurant floor; she took it awkwardly, dropped it as soon as she could and hurried on ahead of him.

After a lunch of curried ginger chicken and banana fritters, Mac wanted a swim, while the beach bunny half of the team was just straggling into the restaurant. Tey changed into the pair of cotton shorts she'd brought along.

Toes massaging the hot sand, she sauntered down to the water's edge. Mac was heading toward Puerto Rico, his overarm stroke cutting crisply through the blue. Far down the shore, Jean wandered alone with the downcast eyes of a beachcomber.

A wave slid up the sand, licking her toes with a silvery tongue. *So nice.* Accepting the invitation, she followed it back to the shallows; knee-deep, she sloshed along, paralleling the beach. Nicer than nice—lovely, but what was Lori doing at this moment? Margie had promised to take her to stay with Margie's mother, north of Santa Barbara, once she was discharged from the hospital. "A strong, funny lady," Margie had described Mrs. Davis, always glad of company since the loss of her husband, a fanatic rose gardener and amateur watercolorist, full of good talk and kind silences.

That had sounded like the perfect solution—a safe, supportive hideaway. And it was also, Lori's lawyer had pointed out, the perfect place to conceal Josh while Margie filed for custody. But first, possession was nine-tenths of the law. *And that's where I come in.*

"That's a bathing suit?" Mac glided toward her with a lazy breast stroke. "They've never heard of God's gift to mankind—the bikini—in Boston?"

"Oh, they have, but I forgot mine." Swimming had been the last thing she'd been thinking about in that frantic rush to catch the plane to L.A.

Rolling onto his back, Mac squinted up at her. "You came to the Caribbean without a bathing suit..." His hands fanned the water, keeping him afloat.

It sounded either suspicious or moronic, didn't it? "I told you, Mac, this is more a working trip than a vacation."

"You did." But he still sounded skeptical. A swell lifted him gently; she stood on tiptoe as it lapped at her thighs. Mac tilted his chin toward the clouds and, closing his eyes, paddled dreamily. "But you also said writing was something you're trying to break into. So what do you do now, for a living?"

"I'm a technical writer...with a software firm." No reason not to tell him the truth when she could. It wasn't pleasant lying to this man; he looked so open and trusting, floating blindly like that. And it was also the perfect chance to feast her eyes on him, come to think of it.

"A high-tech lady, huh?" He opened one eye, checked his position and closed it again.

"An interpreter for the high techies. I write the manuals explaining my firm's software to the people who'll use it, and articles to technical magazines, touting our latest programs.'' He was that same ruddy tan all over; his legs, chest and arms were rough with curly gold. And he had a sprinkling of freckles, she noticed as he rocked closer, on his shoulders, along his biceps, across those nicely muscled thighs. A swell, higher than the rest, rolled under Mac and wet her to the crotch. Darn! Oh, well. Irresistibly, her eyes returned to Mac. His swimming trunks had seen better days; they were a faded blue nylon, held up by a drawstring, their limp material leaving very little to the imagination... And what had she promised herself, after Brian—never to get serious about a man again? But then, who was serious?

"I think," Mac drawled lazily, "that I must have been a crocodile in my last life."

Lord, his eyes were open. How long had he been watching her? The tropic sun suddenly seemed to be beating down just on her shameless head. "Why's that?"

"I'm getting this overpowering urge to come over there and bite your thigh." He rolled onto his stomach and cruised slowly toward her, only his eyes gleaming hungrily above water.

Giggling, she backed toward the shallows, but he was kicking faster now. Her foot caught in the sand and she sat with a splash. "Awp!" But even with full engines astern, Mac was too close to stop. She caught his shoulders just before their heads cracked. "Help!"

Floating in her hold, he left it to her to stave him off as a wave lifted them both. His skin was cool and slippery beneath her fingers. "You don't have a sense of déjà vu?" He twisted out of her grasp and sat beside her.

Another swell lifted them, then dropped them softly on the sand again. The water was breast deep. "A feeling that we've done this before?" No, never. This was easier, different than anything she'd felt before.

"No, a feeling that you were croc bait in your last life."

"Uh-uh." She shook her head slowly, her chin grazing the water as another swell rolled past.

"Never too late to start."

A year ago, had she felt like this about Brian? Surely she must have, and look at all the grief that had gotten her. After she'd moved in with Brian, her independence had started to grate on him. And his ardent devotion had deepened gradually but surely into something so possessive, so humorlessly critical... Once she'd acknowledged that, her love had changed to claustrophobia almost overnight. It was difficult now to remember how she'd once felt. *And who wants to remember?* Giving Mac an enigmatic grin, she held her nose and sank backward beneath the next wave.

It was as good—better—than a cold shower. Delicious, after the hot sun. Arching her back, she shook her head in lazy delight, letting her hair billow back from her face. Surfacing, smiling blindly, she wiped her eyes. "Ah..." Framed by the drops of crystal on her lashes, he looked funny, his expression an odd mixture of surprise and alertness. As if he'd just been goosed. "What's the matter?"

"Um..." Alertness shaded to wariness. Smiling, he shook his head.

"Hey, Mac!" Angie waded toward them. "We're the supper team, remember?"

AND I STILL DON'T KNOW if there's a back gate, Tey reminded herself as Mac parked the van beside its red twin back at the camp. Somehow, she was going to have to make the opportunity to discover that.

"You'll stay to supper?" Mac asked as the others wandered off to their various cabins.

"Ahh...sure, I'd love to." He made it too easy; this wasn't fair, using him like this. *Think of Josh. Is that fair?* And Mac looked well able to take care of himself, after all.

"Good!" Swinging away, he called after Jean, who was following Marty uphill to the largest cabin. "Jean, we've got a dinner guest. Would you show Tey where she can catch a shower?"

So there wasn't time to check the fence before she found herself in the women's damp bathroom, with Jean's earnest warning ringing in her ears not to use too much water. That was no problem. Marty had announced on her way out that she'd finished the last of the hot water, and she hadn't been kidding. Shutting off the icy drizzle, Tey soaped herself rapidly, her skin aching with goose bumps, her nipples outraged and erect.

"Who is it?" she yelled as someone knocked on the door. Probably Marty again; Jean would be too shy to intrude.

"Tey?"

What was he doing here? Blinded by shampoo, Tey tried to recall the shower curtain. Translucent, she decided, and the light from the window above the tub would be silhouetting her clearly. Oh, well, it couldn't be much more revealing than the bikini she hadn't brought. "Yes, Professor?" A little formality couldn't hurt.

"I brought you a T-shirt, since yours is wet."

"Oh—thank you." Anxious to see again, she switched on the water and rotated beneath the shower head.

"This is a full-service expedition, by the way," he drawled after a moment. "Do you need your back scrubbed?"

Smiling, she shook her head. "I've done it already."

"Pity... backs are my specialty." He sounded to be just the other side of the curtain now. "But I s'pose I could be persuaded to try a front for a change."

"Awfully kind of you, but that's done, as well." She shut off the water. Turning toward his voice, she brushed her hair back from her cheeks.

When she opened her eyes, he was shockingly near, his face a tanned blur through the wet plastic. "Too bad," he said quietly. "I'll see you out front, then." The door closed gently behind him.

Hugging herself, beginning to shiver, she stared through the curtain for a long moment, then pushed it aside. *Josh.*

Padding into the kitchen in Mac's T-shirt, she felt righteously clean and awfully small; the blue whales silk-screened across the front of it hit her at waist level rather than across the chest as they should have. Seated at the bar that divided the kitchen from the common room beyond, tears on his cheeks, Mac looked up over a mountain of chopped onions and grinned.

"What can I do?" she asked briskly.

"Umm, you can help me and Marty make enchilada pie, or you can show George a humane way to carve a pineapple."

"Help me!" George pleaded. "Fruit salad with fingertips isn't what I call a good time."

Chopping, stirring, and finally serving for the next hour, Tey found herself slowly being absorbed into the group. Evening meals were taken together, and the expedition members ambled in by twos and threes. Rum and Cokes were mixed from the bottles left out on the counter; Mac's enchilada sauce was sampled by all and alternately praised or reviled, with the women doing most of the praising, Tey noticed. The early birds claimed places at the big coffee table in the common room while the latecomers balanced plates on their laps as they sat on the ragged sofa and easy chairs that lined the walls. The babble of jokes, teasing, and sober scientific debate could not quite drown out the song of the tree frogs beyond the window screens.

"You should have seen the size of him! Five hundred and twelve grams and only type-O teeth. When he's grown he'll be—"

"Mac, tell Gerry to stop lying. Barracudas don't really attack jewelry, do they? I mean not while you're wearing—"

"No, that had to be an ani. The pearly-eyed thrasher—"

"But when they got back to the beach, their clothes were—"

"*Herpestes auropunctatus*, which is Latin for—"

"It's delicious! That's just how we like our men, George. Barefoot, pungent and in the kitchen."

The universal groans that followed this comment were cut short by Mac's tapping his glass with a spoon. His laughing eyes swept the group. "Before you all wander off, we have some entertainment to offer. I owe you a short lecture on the history of introduced mammals, and then Gerry has promised to tell you the thrilling and never-before-revealed facts about the sex-determining chromosome in—''

This was her chance, Tey decided, pausing in her return from the kitchen with more fruit salad. Backing casually toward the counter, she leaned against it, finishing her portion while Mac dragged a stool to the far side of the room and sat, facing the volunteers. There'd been no way to escape his attention during the meal, but now he was trapping himself. She set the bowl aside.

But she stayed on for a moment, curious to hear the professorial side of him, then found there wasn't one. This wasn't a lecture so much as a story; his style was as quietly conversational and wryly humorous as ever. It was just Mac talking, and if dates, facts and a bit of biological jargon crept into the tale, they only made it more interesting. *That is a good teacher,* she realized with admiration, noticing the raptness of his audience. And it was time to get out of here. She edged along the counter, then stopped as his eyes found her. Making an attentive face, she waited for that quizzical gaze to shift, which it did as Lucy asked a question. Sliding out of his line of sight, she tiptoed outside into singing darkness. *Hurry.*

Half an hour later Tey felt her way up the hill again, Mac's T-shirt clinging to her newly sweaty skin. No gate. No spiders, either, thank goodness, but the overwhelming and essential point was that there was no second gate; she'd bushwhacked the length of the fence and back making sure of that. So now what? Josh had looked bigger than she'd anticipated this morning. To get a sleepy, frightened and quite likely uncooperative child over that fence—silently… Always providing that she could steal him away from his bodyguard in the first place.... She sighed, then cursed heartily as her foot caught an unseen root. *How am I going to do this?* She'd told Lori to trust her. Trust her to botch it up was more what it looked like at the moment. *You can't. You cannot botch this up.* For there would be no second chance; Aston would whisk Josh over the horizon again if she made an attempt and failed, or worse yet, make good on his threat to lose Josh. *One try. That's all you get. You've got to do it right.* There had to be a better way than that fence; she would have to think. And right now she was too tired to think; it seemed as if she'd spent her whole life thrashing through guinea grass.

As she approached the main cabin, Tey could see through the screens that Gerry was perched on the speaker's stool now. So where was Mac? She ought to say good-night and thanks before leaving. But seeing her Jeep, she found herself irresistibly drawn toward it; Mac was going to give her a hard time about leaving, she suspected, and she had enough problems without his adding to the load. She put an indecisive hand on the fender.

"Going somewhere?" Mac drawled from the darkness of the passenger's seat.

"Good grief! Haven't you got anything better to do than sneak up on people?" Tey felt her heart drop back into place again.

"Sneaking? I was just sitting here having a cold beer and wondering where you'd wandered off to. I was about to go check the bat nets." He leaned out the window, his forearms crossed on the sill, and lifted a bottle an inch or so. "Have a sip?"

"Thanks." Tilting back her head, she let the beer trickle down her throat like cold fire. Overhead, she could see one big lovely star peeking down through the branches. Looking down again, she was suddenly aware that his lips had touched this glass only a minute before.

"Sorry I bored you with that lecture." Reclaiming his beer, Mac took a swallow, then handed it back again.

"You didn't." Rubbing the bottle absently across her cheekbone, she tried to see his eyes. "But I was so warm in there, I decided to take a walk to cool down."

"That's what you call this?" His forefinger touched the point of her collarbone, then dragged lightly across the very top of her breast; beneath his fingertip, the fabric was drenched.

Feeling as wet and steamy as her shirt, she caught his fingers as they smoothed down the inside of her arm. "Here." She smacked the icy bottle into his palm.

"Thanks," he said wryly.

"No, thank *you*." Moving around the Jeep, she climbed in beside him. "For everything. It's been a lovely day." And it had been, though not too productive. How was she going to—

"It's not over yet. Come have a drink and talk to me." He touched the back of her hand where it now clasped the gearshift. Brushing the soft, fine hairs on her forearm backward, his finger reached the inside of her elbow and circled; it trailed softly down again along the underside of her wrist.

Closing her eyes, letting that caress feather out from the point of contact like the waves from a stone dropped into a warm pool, she smiled. It wasn't talk he wanted tonight, or not just talk. She'd decided not to be serious about love anymore, after Brian. The Kenyon women were unlucky in love, and it all came from caring too much. Look at Lori... Look at her mother... But *unseriously*, what a fling he'd make! If it wasn't for Josh... Sighing, she opened her eyes. "I'm afraid it's over for me, Professor. I'm beat."

"It's tough work till you get used to it, trapping," Mac agreed, but he made no move to go. His fingers came to rest lightly, uninsistently, on the back of her wrist.

Leaning back in her seat, she simply savored their silence for a moment. Why did he make her feel so good? It was more than their undeniable attraction to each other, more than just the fun they had together. Somehow, things added up to more than the sum of their parts....

Mac's hands moved again. Strong fingers curled around her wrist, encircling its fragility as if he were measuring her for handcuffs. "I'm curious about something..."

Her pulse jumped and most likely he felt it. *Don't be curious, Mac. Please don't.* "Mmm?" she murmured warily.

Perhaps he'd caught the tone of that. "What's your middle name?" he asked after a second's hesitation.

Was that what he'd meant to ask? "Tey." She gave him a teasing smile.

"Tey? But—oh..." He grinned back at her. "So what's your first name?"

"Ah, now that's really a secret!" But that implied that she had other secrets, as well, didn't it?

Intent on her mystery, Mac didn't appear to notice. "Bertha?" he guessed.

"Worse than that!" She pulled her hand gently away from him, then wished she hadn't.

"Olivia?"

"Uh-uh. And I never tell anybody."

"But you can tell me," he coaxed, reaching up to brush a wisp of hair back from her cheek. "Your secrets are safe with me."

Their eyes held for a moment. *We're not talking about names,* she decided. *And yes, Mac, I believe you would guard my secrets for me. But these aren't my own secrets I'm carrying tonight.*

"Tell me your secret and I'll tell you one of mine," Mac wheedled, but somehow she knew this was the last time he'd ask.

And suddenly she wanted one of his confidences. Wanted all of them. "Gwendolyn." She wrinkled her nose.

"Gwendolyn?" Laughter quavered in his voice, but he held on to it. "Gwendolyn," he considered gravely, studying her while he pronounced it, as if she'd change to match the sound of it. "G. T. uh-Hargrove?"

She sniffed.

"You're right," Mac decided. "Tey..." He spoke it softly. "Absolutely unique, strong and soft all at once...it's you."

Say my name again like that! But she couldn't ask him aloud. "And your secret?"

Mac cupped his hands and held them out to her. "Which would you like?"

All of them. "You choose."

"Hmm..." Dumping the secrets on the seat between them, he rubbed his jaw. "That's harder...."

"What are you afraid of?" she prompted.

"What am I not?" he countered wryly, then after a moment of thinking silence, sighed.

"Hmm?"

"Well..." He bit a knuckle absently. "I could tell you I'm...scared of...waking one day, to find I'm old with nobody to love me..."

Incredulous, she stared at his face. *Mac, you haven't got a prayer of a chance of that!*

"Or...I could tell you that...all my friends seem to be having kids, and I'm scared—I wish I was, too."

She could see them in her mind's eye, as blond and vital as their father. The boy would carry mice to school in his pockets, and most likely the girl would, too.

"But that's too heavy for a first date," Mac concluded. "Okay...I'm afraid of snakes." He dropped an imaginary reptile in her lap.

Her first impulse was to sling it out the window, but this was Mac's snake. Mac's secret. Catching it just behind its head, she held it up to peer at it, nose to nose. "Lots of people are," she ventured finally, suppressing a shudder.

"Try bein' a zoologist who specializes in small, tropical mammals and not liking snakes!"

"Hip boots?" she suggested.

"Hip boots up to the ears!" he agreed fervently. "But that's too hot and not macho. Try heavy boots, constant prayer and tap dancin'."

Picturing him tiptoeing through the jungle, she had to giggle. "How'd it happen?"

His shoulders jerked in what was almost a shiver. "I was working down in this camp in Panama, and I was sharing a tent with a herpetologist—guy with a really sick sense of humor..." He shrugged again, nervously, then laughed under his breath. "Can I tell you this some other time, Tey? I don't like to tell this one just before bedtime."

She nodded in rapid agreement.

But the memory wouldn't quite let go of him. "What it all comes down to is: south of the Rio Grande, don't *ever* put your boots on without shakin' 'em out first."

They shivered together this time. "Ugh!" Dropping his snake out the window, Tey leaned out after it. "Go find a mongoose," she commanded and turned back to smile at him. *I've got to go. I could talk to you all night, but I'd better not.* "I've got to go, Mac."

Silently, his eyes asked her to stay.

She met his gaze squarely and smiled her denial. *There's a million reasons I can't, Mac.*

"All right." He half opened his door, then stopped. "What about tomorrow?"

What *about* tomorrow? She couldn't storm Aston's fence in broad daylight, couldn't just hang around outside his front gate. The beach where Josh and bodyguard swam was restricted. But then, the expedition had beach rights, David had said. That was the place the team swam most days, he'd said. What other choice was there? "I don't know..." she drawled finally. "Are there really mongooses on St. Matthew? I'm beginning to suspect I'm on an extended snipe hunt."

Mac laughed. "You've been on one of those, too? My cousin took me huntin' for snipe when I was eight. We carried baseball bats, I remember. 'Watch for their red eyes in the bushes,' he told me."

"I thought that was just a figure of speech!"

"More like a rite of passage, in my family. I chased him all the way home with my bat, once I figured I'd been had. Lucky for him his legs were longer.'' He laughed again quietly and slid out of the Jeep. "As to your question, there are mongooses on St. Matthew— cross my heart and hope to choke, there are. Come to-morrow and I'll prove it.''

"I've heard that line somewhere before.''

"Ah, but this time I mean it.''

"That's what they all say!'' She flicked on the headlights.

"You may not have figured this out yet, Ms Har-grove, but I'm not they.''

"I'm awfully glad to hear it,'' she said mockingly. "Split personalities are out this year, I hear.'' Shifting to neutral, she didn't bother to start the Jeep; it rolled slowly forward and began to gather momentum. "Night.''

"Sleep tight,'' Mac called after her.

She leaned out the window, glorying in the coolness of her speed-created breeze and the soft rush of gravel beneath the wheels. She'd start the Jeep at the bottom of the hill.

No, he was certainly not they, but he might be something else....

CHAPTER FIVE

"ANYBODY SEE IT?" Mac asked without looking behind him.

Squinting through the blaze of light, the members of Team Two shook their heads in sweaty silence. The A-3 marker had to be near, but the thickets of sea plum ahead were flecked with random leaves of orange gold; the markers didn't stand out as they had in the lush greens of yesterday's mountain site. And the coarse, cream-colored sand underfoot didn't help matters; the sunlight glanced off it to half-blind them. The air was as hot and bright as burnished metal.

"Those turkeys," muttered George, presumably referring to Team One, which had set the traps on this desolate point the day before. "No wonder they agreed to trade with us!"

It had been Mac's idea to trade sites today—to give Tey a look at another of the island habitats the expedition was trapping. And a new site was all she'd seen so far; traps one and two had been empty of all but the sun-dried bait. But he made no apology now. The sun turned his hair to spun gold as he scanned the scrub again.

"Is that—" Jean murmured just as Marty broke rank to forge off to the right.

"I've got it!"

"What's it doing over there?" George grumbled as they threaded single file through the brush after her. Mac had kept the team together to run the traps; it was the best way to avoid confusion and make sure no trap was overlooked. That was the cardinal sin, apparently.

Screeek!

"We've got one!" Marty cried. She plunged through a screen of beach plum and disappeared.

Reeeeek! It sounded like a Siamese cat being dipped into boiling water.

As the professor drew alongside, Tey shot him a doubtful look. "He doesn't sound very frightened."

"He's not," Mac assured her cheerfully. "Just hoppin' mad."

Hopping wasn't quite the word for the small, coffee-colored creature that moved back and forth in the trap. Fascinated, Tey joined the others in a circle around its cage. The mongoose looked like a small weasel, perhaps eight inches long. Its tail, nearly as long again, was fluffed like an enraged cat's. Stopping its sinuous prowling for a second, it glared up at them with red-tinged, feverish eyes. *Phffft!* It spat like a cat, then resumed its weaving exploration of the cage mesh.

"I take it that's mongoose for 'drop dead'?" Tey leaned down for a better look. "I can't believe he's not afraid of us!"

"You've got to remember that these guys are the thugs of the island," Mac drawled as he slipped the hook of a portable spring scale into one corner of the cage. "Most of 'em go through life without meeting one critter they can't invite home for supper." Lifting the trap, he studied the needle on the face of the scale. "A thousand and four grams." This was directed at

Jean, who nodded and scribbled it down on the clip-board she carried.

"Who's handling?" he asked as the mongoose gave its war cry and bounced off the ceiling of the trap. Grinning when no one leaped forward, Mac knelt by the cage. "All right." Accepting the cotton sack that David held out to him, he drew the mouth of it around the door end of the trap and twisted it tight. As the mongoose hissed and retreated to the far end of his cell, the professor lifted the door.

But the mongoose had no intention of crossing into the rumpled shadows that now awaited him; bobbing like a tiny prizefighter, he stayed where he was.

"I'll fix him!" Crouching at the back of the cage, Angie blew on the mongoose. Without a backward glance, he whipped into the pocket, and Mac gathered the mouth of the sack tight behind him.

"Got 'im." Gently he maneuvered the wriggling form until its snout was facing the neck of the bag. Wrapping thumb and forefinger around the back of the mongoose's shrouded neck, he lifted it off the ground. Tey knelt beside him. "Ms Hargrove?" Mac peeled the fabric slowly back from his captive, revealing the out-raged tail and two helplessly dangling, absurdly pink, back paws, the soft belly fur, the front paws grasping at air. "I'd like you to meet *Herpestes auropuncta-tus.*" The last fold slipped away, revealing a gaping maw lined with needle teeth. Brownish-red eyes gleamed wildly up at her. "The gold-spotted mon-goose." Mac cradled his other hand beneath the ani-mal's back and looked down at it with affectionate interest.

"Pleased to meet you, I think." Tey touched a front paw, and the mongoose hissed a foul-tempered reply.

While she watched, Marty covered the animal's eyes with a fold of the sack—"To keep him quiet," David explained. Those razor-sharp teeth were inspected by all and judged to be type one—young adult—and so noted in the field notes Jean was keeping.

On examination, the mongoose proved to be female. "It figures," George remarked, blithely ignoring the feminine scowls that turned his way.

"Not lactating." Mac looked up from her belly. "And now—" he glanced at Tey "—I seem to have left the tags in my pocket."

"Oh?"

"Left shirt pocket." He gave her an extravagantly innocent smile.

It could be worse, Tey decided resignedly. He could have chosen one of the front pockets on those snugly fitting jeans he was wearing again today. Standing, she braced one hand on his right shoulder. From behind, she ran her left hand down his shirt and into the designated pocket. Palm flat against the damp warmth of his chest, she could feel his heart thumping. Its soft cadence seemed to seep through her skin, shudder slowly up her arm. Her hand tightened on his shoulder and the beat accelerated. *Got to get out of here!* "I can't... There isn't any—" Her groping fingers touched bits of hardness. "Is this—"

"Yup," Mac agreed huskily as she pulled them free and backed away.

Face more than a little warm, she found herself holding a metal safety clasp on which were strung a collection of triangular metal clips, each with a number engraved along one flattened side.

"Thank you." David claimed them, chose one and read its number to Jean. Fitting it into the specially shaped jaws of a pair of pliers, he crouched beside Mac.

Marty was there before him with a leather punch. Carefully she slid the delicate, rounded ear of the mongoose between the jaws of the tool.

"Oh, no!" Tey protested, just as the punch made a snicking sound.

Above Marty's blond curls, Mac met her eyes. "It doesn't hurt much—honest. They don't have many nerve endings there."

"That's what fishermen say about worms!" But it had been she, not the 'goose, who had jumped when they did it.

"I expect it hurt you more than that, when your ears were pierced." Mac's eyes lingered on her earlobe for a moment, and somehow she knew he was touching her there in his mind.

Her own ears tingling pleasantly, she watched David slip a side of the triangular tag through the hole Marty had created. The point on one end of the tag fitted through an opening in the other end; by squeezing the pliers, David closed the triangle. With the point crimped over, it made a permanent earring.

"Stylish!" Mac decided, checking David's work. "She'll be the rage at the disco next Friday night." He glanced up at Jean. "Got everything?" At her nod, he set the mongoose on the sand. Rippling into the brush, she was gone between one blink and the next.

The team moved on, carrying the empty traps. "What good are the ear tags?" Tey asked as Mac fell back to walk beside her.

"This is a continuing study, remember. We're trying to learn things like life expectancy in the field, how many mongooses there are on St. Matt, how that var-

ies with habitat. And the sixty-four-thousand-dollar
question is, have they reached a stable population
density yet, or are they still multiplying?'' They paused
as they caught up with the others, who were milling
around the A-4 marker. George found the trap—
empty—and they trudged on. ''Knowing each time we
catch a mongoose if it's the same ol' mongoose they
caught last year, or a new one, helps us to estimate the
answers.'' Pushing a thigh-high, thorny branch out of
his way with the trap he carried, Mac held it aside for
her. ''You keep this all in your head?''

Startled, she pulled her gaze away from the play of
muscles in his forearm to meet his eyes. ''What?''

''I thought writers took notes?''

''Oh...I do. I write everything down each night.''
Oh damn, she didn't want to lie to him! But once
started, one lie followed the next like links on a chain.

''I see.'' Stopping, Mac nodded at the scruffy tree
they'd been skirting. ''Look there.''

A clump of green, strap-shaped leaves sprouted from
one branch of the tree. Standing on tiptoe, Tey saw the
spray of delicate flowers rising from those leaves and
sucked in her breath. Orchids—exquisitely tiny and
creamy yellow, with brownish centers spotted in pink
and red. Turning to Mac, she beamed her delight.

''I don't like to pick them,'' he murmured ruefully.

''No, don't—'' But he was reaching for them already.

Stopping just short of their stem, his fingers closed
precisely on thin air. But this imaginary stem appeared to be tougher than he'd expected; gentle tugs
turned to determined yanks. A final two-fisted wrench
attained the prize, and Mac's scowl of frustration
changed to smug satisfaction. Gravely, he held the in-

visible flowers to his nose and sniffed. "Not much scent to them, I'm afraid. They're all for the eyes." He held them out for her inspection.

"I've never seen anything so lovely," she agreed.

"I have." The air flowers poised in one hand, he smoothed the hair back from her ear. Face up-tilted, she stood hypnotized by his touch, by the nearness of his mouth to hers. But even as Mac fingered her ear, he changed his mind. "I guess corsages go on the chest, don't they?" Resting the bouquet just above her right breast, he started to pin it. "Or...maybe it'd look better here?" He tried it above her other breast.

"I—" Light and warm, his fingers rose and fell as she breathed. "I liked it better the first place."

"So did I," he agreed, misunderstanding her. He moved the orchids back to her right breast, rather than her ear. His fingers weren't so sure now; he seemed to be having trouble with the pin. The blackness at the center of those sky-blue eyes steadily widened as he frowned down at her breast. "I can't seem to—"

"Ouch! Watch that pin, Mac!" *Lord, what had made her say that?*

"I got you?" He looked stricken. "Did I draw blood?" Two fingers touched her skin where her collar parted. Delicately, almost fearfully, they slid beneath the fabric, searching for the imagined wound.

Her breast rose again with her breath, slowly, as if his hand was an unbelievable weight.

"Mac?" It was Marty's voice, coming from somewhere beyond their sheltering bushes.

"Damn." His fingers retreated softly, then lingered in the hollow beneath her throat. "I didn't hurt you?"

"Mac?"

Tey managed a shaky smile. *Keep it light.* "Not at all." Her fingers stroked just above her shirt, brushing petals made of air. "They're beautiful. Thank you."

That expressive, oddly tender mouth curled in a truly beautiful smile. "My pleasure, ma'am." He bent down to collect the trap he'd been carrying, then turned in the direction of Marty's voice. "Comin'!"

Two trap sites away, the volunteers were waiting for them. "We thought you'd gotten lost," Marty explained brightly.

"Found an epiphyte," Mac drawled.

"A what?"

"An orchid." He crouched by the trap. "By gosh, a recapture! Why didn't you say so?" A mongoose, larger than the last, stood quietly in the cage. A tag gleamed in its left ear.

"That's the last of them," Mac announced one hour and seven mongooses later as they collected the trap at the F-6 site. "Gerry said they couldn't find the F-7 marker yesterday, so there's no trap set for it."

"That's funny," George wiped a forearm across his brow. "I helped lay out this grid the first day we worked. F-7 was the one next to the road."

"Maybe it blew away."

Traps clanking against their legs and catching in the brush, the team stumbled behind Mac toward that winding track. They'd crossed it several times already, following the lines of the grid. Stepping gratefully out onto its barren ruts, Tey was completely turned around. The van might be either direction; she could only pray it was close. Eyes squinched to slits, she trudged after Mac's sweat-darkened back.

"There it is!" His hands full of traps, George nodded with his chin. A few feet beyond the road, the tip of a red-orange streamer lifted in the faintest whisper of a breeze. The rest of it was wind-snarled around the branch of a sea plum.

"But there's nothing there," Marty objected as he put down his load. She sounded as hot and cranky as Tey felt. "They didn't find it yesterday."

"So I'll fix it, and we can find it next time," the Southerner called over his shoulder. Reaching the marker, he stood on tiptoe to untangle it, then turned. He stopped short.

"What is it?" Mac set down his traps.

There was a trap at F-7, after all, complete with a mongoose who'd seen better days. The team looked down on its stiff-legged, bloated body in sick silence for a moment; as the smell hit them, most of them retreated to the road.

"But if they didn't set a trap here yesterday—" Jean looked confused.

"He's been here since last Saturday." Mac's voice had lost its soft drawl. His words were dry and hard as the sun-baked soil on which they stood. "Team One trapped here last week."

Five days. Without water. In this oven country. Light-headed, Tey shut her eyes for a moment. When she opened them, Mac was shaking the mongoose out of the trap. The small, rigid shape dropped into the bushes.

Silently, Mac led them back to the road. He didn't speak again till they caught up with the rest of the team at the van.

"Let's go swim!" Marty suggested as she brought Mac one of the gallon water jugs. She had already stripped off her T-shirt to reveal an expanse of pink curves and a scrap of bikini.

Removing the cap, he handed the jug on to Tey. She spilled almost as much as she drank; the water trickling down her cheeks and throat was blessedly icy. In the silence she could hear the waves thumping ashore. The beach must be just beyond that line of white dunes to the west.

"You can swim back at camp." Mac climbed into the van and waited, his face expressionless. After a moment, exchanging rueful glances, the volunteers scrambled aboard.

The drive back to camp seemed much swifter than their earlier outbound journey. The van slammed through the potholes that Mac had eased it through on the way in to the point. When they bounced out on the paved road, the van whirred for home with the hellbent haste of the island taxibuses. The lush fields of the central valley whirled past, punctuated with distant views of rows of royal palms, the dark green mountains, a gamboling herd of brown and white goats. They slowed for the wide, lazy streets of Thisted, but they didn't stop.

"You can let me out here," Marty announced as they reached the foot of the drive up to camp.

Mac nodded and pulled over. Most of the others slid out as well. "Coming swimming?" George asked as he climbed over Tey.

If she was anyone's guest here she was Mac's. But he looked in no mood for company at the moment. And this was what she'd come for, after all, to gain access to this beach. "Sure," she said casually. But she stopped by his window. "What about you?"

His face softened for a second. "Maybe later."

In uneasy silence, they watched the bus snarl away uphill. "I wouldn't want to be Gerry 'bout now," George declared finally. The team headed for the gate to the beach.

"Why? It's not his fault," Marty protested. "I bet Gerry didn't lose the trap."

"He was the boss. It's up to him to keep count of the traps." Producing a key from his pocket, George unlocked the gate.

Tey's waiting was over. Down the beach, a hundred yards or so, a red blanket gleamed in the shade cast by the palms. Two figures, one a broad-shouldered adult, the other so small as to be barely visible, sat facing each other, their eyes on the space between them.

A direct approach would never do. Heart thumping, Tey followed her companions down to the water. With pants legs rolled high, she sauntered through the shallows; it took all her willpower not to break into a run, but rather to stop occasionally to collect a shell or stare blindly out to sea. For all the attention the pair paid her, though, she might just as well have charged directly at them. The bodyguard moved some object across the blanket. Josh countered by snatching something to his shirtless chest. The man spoke—as near as she was now she still couldn't catch the words—and her nephew shook his head violently. The guard spoke again, unemphatically, and after a moment of frowning consideration, Josh set what he held between them.

It would have to be a direct approach, after all, Tey decided. They were too engrossed to notice her otherwise. "Which one are you going to chase, partner?" the guard asked as she came up behind him. On the blanket was spread a cloth checked in five-inch squares

of white and black. It looked homemade, as if someone had filled in a scrap of bedsheet with a felt-tip pen.

"That one!" Seizing the chess piece before him, Josh
brought it swooping down on his opponent's bishop.
"Gotcha!" He laughed—the rippling giggle of an excited child—and Tey stopped, her mind suddenly filled
with an image of Lori holding her Bogie up to a cage
full of rabbits. "Gotcha, gotcha, gotcha!" Josh
chanted, bouncing his chessman on top of his victim.

"There's just one problem, Josh," the man pointed
out. "How does a black bishop move?"

"Goes   blackity-blackity-blackity-black!"   Josh
glanced at Tey and back to the board again.

"Well, my knight was here, and your bishop was
there." The guard repositioned their pieces. Besides the
two in dispute, the chessboard was bare except for the
second bishop of either color. "Okay, let's see if you
can get my man and stay on the blackity-blacks at the
same time."

Josh   nodded   solemnly.   "Blackity-blackity-
blackity..." Reaching the black square closest to the
piece that waited on a white, Josh's bishop pounced
again. "Gotcha!"

Head bent, the man contemplated this misappre-
hension with such a thunderous silence that Tey
laughed aloud. "Who's winning?" she asked as he
turned.

That square, perplexed face broke into a grin. "Josh
is, hands down. He hasn't discovered the concept of 'ya
can't get there from here' yet."

"Never underestimate the power of logical thinking!" Folding her legs, she dropped down beside them.
"Mind if I watch?" she asked, now that he had no
choice.

"I need all the help I can get," he assured her. "You're one of Mac's gang?"

"That's right. Tey Hargrove." She held out her hand.

He didn't reciprocate. "I'm afraid I'm not shaking hands this week." Reversing his hand, he showed her the splint taped to his little finger. "I'm Bo—Beauregard Lee, and this is Josh, who's an expert hand shaker."

"Hi, Josh," she said casually. "I'm Tey."

Ignoring the hand she offered, he looked up at her with Lori's eyes. "I know." He bounced his bishop on top of Bo's long-suffering chessman again. "Gotcha!"

Tey swallowed carefully. Did he know? Or did he just mean—

"Josh, let's try it this way," Bo decided. "Let's see if I can catch *you*." Replacing the chessmen, he put a hand on his bishop. "Aha, I'm a white bishop," he announced in an evil, hollow voice. "And I'm going to go get that black bishop over there!" Lifting his piece, he began hopping it with deliberate menace toward Josh's waiting man. "Whitey-whitey-whitey—ummm, I can taste him already—whitey..."

Giggling in delicious terror, Josh grabbed for his man.

Bo caught his hand and held it. "No, Josh, leave him there. He's safe." Reverting to his bishop persona, he brought the bishop to the neighboring square. "What's this? The sucker's on a black square! I can't get to him! Arrgggh!" Quivering with rage, the bloodthirsty bishop leaned out from his square, but his feet stayed planted firmly on the white.

As entranced as the child, Tey watched while the muttering bishop hopped off to solicit help from his

partner, a specialist in black squares. The director of
this educational drama was a rather heavyset individ-
ual—not fat by any means—but comfortably solid.
Thirty, she guessed, or perhaps a year or two under
that. That squarish, pug-nosed face would look much
the same at fifty as it did now, but his short, grizzly-
brown hair and those wire-rimmed glasses added a few
undeserved years to the first impression he made.

"Okay, it's your turn, Josh," he was saying. "You
can run or you can chase my man, but you've got to
stay on the blacks."

"Blackity-blackity—" Skipping three squares at a
bound, Josh's rebel bishop leapfrogged across the
board—landing only on blacks—to finish feet-first
atop Bo's hapless chessman. "Gotcha!"

Frustration warred with hilarity in his opponent's
face. "Now that . . . was an interesting approach," he
said mildly.

"I got you," Josh reminded him.

"You sure did." The bodyguard ran one hand ab-
stractedly through his wiry hair. He squinted beyond
Tey's silent amusement and turned back to his charge.
"Hey, Josh? Did you see that coconut down there?"

"Where?" Josh stood.

"Way down thataway. There's a coconut. Do you
think you're big enough to carry it?"

"Sure!" Josh put down his lawless bishop.

"Well, if you can get it back here, I bet we could
crack it open," Bo drawled with a calculated indifference.

Josh was off and running. Breathing a sigh of relief,
Bo swung around to watch. "God bless the house-
wives, each and every one," he muttered. "How do
they ever do it?"

His hair still stood in rumpled points, reminding Tey of someone. Or maybe it was those brown, clever eyes. "Your son is a doll!" she said deliberately.

"My—" Bo smiled and shook his head, his eyes still monitoring the child's stumbling progress. "He's not mine. I'm just the baby-sitter and self-appointed tutor."

"Oh... Where are his parents?" And just how far did she dare pump him?

But Bo found nothing unusual in her question. "His father's off island on business right now. And his mother's somewhere in California. They're separated—divorcing." The bodyguard stood as Josh trotted down to the water's edge. "The other way, Josh," he called, waving the boy back toward the trees. "Just a little farther. That's right. Keep going."

So he knew that much of the truth, anyway. "The father has custody? That's a bit unusual, isn't it?"

He sat again, face still turned to his charge. "Not when the mother's not fit to—" His voice faded away and he shot her a guilty glance. "Not in this case," he amended, turning back to Josh.

Stop right there, she warned herself, *or at least change tacks.* So that was what Aston had told him; it figured. Where was Aston? And gone for how long? But she couldn't ask those questions yet. What *could* she safely ask?

Josh's wavering trot changed to a burst of speed as he finally sighted the coconut. He pounced on it and stood again, the dark bulk hugged to his chest.

"Gotcha!" Bo murmured with satisfaction.

Perhaps the angle to take was to ignore Josh. Put the focus on Bo. "Now how did you get a soft job like this, Bo?" she asked as they watched Josh's staggering return. "Getting paid to sit under a palm tree playing chess?"

His smile was wry as he glanced down at his splinted hand. "It's not always so soft."

It would do Mr. Kopesky and his aching jaw a world of good to hear that, Tey suspected. She stifled a grin.

"I just lucked into it," Bo continued. "A friend of a friend knew I was looking for a kid to experiment on, and a friend of his worked with Aston—Josh's father—and knew he needed someone to look after Josh. It couldn't have worked out better if I'd planned it."

If her hair were any shorter it would have been standing on end. "Experiment on?" Tey echoed weakly.

Bo laughed outright. "Geez, that does sound sinister! I'm working on a doctorate in early childhood education," he explained. "Experimenting with a method to teach children to read and write, using computers. It's something I got interested in while I was in Africa with the Peace Corps."

"Bogie, Bogie, Bogie..." Josh was approaching. Encumbered with the coconut, he couldn't skip, but he managed a triumphant sort of jigging, as he chanted his bodyguard's name. "Bogie, Bogie..."

But that wasn't his name, Tey realized with a jolt. She turned to stare at Bo as Josh dumped the coconut at his feet—just missing his bare toes. Josh was right. Bo did look exactly like his cuddly friend!

Beaming like a nearsighted teddy bear, Bo inspected the nut. "This is a beauty, sport! A veritable humdinger!"

"A what?" Josh cocked his tow head attentively.

"Hum...dinger. The best of the best. Now all we have to do is open the sucker."

"Hey, Tey!" Far down the beach, David waved an arm. Beyond him, the rest of her abandoned friends were straggling toward the gate. "Coming?"

"Be along shortly!" she yelled back, motioning him on. He nodded and turned uphill.

"Show Tey how you'd write coconut," Bo suggested as she swung back to the pair.

Eyes on his toes, Josh shook his head.

"Well, you're probably right." Bo smoothed the sand beside their blanket. "Coconut is pretty tough. It's probably a grown-up word. Let's see now... *Cuh...Oh...*" Tracing a large *C* and then an *O* in the sand, he ignored the child now hovering at his elbow. *"Coco..."*

"Coconut!" Josh exploded. *"Cuh-oh...cuh-oh..."* He added a lopsided *C* and an *O* to Bo's letters. *"Nuh...uh...tuh!"* he sounded out, looking a little less certain now. *"Nuh—"*

"That's right," Bo assured him. "You've got it."

"Nuh...uh...tuh!" Tongue clamped between his teeth, Josh completed the word in shaky capitals.

"Josh, that is super!" *If only Lori could see you now! By God, Lori will see you...soon. Very soon, Lori, I promise.* "Can you write 'Josh'?" she asked while Bo folded the blanket around the forgotten chessmen.

"Sure!" He didn't have to sound that out.

"Boy, I'm impressed!" Tey assured him truthfully as they started toward the gate, Josh clutching the coconut. After a minute, he toddled on ahead. "How many words can he spell?" she asked Bo in an undertone.

"He can spell anything he can pronounce, but it'll be spelled phonetically." There was more than a trace of pride in this announcement. *"Rough* would be spelled R-U-F, for instance. He wrote a story about a ruf, tuf tomcat yesterday."

"He's writing stories? I'd love to see one!"

But Bo didn't take the hint. "I'll try to remember to bring one next time we come to the beach. Will you be there tomorrow?"

"I think so." Yes. Come hell or high water, she would be. Somehow. She stopped as Bo let them through the gate. On the other side, he put a restraining hand on Josh's small shoulder while he checked for cars, then steered him across the road.

"Bogie-coco-coconut," Josh chanted contentedly. "Bogie-bo-bo-bobonut."

"How, by the way, do you crack a coconut?" Bo wondered.

"A hammer?" Mac would know. "Want some help with it?" she asked hopefully as they reached the estate drive.

Bo shook his head regretfully. "I'd love some, Tey, but that's one of the few disadvantages of this job. I'm not allowed to bring home guests." He looked embarrassed.

"But why?" she asked, knowing the answer perhaps better than he did.

Bo shrugged. "Don't know. I suppose my boss is a bit of a recluse. And there's another reason..." His voice trailed away.

"Well, what about coming out?" she asked jokingly, feeling her way through the hedge of his loyalties. "Surely you and Josh are given town leave once in a while, aren't you?"

Bo shook his head glumly. "Not really... Not since Switz—he's been tougher recently. I mean, I could go, as long as there's someone at the house to take charge of you-know-who here.'' He tousled the boy's silky hair and shrugged again.

"That's awful!" Truly awful. It would be so much easier if she could get them into town and then separate them. How was she going to snatch Josh out from under Bo's watchful eyes out here?

"It sure is," Bo agreed cheerfully. "But the pay's great. And the short one's good company." He drummed his fingertips idly on her nephew's head and grinned when Josh looked up at him. "And I get a week off for Christmas." Fishing in his pocket, he pulled out a ring of keys.

A lot of good that would do her! The line of credit on her charge card wouldn't last till Christmas, and Aston would surely return before then, as well. No, it had to be soon. Very soon. But not today, Tey admitted, swallowing a sigh. She ruffled Josh's hair and was rewarded with a shy smile. "Well, nice to meet you, Josh...Bo..." She backed away toward the camp turnoff. "I guess I'll see you around."

"If you go to the beach, you'll see us, believe me," Bo called after her. "It's the only game in town."

"Then I'll see you." Somehow. And trudging up the lane to camp, she could think of only one way.

BLAST ASTON and his rules! Bo thought. Aston was probably surrounded by women down in Rio—that must be why he'd left them here, come to think of it—and he couldn't invite a girl home to help him crack coconuts.

"Oop!" Josh dropped the coconut and Bo stumbled over it and nearly went sprawling.

"Careful, Josh!" The words came out close to a snarl. He stole a glance at the boy and found he'd caught the tone all right; his eyes had that wide, startled look that he usually saved for Aston. Damn. Crouching, Bo scooped up the coconut and held it out to his charge. "A coconut's a lethal weapon," he told him in a gentler voice—the words didn't matter much, it was the tone that counted. "Grenades and coconuts—you can't just go dropping them, Josh. You either do it on purpose or you hold your fire."

"What'sa grenade?"

Me and my mouth. "A toy for big boys. You want me to carry it?"

"Uh-uh."

"Okay, but hang on to it." Rising, he kept his hand on the child's shoulder for a little way. Most likely she was just being friendly, anyway. A nice, friendly sort, the way she'd come right up to them. A little...intense... Was that the word he wanted? Not really—it was more just a feeling he got, as if her casual smile was stretched tight over some stronger, bigger emotion. A bit like Mac maybe, someone who cared deeply and kept it under wraps. "You've got a great imagination," he said aloud.

Josh peered up at him.

"I feel a story coming on," he explained. "I'm going to write a story about a guy who cracks open a coconut and finds a princess. What are you going to write about?" He'd found the best way to keep Josh writing was to write along with him. Make it play, not work.

"Umm... I gotta think...."

"What about that lizard we saw on the tree this morning? The green one with the red throat? Do you think you could spell lizard?"

"Sure!"

CHAPTER SIX

HALFWAY UP THE HILL, she saw him coming. With that long, soft-stepping stride of his and his hair gleaming red gold in the late slanting sunlight, Mac was unmistakable at any distance. Heart bumping from the steepness of the road—and only from that, Tey assured herself—she stopped and let him come to her. An unbuttoned shirt flapped against his swim trunks, and the towel he'd slung around his neck framed a muscular, gold-hazed chest. His skin caught and reflected the red of that towel in a ruddy glow; her hand pressed to the hard swell of his pectorals would look almost white in contrast. Making fists of those tempted hands, she found her palms were tingling as she met his eyes.

"I saw the others come back without you," he explained. "I was afraid you might be swimming alone."

"No... just wading." Among other things.

"I'm going to take a quick dip. Want to come along?"

Yes. No. Not with his shirt unbuttoned like that; the view made it too hard to think. She could set both hands against his chest, drag them slowly down across his ribs. "Ahh, I'm awfully hot and sticky right now, Mac." *What was she saying?* "I think I need a shower." An ice-cold one. And perhaps a gag.

The line of his lips quivered and straightened as if with an effort. "All right. But don't run away before I come back, will you?"

"I thought...maybe I could buy you supper in town tonight?" *Wear clothes. I've got a proposition to make, and I don't need distractions.*

But Mac was shaking his head. Reaching out, he caught a lock of her dark, springy hair and looped it around his finger. "Could I have a rain check on that? I've been rantin' and ravin' and foaming at the mouth about responsibility for the past hour. I don't think Gerry would take it too kindly if I skipped out tonight."

"Oh..." Suppressing a shudder of pleasure as he tugged gently at her curl, she tried to reorganize her campaign.

"Why don't you eat with us?" he suggested. "There's always room for one more."

That was exactly what she'd been hoping. "If you're sure it's okay."

"I'm sure." He lifted the curl, held it tickling just beneath her nose and studied it critically. "You'd even look good with a mustache."

Laughing, she backed away from him. "Not my style." Her hair stretched like a dark and twisted chain between them and, for a moment, she thought he'd hold her there.

"Maybe not." He let her go. "See you shortly."

"See you." She backed away another step, then turned uphill. She could feel his eyes on her back till the trees gave her shelter.

An icy shower was what she needed, and that was just what she got; there was no hot water left at the main cabin. Changing into a pair of shorts and the last of her clean shirts, she rolled up its sleeves, gathered the shirttails and knotted them above her waist. The air was sultry and still tonight. Tey twisted her hair into a knot. Holding it at the back of her head, she inspected herself in the damp mirror. That would be coolest; all she needed was her barrette to keep it in place. And Mac must still have that, probably in the same drawer from which he'd taken her earrings.

From the chopping and kibitzing in the kitchen, it sounded as if Team One had a way to go on supper. Tey drifted outside and, after a moment's hesitation, padded downhill toward Mac's small cabin. Most likely, he'd still be swimming.

But he was back, she realized as she stepped up onto the deck; from beyond the dark screens she could hear the steady trickle of his shower.

So now what? Retreat to the main cabin, or wait out here to demand her property? There was no way she'd walk into his bedroom now. In the hibiscus bush below the porch, an invisible frog cleared his throat softly, tried out the first sweet cries of evening. No one took up the call and he stopped in midpeep, abashed by his own boldness. Caught by the velvety, gathering twilight, she sank into the hammock that hung beneath the eaves.

Against a lavender sky, the leaves of the encircling jungle were black and knife-edged. High up in this serrated mosaic, a firefly lit his frail lantern, and seeming to answer that signal, the light in Mac's bedroom switched on. Through the hammock's webbing she could see the bright rectangle of his open door. As if stepping onto a stage, Mac appeared in that doorway and stood buttoning his shirt; with his head cocked slightly, he might have been thinking hard or merely listening.

The light went out. *But he won't see me,* she told herself, lying very still as movement flickered beyond the screens. Heading for the kitchen, he passed within feet of her; she couldn't hear a footfall. The kitchen light went on. The refrigerator door opened, then closed and ice clinked against glass. Darkness swallowed the light, and then the screen door creaked.

If she didn't move, he wouldn't see her. Eyes on that tall approaching shadow, Tey didn't question why invisibility was important. But now he was looming over the hammock. It was time to make herself known and she couldn't do it, not and hold her breath at the same time.

A long leg swung up out of the darkness, and Mac sat astride her ankles.

"Hey!" she exploded on a released breath, whipping her feet out from under. "I'm in here!"

"So I see." Mac settled down gently between her calves. Leaning back, he swung his legs carefully up into the hammock. His feet settled to either side of her ribs, effectively pinning her in place. "I thought you were just a possum."

Tey wriggled backward, striving for a sitting position, and the hammock rocked ominously. "This'll never hold us both!" Turning, she put a hand to his leg and pushed.

He didn't move it. "Sure it will, if you'll be still." Ignoring that advice himself, Mac leaned forward. Two round, freezing shapes were pressed lightly to her bare stomach—glasses, she realized as her muscles contracted. "Gin and tonic or rum and tonic?"

So he'd known she was here all along. It figured. "Ahh, gin and tonic." Closing around one glass and the fingers holding it, her hand grasped sinewy warmth, icy smoothness.

"The other one," he murmured huskily.

"Oh. Thanks."

"*¡Salud!*" His glass clinked against hers, and he leaned back again.

Savoring the burning, bittersweetness of the drink on her tongue, Tey tried to ignore the rest of her body. Difficult. No, impossible. The sides of her feet tingled where they touched his shirt, and as that sensation climbed, it changed to long, shivering waves of pleasure rolling slowly up her thighs. It was astounding how vulnerable she felt with her legs spread this way; in the daylight such an arrangement would have been unthinkable. But if her body was symbolically open to him, her face and all its thoughts were cloaked in shadow. The anonymity of the dark balanced the intimacy of their bodies, and they swayed in an uneasy equilibrium.

But Mac wasn't content to leave it that way. "Talk to me."

"About what?"

"With your voice, I'm not sure it matters. Try the multiplication tables."

"What's the matter with my voice?"

"Nothing, it's seductive as mink sheets. Deep and dark and smoky."

"Oh." No one had ever said that before.

"How old are you, Tey?"

"Ninety-two, going on twenty-six." Tilting back her head, she took another icy swallow. Those first waves of awareness had changed to a warm, all-over feeling of floating.

"Good."

"Why's that good?" It would be so easy to slide her fingers around the underside of his calf, to feel the bunched muscles there. Instead, she reached overhead to hold on tight to the hammock strings.

"Well, it beats twenty-one or twenty-two, which is what I'd have guessed."

Tey snorted. "If you can't tell the difference between twenty-one and twenty-six, *you've* got to be ancient!"

"I'm thirty-four!" he protested.

Just right. "Ancient," she agreed with a grin he couldn't see.

A thinking silence was followed by soft laughter, and Mac dug a toe gently into her ribs. "Baby-face Hargrove cuts another one off at the knees!"

He wasn't going to be put off that easily, Tey admitted as she squirmed away from his toes—which simply pressed her against his other foot. "I thought I reminded you of your mother?"

The change of subject didn't lose him; she had the feeling they were on the same wavelength tonight. "Yesterday?"

Yes, when you kissed me. Tey rubbed her glass slowly across her lips. "Uh-huh."

"Well you did, sort of, in spite of the fact that she's nearly a foot taller and blond." Mac leaned down carefully to set his glass on the deck. "She always brings my dad a cup of coffee while he's shaving."

And then your dad kisses her, Tey completed the tableau mentally.

"I expect your parents have some rituals like that, don't they?"

"Maybe they did once, but my father left my mother when I was eight." *And she never got over it, not till the day she died. He was a jerk, and she never stopped loving him. Who says true love brings happiness?*

"I'm sorry." His hand closed gently around her ankle.

She shrugged and pulled her foot away, but his hand came with it. "We got along fine without him."

"Who's we?"

"L—my older sister, my mother, and I."

"Where are they now? In Boston?"

She shifted restlessly. "My mother died the year I graduated from college—heart failure. And my sister's ... out west."

"So you're on your own," Mac concluded quietly. His hand slid caressingly down the top of her foot to her toes. "Or are you?"

"Meaning?" she asked, though she knew very well.

"I'm asking have you got a lover, possum."

"Not at the moment." *And don't need one, Mac, don't need one in my way, at the moment. If I did ...* "What about you?" she asked as casually as if they were comparing mileage on their cars.

His fingers laced between her toes in an odd and endearing hand-to-foot clasp. "Not at the moment. There's been nobody ... special ... since my divorce."

So that explained it. There was no way this one could have made it to his thirties without someone grabbing him. But what had ever possessed her to let him go? "How long ago was that?" she asked hesitantly.

"'Bout two years." Now it was his voice that had gone remote. Swinging one leg out of the hammock,

Mac slowly disentangled himself and somehow stood without dumping them both. "Want one more of the same?"

"If you'll make it weaker, sure."

"One feeble G and T comin' up." The screen door squeaked behind him.

"Oh, and Mac?" she called after him. "Have you still got my hair clip?"

"Hmm? Oh, yeah. I do."

Eyes closed, her body floating and swaying gently in the hammock, Tey listened to the frogs. The chorus was in full cry by now, the black velvet air alive with their counterpoint. The screen door complained again, and her body rippled in sensual anticipation. *Of what?* she chided herself.

"My barrette?" she asked as Mac set the glasses down on the deck.

"Right here." He moved to stand beside her. "Don't know why you want it, though." Sliding slowly into her hair, his hands framed her face. "It's nicer all fluffed up around your face like this. Like a cloud." His fingers combed into the silken stuff, spreading it out, tugging gently at her scalp.

Think of Josh, think of Lori, don't think of how your body's responding. "Keeps it out of my eyes," she murmured in a drugged, husky whisper.

"It'll just get caught in the hammock strings." One hand curled around the back of her neck, while his other pulled the clip from his shirt pocket. "Don't wear it tonight." Slowly, deliberately, Mac tucked the barrette into the breast pocket of her shirt.

Arching her back as that slow, teasing stroke dragged across her waiting nipple, Tey sighed deeply, contentedly. Tilting her head lazily back against the palm of his hand, she stared up into his shadowed face with half-closed eyes. Warm and gentle, his fingers shaped to her breast as his mouth covered hers. Eyes closing, suspended in space, she could hear her own heart adding its bass to the song of the tree frogs. Her body seemed to be shimmering, throbbing along with that sound, all her senses spiraling slowly inward around the insistent and deepening stroke of his tongue. Meeting that soft exploration with her own, Tey found that the hand cupping her breast was not enough; she needed more than that—she needed friction.

Mac dragged his mouth away with a breathless laugh. "I'm goin' to break my back like this, darlin'. Let me—" Swinging a leg over the hammock, he stood astride her, his taut thighs gripping her waist. His fingertips feathered delicately, restlessly, across her face, her throat, her shoulders.

Lord, what were they doing? What was *she* doing? She hardly knew this man. As his hands claimed her breasts, Tey captured his wrists. "Mac—" And then what? To know what to say, she had to know what she wanted. And all she knew at this moment was that this felt so right. So right. Beneath her fingers, his blood surged in a silent, thundering echo to the beat of her own heart.

"Must be in his cabin." A woman's voice reached them faintly, but all too clearly, from the hillside above. A screen door—the main cabin's—banged open.

"Damn!" Mac whispered emphatically.

"Mac?" the woman yelled. It sounded as if she were approaching.

"What's up, Lucy?" he called. Obviously meant to be casual, his words ripped out on an unexpectedly deep and ragged note, and Mac groaned under his breath. Laughing silently, Tey lifted his hands off her breasts.

"Suppertime! If you don't come up soon, there's not going to be any left!"

"Thanks... I'll be right up." He looked down at Tey again. "Thanks a lot," he added in a low growl. "The goddamned pleasures of communal living!" Balancing himself by spreading a warm hand on her bare stomach, Mac swung his leg over the hammock again. And kicked one of the glasses he'd left on the deck. "Damn!"

Laughing aloud this time, Tey sat up and quickly got her feet on the ground—where they should have stayed all along. Was it Lucy's interruption that was bothering him, or the fact that she'd called a halt to the lovemaking the moment before that interruption? Standing, she pulled back her hair, twisted it into a knot and pinned it off her neck while Mac watched. "Want me to wait down here a few minutes before I follow you?"

Mac shook his head. "They're all adults...or so they say. I don't ride herd on them. I don't expect them to ride herd on me." His hand curled around the back of her neck, urging her forward.

But this had been a mistake. She hated to ask favors after letting him touch her like this. If Mac concluded that she'd been softening him up, offering herself as payment for what she'd yet to ask, she was going to be ill. Shaking her head gently, Tey backed away a step.

His hand dropped away. "Come on, then." If there was irritation in that quiet voice, she couldn't detect it, and Tey felt a sudden fierce surge of liking. And an answering surge of loathing for herself. To use him this way...

"How's the writing comin'?" he asked as he guided her toward the boardwalk.

Here was the opening she'd been waiting for. She didn't want it now. Not yet. It was too soon after their touching. But then, would she get another chance tonight? *Think of Josh, dammit, and stop being so squeamish!* "Well, I'm only taking notes so far, but I think there's real material here, Mac."

"For what kind of article?" Catching her hand, he preceded her, lifting the clutching branches and vines over her head as they walked.

"For a book, actually, I've decided. For young adults. They're interested in animals at that stage, and outdoor adventure, exciting careers. I think this is a natural. What do you think?"

"I think I'll try and remember tomorrow, while I'm chopping rancid fish for bait, that I'm in the midst of an exciting career."

"Seriously, Mac! Ouch!" She stopped short as a vine caught her hair.

"Well, seriously, it sounds like a good idea." Turning back, he moved her hands aside. "It's the outdoor adventures that this kid goes for." His face nearly in her hair, he separated her deftly from her crown of leaves. "And the wildlife." His lips brushed lightly across her cheekbone. Were gone even as she looked up in protest. "Have you taken enough notes to write a book yet?"

"No, of course not. I'm afraid it'll take more research than I can do in just a day or two, so I was going to ask you—" *Oh, dammit, Mac, why can't I just tell you the truth? Right.* She answered that herself, silently. *Professor McAllister, may I just use your expedition as my base of operations while I stage a kidnapping?* He'd go for that, wouldn't he?

"If you can hang around with us for a few more days and take notes?" His hand on the door to the main cabin, Mac stopped and smiled down at her.

"Well, more than that. I'd like to see this expedition through from the inside out. Could you use another volunteer?"

"Personally?" His expression said it all, but that sexy, devilish grin faded to a look of consideration. "But I'm afraid from the perspective of project head, I can't just offer you a free berth, Tey. Not when everyone else has paid to be here."

She let her breath out slowly. "Can you take a check, Mac? With the understanding that it won't be good till I get back to my bank to cover it?" Margie would loan her the money, if necessary.

He gave it his best cowboy drawl. "Ah reckon we can trust you, ma'am." Opening the door, he ushered her in before him. "So welcome to the campfire, Ms Hargrove!"

The kitchen was crowded with the dishwashing crew and a hearty few coming back for third helpings. Mac whisked a serving bowl out from under George's descending spoon. "That's okay, George—we can serve ourselves." He split the last clump of macaroni and cheese and raked half onto Tey's plate. "Salad?"

"Please." Accepting the end of a loaf of bread that George was now passing with an ironic bow, she tore it in half. "Bread, Mac?"

"With lots of butter."

From the end of the counter where she was mixing a drink, Marty turned her way. "Fast work, Tey!"

It was the first time the woman had addressed her by name. Balancing a pat of butter on a knife, Tey looked up, smiling. "Huh?"

"You certainly hit it off with Bo, back there," the blonde observed pleasantly. "At the beach."

"Oh..." *And butter doesn't melt in your mouth, does it, sweetie?* She set the knife down deliberately. "Yes, he's a nice guy." Turning, she balanced the hunk on Mac's plate and looked up to find he hadn't missed a word of this exchange. The easy pleasure of a moment before had been replaced by a look of not quite shock, certainly not hurt—surprise, that was it. It shaded into wary blankness as their eyes met.

"Nice guy?" Marty exclaimed behind her. "He's a doll!"

Subtle, Marty. Really subtle. But she could feel her face warming in spite of her contempt—perhaps because of it. Because of that and her guilty conscience. To have this jealous ninny see through to her real purpose in being here... Was it that obvious, her interest in Bo? And far more important, could it have been obvious to Bo that that had been more than just a chance and friendly encounter at the beach? Surely not!

And in the meantime, Mac was still appraising her flushed cheeks with that look of almost scientific objectivity. As if he hadn't seen her before. Wheeling away from his inspection, Tey collected the butter knife again and took a vicious swipe at her own chunk of bread. *What did you expect, Mac? That after one kiss—okay, two—you'd own me?* Brian had been like that toward the end, ridiculously possessive, absurdly jealous. It had been as silly as it was painful.

"Tea?" he asked at her shoulder, his voice quietly neutral.

"Please." She was making a mountain out of Marty's nasty little molehill, Tey decided, following Mac into the common room. But something had changed. The sense of connection and trust they'd been building slowly between them was gone. Mac was unfailingly polite, but he devoted himself primarily to a technical discussion with Gerry, who sat down on his other side. Or perhaps he was simply being politic, mending fences with his second in command after this afternoon's chewing out. Perhaps it was no more than that. But the sparkle had fled from the evening somehow. Tey made halting conversation with Jean, who was nursing a cup of coffee as if she had nothing else planned for the night.

"Ladies?" David came up behind them. "I've decided that tonight's the night for our first game of Trivial Pursuit. I've got the Hoffmans and Vivian, and if I could recruit you two—"

Standing, Tey shook her head. "Some night I'd love to, David, but tonight, I'm pretty pooped." Collecting her empty plate, she drifted toward the kitchen. Mac didn't even look up. Suddenly she was not only dog-tired but depressed. What was she doing here? Josh might be only down the hill, but he might just as well be in Arabia, for all the good she was accomplishing.

A long arm reached past her cheek to swing open the cabin door for her. "Heading back to the hotel?" Mac asked quietly.

"Yup." And tonight he didn't invite her back to his cabin for a drink, she noticed. Not that she'd have gone....

"You ought to check out of the Dolphin in the morning so they don't charge you for tomorrow night. There's a sort of couch at the end of this porch, away from the kitchen, that you can have." He jerked a thumb over his shoulder at the main cabin. "I'll rustle you up some sheets and a blanket by tomorrow."

"Thanks." An hour ago, he'd have offered her half of his bed—jokingly—but he'd have offered. Well, at least their agreement was still on; that was what counted, after all. It might be a roundabout way to her small nephew, but it was the only way she'd figured so far.

Mac shut the Jeep's door behind her. What had come over him? With her hand on the ignition key, Tey turned to study his face. No clue. He looked as somber as she felt. "Night, Mac."

His mouth twisted suddenly. "Night, possum." Reaching out, he smoothed one fingertip along her lips.

His hand dropped away before she could kiss it—had she even intended to? Like a shooting star, the impulse was there and gone so suddenly that it might never have been. "Night," she repeated without looking at him. If he replied, the engine shut out the sound.

LOUNGING ON HIS BED, his shoulders supported by two pillows stacked against the wall, Bo looked up from his book and listened. Had he heard something? Wasn't the frogs; your mind shut them out in no time. He turned suddenly and scanned the wall. No, no chameleons sneaking up on him, or worse yet, one of those granddaddy-of-all-roaches. Something outside on the window screen, maybe. "Just stay out there," he warned it, glancing at the black square with its drifting, gossamer curtains. Since he'd spent two years in Africa, his ideas on the sanctity of life had contracted sharply to exclude the insect world.

He looked down at his book again. "The mean vocabulary of the preliterate three-year-old..." "Why can't you guys speak English?" he growled. Shutting the text on his thumb, Bo stared at the white-washed wall across the room. In the lamplight, the plaster glowed a warm, rough golden. Shining through the curtains when they belled out into the room, the light threw shadows across the wall, making rippling, translucent creatures that capered and beckoned and vanished as he watched.

His chest lifted and sank again in a long sigh. What would it be like to have someone here? Just to be able to say, "Look at the wall. Isn't that beautiful?" Somebody who wouldn't laugh if he said that?

After marking his place in the book, he stretched across to deposit it on the bedside table. *Should I invite her to come to town?* Or would that be rushing things? Lord, he'd agonized over exactly the same questions with Janie Ashwood, back in tenth grade. Didn't a man ever make progress? Most men were married by twenty-nine; they had wives, mortgages, flea-bitten collie dogs, kids on the way. What was wrong with him?

Rolling stones gather no moss, he reminded himself wryly. Checking the floor for critters, he swung his legs off the bed. Backpacking around Europe, those two years in the Peace Corps, then grad school—Anna had nearly gathered *him* there, but that would have been all wrong. That kind of moss a man could live without.

Without rising, he tugged his shirt from beneath his belt. *I need a woman.* Pulling the T-shirt over his head,

he got a good whiff of it. *What you need is a shower!*
Wadding it into a ball, he lobbed it into the basket in
the corner. *And a woman.*

But not just any woman… He could almost see her,
all but the face… She was a shape as substantial, as
unholdable, as those shadows on the wall… The soft,
sunny hair curling around that unimaginable oval.
Softness, kindness, intelligence… Someone who
needed him. Was that too much to ask?

Maybe. His shoulders rose in a tight shrug. It never
paid to think late at night. Not by yourself, anyway.
Now where the hell were his pajamas?

"Mmmmmma?" The wavering, sleep-choked cry
carried clearly from down the hall, snapping his head
around.

Oh, no, Josh. Another one? His slippers—where?
There—jamming his feet into them, he headed out the
door.

"Mommie, where's—*Mommie*?"

*That bastard back in Switzerland. I should have
punched his lights out!*

"Mmmmmmmmm!"

Someone should punch Mrs. Aston's lights out! he
thought, groping for the light switch in the hall. *Lady,
if you could hear him right now, I wonder how proud
you'd be of yourself?* Careful not to rattle the door-
knob, he swung the door open gently.

"Mommie, where's Bogie?"

"As if she would know!" he growled under his
breath. Padding across the room, he sat on the edge of
the bed. "I'm right here, partner."

CHAPTER SEVEN

"THE TAXI BUSES STOP over there." Mac pointed to a building across the square. "Make darn sure that the fare back to Thisted is a dollar before you get aboard. Most of these guys moonlight as taxi drivers when they're not driving the scheduled runs, and if they charge you the tourist taxi rate, it'll cost you twenty for the same ride in the same van."

"Yes, Papa," Marty chanted dutifully as she followed George and three other volunteers out of the van. "What about white slavers?"

"You tell George that, as head of this expedition, I'm co-brokering. I want fifty percent of whatever he gets for you." He grinned as she stuck out her tongue and slammed the sliding door shut. "And God help 'em!" he murmured, watching the group pick its way through the mud puddles and the darting traffic.

The rain had stopped just as they reached Julianasted. Above the pale yellow buildings that edged the harbor, the clouds gleamed pearly gray; an early morning tropic sun would be gnawing at the other side of them. To the west, toward Thisted and the camp beyond, the sky was still an ominous, swirling purple; so there was no reason to feel guilty, Tey reminded herself while the professor parked the van. Mongooses don't hunt in the rain, Mac had explained when she'd arrived in camp that morning. Neither, presumably, did bodyguards take their charges to the beach, so there'd been no reason not to join this foray into town.

Besides... "Now what did you need help with?" she asked Mac as they sauntered down to the water. His mood of last night had vanished; he'd been cheerful but a bit impersonal on the drive into town. But then they hadn't been alone till now.

"Shopping." Stopping on the concrete walk that rimmed the side of the harbor, Mac scanned the fleet of sailboats anchored there as if his prospective purchase might be nautical. "It just hit me that it's my youngest sister's birthday next week. I've got to get something in the mail today."

"What's she like?" The same breeze that held the boats to bobbing attention was combing through the palms in the green little park at their backs. As Tey watched, the wind ripped a gash in the clouds; sunlight poured through, turning the cobalt blue waters to outrageous turquoise for one gleaming second. Far out, a necklace of white marked the reef that cut off Julianasted's harbor from the open sea.

"Betsy?" Touching her arm, Mac drifted on toward town. "She's the driver in the family. My other sister and I just cruise through life, with detours to smell all the roses. Betsy's the empire builder—a stockbroker in New York. If I ever get rich, it'll be because I send Betsy all my spare cash and she invests it in pork-belly futures or God knows what-all."

"Sounds like quite a girl." Odd how decisive he was in most ways, and then to entrust his kid sister with his finances... That showed either supreme indifference to money or supreme confidence—the certainty that he'd always be able to make his way whether the bottom dropped out of the pork-belly market or no. Somehow she suspected it was the latter. She tried to imagine Brian entrusting his financial future to another—and a woman, at that—and failed. He'd been better at supervising than entrusting.

Winding their way through lush green and shaded alleys, staying always near the water, they entered the historic district. Julianasted was a town of cool stone, its low two- and three-story buildings constructed of lacy gray coral block, or whitewashed or yellow stucco. It was a town of shadow, built to withstand the tropic sun and the sudden downpours while it welcomed the cooling trade winds; the upper levels of the blocklike buildings often overhung the first, providing covered galleries that opened to the street through graceful colonnades. The floors above were also galleried, or pierced by arching, unscreened windows.

It was a town geared to tourism, its small shops bright with coral necklaces, seashells, T-shirts, watercolors. A shop front full of polished wood animal carvings caught Tey's eye, and she grabbed Mac's hand to stop him. "Would she like something like that dolphin?"

"Maybe." He studied it critically. "Let's have a look at it."

On closer inspection they decided it was too heavy to ship airmail. While Mac patiently admired the antelope and then something that might have been a goat that the salesclerk brought forth, Tey scouted the cluttered aisles. On a shelf near the door, a brown furry shape crouched among some conch shells. Smiling, she lifted it down. The mongoose wasn't stuffed as she'd first thought; soft fur had been sewn around something hard—a core of wood perhaps. His tail was properly puffed, however, and his expression something between indignant and pugnacious. "Screek!" She feinted the toy at Mac's nose as he loomed up beside her.

"Reckon I've been working too hard, Doc," he drawled, eyeball to beady eyeball with the toy. "I see mongooses everywhere...in the shower...in the best shops in Julianasted.... Last night I was in the middle of this *fine* X-rated dream, and damned if a mongoose didn't come sit on my chest and tell me to cut that out. What should I do?"

"Take three aspirin," she lisped on behalf of the mongoose—in what she hoped was a suitably Freudian accent, "und come lie down on my couch."

"Lie down on your *what*?" he repeated in dazed delight as his eyes shifted to her.

"Couch," she enunciated precisely, and bit her lip to stop the laughter.

"Oh." He sounded like a polite child receiving the news that there is no Santa Claus.

Her cheeks were a bit too warm. She looked down at the mongoose. "That's not real mongoose fur, is it?"

Mac ran a finger along the toy's back. "Nope. I'd say that's real, cuddly bunny fur. That make you feel better?"

"Brute." She checked the price tag on the mongoose's belly. Affordable. It hadn't the comforting squishiness of a stuffed animal, but all the same, she knew someone who might like it.... "I'll take him," she decided, turning to the clerk.

Prowling on, they ventured into an arcade—a square block of shops all opening onto a central courtyard. Tey found a stationery store and bought two spiral-bound notebooks and a couple of ball-points.

"What are those for?" Mac wanted to know.

"I filled my last notebook last night," she lied, hating herself. "These are for notes."

"I see." Studying the shops ahead, Mac nodded to one and caught her arm. "Now this looks like what we want!"

Mac's discovery was a boutique that specialized in Indonesian batik fabric. Racks of brilliantly dyed blouses and swimsuits beckoned from every side.

"What's this?" Tey wondered, fingering the vibrant scarlet of a long rectangular piece of fabric. Stylized hibiscus blossoms in turquoise and yellow were stenciled across it. "A tablecloth?"

"That's a java wrap," the elegant, dark-skinned woman attending them explained. Removing it from its hanger, she held it up for their inspection. A simple seam joined the two long sides of the cloth for most of its length, creating a tube. The last foot at each end of the seam was left unsewn. "You just slide inside and knot these two corners above your breasts. Or around your hips, if you want a skirt. It's like a pareu, but with a slimmer silhouette."

"Try it on," Mac suggested.

"I'm afraid it's not in the budget." She'd stacked up the debts on her Visa account this past week, jetting back and forth across the continent; it was imperative that she leave herself enough credit to buy two one-way tickets to California. And who knew what other expenses she might incur before she'd won this game? But that scarlet was gorgeous.

"Well, would you model it for me, anyway, possum? This might be just the ticket for Betsy."

In the dressing room, she stripped to her bikini briefs and stepped into the tube. Against her thighs the cool cotton felt soft as silk. Knotting two corners above her breasts in front, Tey stopped to study herself in the mirror. *Not bad,* she had to admit. It was an utterly graceful, incredibly feminine style; below the knot, the cloth fanned out in smooth, clinging folds to frame her slender hips. Through the slit at the bottom of the seam, her thighs glowed brown, then disappeared as the fabric swayed. In back, a series of looping folds created the softest suggestion of a bustle, then molded her hips like a second skin. As light and loose as it was, it was the next best thing to being naked—better; it added vivid color, suspense—would the wrap stay up or would it drop at her first hiccup?—and promise; that big, simple knot in front was all that stood between her and . . .

"Let me guess," Mac drawled from beyond the dressing room curtain. "You've bumped into a bat net and you're too shy to tell me."

"Wise guy." She edged out from behind the drape.

He fell back a step, as if he'd been slapped. Blue eyes widened, then stroked slowly across her bare shoulders and down. He backed away another step.

"Well?"

"I think I'm 'sposed to beat on my chest. Or swing from the chandelier, but I'm afraid I'm having a heart attack. Do you know CPR?"

"You like it?" No one had ever looked at her like this before. She'd stand there all day if he kept on looking like that.

"Do I like..." Mac shook his head, as if words failed him at this absurdity. "Turn around. I think I can take it."

"Get this for Betsy!" she commanded as she turned. "Any woman would love this."

Mac shook his head dreamily. "Uh-uh. This'll be for someone else."

She couldn't let him give her something like this, just couldn't. But, Lord, did she want it, and from him.

"This'll be for Betsy's boyfriend," Mac declared firmly. "I'll send Betsy a card, or something."

Aaaagh! Feeling the blush rising up from just below the knot on her breast, she nodded stiffly and ducked behind the curtain. Another second and she'd have been making an acceptance speech!

Ignoring the reddening image in her mirror, she peeled out of the wrap and hung it on the hook outside the dressing room.

"Knock, knock," a beguiling male voice chanted from the other side of the curtain.

To heck with him. She reached for her brassiere.

"Knock, knock," he tried again after a long pause.

And he'd stay there till she answered, wouldn't he? "Who's there?" she responded grudgingly.

"Doncha!"

Her lips quivered at the laughter in his voice. "Doncha who?"

"Doncha-think-it's-time-you-got-a-bathing suit?"

His hand pushed around the edge of the curtain to wave a hanger seductively.

The bits of cloth dangling from the clips were a rich purple sprinkled with tiny blue-green and lavender flowers. Orchids. "You call that a bathing suit? I've got hair ribbons wider than that!"

"Most modest one they've got. Honest."

With a sigh of resignation, Tey accepted it. He was right. She needed something for the beach. But no way would she model this for him, not if he got down on his knees outside the curtain.

"Tey? While you make up your mind, I'm going to run Betsy's present over to the post office. I'll be back in fifteen or twenty."

Ouch! Humiliation complete. "Take your time," she mouthed silently at the mirror. And crossed her eyes for good measure. So he didn't even want to wait and see it.

It was closer to half an hour later when he met her at the door of the boutique. "What'd you get?" He nodded at the package she was stuffing into her shoulder bag.

"Bow tie." Sweeping around him, she stopped on the pavement. Where to now?

A big hand on her shoulder turned her gently to the left. "Did you get the purple one?"

"There was this fetching little number in puce and polka dots. I couldn't resist it." Actually, she had bought the purple bikini, after trying on half a dozen maillots. Mac had lied about it, however; it was not the most modest suit in the store, but the most daring. It had a nice cut, though. Proper attire for an adventuress.

"Where are we going?" she asked after a few minutes' silent walking.

"You hungry yet?"

"Not really."

"Well, come watch me eat, then." He led her down a green, shady alleyway to a small bar with a few outdoor tables arranged along the stone edge of the harbor. Having ordered twice as much food as he needed, he slid the plate of conch salad in front of her when it arrived. "Try this."

Marinated in a peppery vinaigrette, the conch was fresh, delicious and rubbery. "Conch always is," Mac assured her, helping himself to a forkful. He fed her bites of his fried rockfish sandwich, holding the bun for her as she bit into it. Her lips grazed his fingers, and their eyes met and held above it till she retreated and looked for her napkin. *This is so different.* So different and yet so good. Brian had never liked to share food off his plate. This man seemed to share everything.

He shared bits and pieces of his life with her while they lingered over coffee—told her of his graduate work with coatimundis in Arizona, of collecting bats in Panama. How much fun it was to teach college freshmen; how he had to tease and beguile and bully them into thinking for themselves. How exciting it was to discover a "good 'un," who might someday contribute something to his field.

And Mac coaxed words from Tey, as well. She didn't want to talk of Lori and her troubles, but she told him about growing up in Boston; she told him about her job, of working with the brilliant, often hilariously obsessive characters who could speak computer, but not English, and how she translated their programs into user manuals that mere mortals could comprehend.

"You make it friendly," Mac decided, and caught her napkin as the trade wind snatched it away.

"I make it friendly," she agreed, accepting the napkin back from him. His blue eyes were friendly and so much more. *Josh, remember Josh?*

But Mac was consulting his big diver's wristwatch. "'Fraid I've got to get back to camp, possum. It's my day to collate field notes. Want to tag along, or would you rather come back later on the taxi bus?"

So much for her jaunt into town. There was so much more they could have explored: that neat little fort painted an astonishing yellow ocher that loomed over the harbor—she'd noticed it when they walked through the park. Or that shop that specialized in imported, duty-free gemstones. And they hadn't inspected the boats properly yet, but it wouldn't be as much fun without him. Looking over her shoulder, she checked the sky. Clearing all over. Bo and Josh were probably at the beach already. Her shoulders lifted in a silent sigh. "I'll come with you."

But they didn't take the direct route back. Halfway home, Mac turned off to the right onto a lane not much wider than the van. Winding and swooping through lion-colored pastures dotted with low, spreading, flat-topped trees, they headed north. Toward the mountains. Leaning out the window, she unclipped her hair and let it blow in the hot wind. "What are those trees, Mac?"

"Acacias. Looks like Africa, doesn't it?"

Exactly what she'd been thinking. She darted a startled glance at him. *You mind reader!* Or maybe they just thought alike.... "I always wanted to see Africa," she murmured wistfully.

"You, too?" His lips curled in the faintest of smiles, Mac was intent on navigating an unbanked curve. "And these are mahogany," he added, returning to the botany lesson as they hummed up a flickering tunnel of shade. The massive trees to either side were clothed in a scruffy, ragged bark that belied the solid red beauty of the wood at their hearts.

"And where are we going?" she turned to ask him.

"We're taking the scenic road home. You can't write about St. Matthew if you haven't seen this."

Climbing into the green, knobbly hills, they passed rows of roofless, barracklike structures built above a valley. Their walls were a sun-bleached coral block the color of old bones. "What are—were—those?"

His lips tightened. "Slave quarters."

Slaves to work the cane fields, of course. She shivered and turned to stare back at them. "When were they given their freedom?"

"Guess you could debate whether they were given their freedom or they took it. There was an uprising in 1851. Not much bloodshed, but some burning of the cane fields and the planters' Greathouses. The Danish governor made the freedom proclamation from Thisted."

"I see." They topped the ridge, leaving the ruins and the past behind like cloud shadows across the valley. Crimson hibiscus gleamed in the ditches. The trees were closing in as the road angled up into the foothills. Rounding a bend, Mac slowed the van. A dark-skinned boy—not much older than Josh—straddled a bareback dun mare. The red colt tagging free at her heels bolted. Bucking for the fun of it, his switch of a tail on high, he capered across the road ahead of them. Laughing, they returned the child's wave.

Pavement gave way to orange dirt and still they climbed—in lowest gear now. Looking back, Tey could see the south side of the island. Against a backdrop of pristine blue, the giant refinery along the coast looked like a dingy Emerald City for some tropical Oz. The van lurched and she turned around.

The runoff of many rains had scoured a ragged ditch down one side of the track. Frowning, Mac edged their wheels to the high side of the trail. "Looks like they had a gulley washer up here." He slowed still more as they bounced through a puddle. Dark brown butterflies with wings edged in scarlet fluttered up around the windshield, then settled behind them again.

"Do you think we should turn back?" she asked when they came to a wider puddle. The wheel ruts dipped into it, then reappeared half a car length beyond.

"Probably." But the van took the pool steadily and splashed out the other side. "There's just one problem."

"Which is?"

"See any place to turn around?" As if to emphasize that point, brush clattered along the flanks of the van.

"What happens if we meet a car?" She bit her lip as the gulley to the left zagged toward the centerline of the track.

Bushes snapping under its right-hand tires, the van skirted the little drop-off. If their wheels slipped into that, they'd tip over. Possibly keep on rolling down the mountainside. No, the trees would surely stop them. Sooner or later.

"Somebody's got to back down. And today, I promise you, it won't be us." Mac shot her a narrow-eyed glance, reminding her of old cowboy movies, the final showdown on a red dust main street. He'd look wonderful in a Stetson, wouldn't he? "Not likely to happen, anyway," he added comfortingly as he misread her wide-eyed look. "Three cars a day is major traffic up here."

Inching up and around a hairpin turn, they were suddenly on level ground—the top of the ridge, Tey realized as she caught a flash of blue far out beyond the thickets. Beside her, Mac heaved a sigh of relief. "That should be the worst of it." They rolled slowly through another puddle, but the ditch that had threatened to wash out the road below had petered out.

A wet and bumpy half mile farther on, Mac stopped the car on the track. "This looks like a good place." To the right, the scrub had thinned; more blue gleamed between the leaves.

Following him across a pocket meadow toward the line of bushes, Tey was struck by the silence. No sound of surf, no traffic, just the swish of their legs through the grass and daisies. No one around for miles and miles but the two of them. A tickling shudder shook her shoulder blades and rippled down to the backs of her knees.

Holding a branch aside, Mac was waiting for her. Expecting a trail just beyond, she started around him, giving him a smile of thanks.

"Whoa!" A hand clamped on the back of her belt just as she looked forward and yelped.

There was nothing there. Just a blue canyon of space, with the ocean glittering at its bottom, then stretching away to the empty horizon. Far below—so far below she couldn't hear them—waves shredded themselves endlessly against a ribbon of beach. Leaning back against Mac's wonderfully solid chest, she found his other arm was now wrapped around her. Good. Much better than good. She took a deep breath, and that was so nice that she tried another. Nice, to keep on breathing.

"God," Mac growled at her ear. He sounded as if he'd just resumed breathing himself. "See if I ever take you to see the Empire State Building. God!" The arm around her tightened.

"Have you been there?" she asked irrelevantly when she could breathe again. Tilting her head back, she rested it against his throat.

"Joanne took me once. Was too smoggy to see much."

She could feel the beat of his pulse through the back of her head. "Who's Joanne?"

His hand was still on her belt. Warm, broad knuckles rubbed slowly down the slope of her hip and back up again. This absent caress tightened her shorts at the waist and crotch and she shivered, a long, liquid, rippling shudder, and caught the hand behind her.

"My wife," he said flatly.

"Oh." She lifted his fingers off her belt.

His fingers curled around hers and held on, trapping her hand between them. "She was at that time, anyway."

"Oh." And he'd loved her. It was there in his voice—that and something else—bitterness? None of her business, anyway. But suddenly, fiercely, she wanted to know. *How did she hurt you, Mac, and why?*

None of your business, she reminded herself. Leaning out as far as his arm at her waist would allow, she concentrated on the view.

Fold after fold of green mountain wrinkled down to meet the sea. At their feet, white-fringed blue rollers faced a wave of arching palm trees across a narrow dividing strip of sand. Deserted sand. No one moved down there; there wasn't a house or even a road in sight. As the waves retreated, the shallows boiled brown and turquoise beneath their lacing of white. The brown would be coral. Not a friendly coast. And the turquoise shallows shaded to midnight blue in a few feet; so these mountains didn't end at the beach; they went on plunging down into that fathomless blue, she realized, and shivered again.

"Cold?" Mac murmured in her ear.

She shook her head against his jaw. "Not even a boat down there."

"See the reefs?" He let go her hand to point. A quarter mile out, white teeth cut the blue. Brown gleamed for an instant and vanished. "That's why."

"And what's that?" This time she pointed, to a soft, white patch in the water far out beyond the reef. And just beyond it, a rich purple stained the blue. "Coral of some kind?"

Laughing softly, he rubbed his lips along her cheek. "Look up, darlin'." Looking, she found one of the monster trade wind cumulus clouds wafting above the discoloration. "That's the reflection in front—the white. And the purple's the shadow. You've got to be high up ever to see that." His free hand found her shoulder, cupped its curve and stroked restlessly down her arm.

"So was Joanne a New Yorker?" she asked in spite of herself. As his grip slackened, she turned gently out of his hold and took a step back toward the van.

Hands jammed into his pockets, he stayed where she'd left him, facing out to sea. "Not a native New Yorker," he murmured at last. "But sometimes I think the adopted ones are worse. That city's like a disease. It gets in the blood. Money, concrete, crowds, and money..." His shoulders jerked in a tight little shrug. Turning, he led the way back to the road.

Two miles farther on, they came to the biggest puddle yet. "We'll never make that!" Tey declared. It was perhaps three times as long as the van, and there was no way to drive around it. The brush grew close to either side. "And for all we know, it could be a half a mile deep."

"Or full of alligators," Mac agreed, eyeing its opaque surface. "Maybe we should camp out here till it dries out. We can thumb wrestle to pass the time, or something." Stroking slowly across her face, those blue, devilish eyes seemed to be voting for the something.

"I'd die of boredom," she told him gravely, biting back a smile.

"Would you?" He didn't look convinced. Looked damned confident she'd be well entertained, if anything.

"You did this on purpose," she decided.

"On your sweet mongoose, I swear I didn't! See if I ever help *you* do research again."

It was best to keep on attacking. The minute she let up, it would be his turn. "And what's Gerry going to think about your professionalism, your responsibility, if he has to come rescue us?"

Mac flinched as that hit home. "True." Kicking off his tennis shoes, he started to roll up the khaki pants he was wearing.

"What are you doing?"

"Guess I better make sure it's not a bottomless pit. For all we know, that's a Matean car trap. There's probably sharpened stakes under there." After opening his door, he waded gingerly into the pool.

"Now everyone I've met has been very friendly," she pointed out, leaning out her window.

"Friendlier than I'd be to a pack of tourists," Mac agreed over his shoulder. The water rose to his ankles, then halfway to his knees as he shuffled carefully along one rut. Holding his arms out to either side, he seemed to be having trouble keeping his balance. "Whup!" He slithered sideways, wobbled and nearly went down.

"Awwww."

"Thought you had me that time, did you?" At the end of the puddle, he turned and sloshed slowly back again, along the other rut. "It takes more than that to bring a good man down." With this declaration, he slipped again, but somehow stayed upright in spite of her delighted whooping.

After knocking the worst of the mud off his feet, he slid in beside her. "You're a liberated female, aren't you?" Starting the van again, he aimed it slowly into the puddle.

"Does that mean I push, if we don't make it?"

"And a mind reader! Just think what we'd be like in bed together." They were past the halfway mark now.

She didn't seem to be thinking of much else today. And that was a big mistake. *Josh, think of Josh.* "Shouldn't you be going faster? If we bog down . . ."

"Don't want to drown the engine." His jaw muscles tensed as the van sideslipped, then straightened again. "Can't splash." The tires slipped again, and the van swerved greasily to one side. "Damn!" Spinning the wheel, he stepped on the accelerator as the vehicle seemed to settle. "Dammit, come on, baby!"

Like a hippo easing in for a beauty pack, the van sank another inch. Water lapped in under the door just as the engine wheezed and died.

"That tears it!" He turned the ignition key off and back on. The engine gave a disheartened whir and coughed into apologetic silence again. With a shrug, Mac pocketed the keys. He swung around to collect a paper-wrapped parcel off the seat behind him, shoved it under his own seat, then slid out into the puddle.

By the time he'd sloshed around to her side, she had tucked her shoes into her shoulder bag along with her purchases. Swinging open her door, Tey contemplated that murky first step. At least all she had to worry about was alligators. Spiders weren't that keen on water.

"Sir Walter Raleigh at your service, ma'am." Mac bowed and reached for her.

"Oh, no. I'm liberated, remember?" Spreading her fingers against his oncoming chest, she found he was brick warm and quite determined; he scooped her up, anyway.

"I'll remember that." He nudged the door shut with his shoulder. "The next time you bog down the van, you can carry me."

There was only one logical place to put her arm, and that was around his neck. But that brought her breast in contact with his chest. Mac stopped, looking down at her, his arms tightening, molding her closer to his damp warmth. "Dry land's thataway." She pointed with her chin. He was so beautifully, satisfyingly firm—his arms, his chest . . .

"So it is." He started wading again. Slowly, toward the shore they'd been trying to reach. "So which bikini did you buy?" he asked after a moment, nodding at the bag she held. "The purple one?"

"It's a secret," she told him smugly. What wasn't a secret was what his heart was doing, just below her breast. Or could that be hers, thumping like that?

"I won't tell anybody." His arms squeezed her hard as he slipped; once he'd recovered, he didn't ease them again.

"A secret." She gave him a Cheshire cat grin. The thought of wearing it for him made her even warmer.

"I'll get it out of you somehow," Mac promised. "What if I threaten to drop you?" His legs wide for balance, he had slowed to a deliberate shuffle—whether to prolong this portage or to stay upright, she wasn't sure.

"I wouldn't do that, if I were you. I respond badly to threats."

"Oh?" He stopped to stare down at her again. "How do you respond?"

One look at her breasts would have told him—it should have been plain with the thin T-shirt she was wearing—but his eyes were locked on hers.

"Ohh...I'd probably start by ignoring you." *Impossible, Mac, but I could try.*

"That wouldn't work. I respond pretty badly to being ignored." He started moving again.

They were nearing dry land now, and not a moment too soon; she felt like a chocolate bar at high noon. "Well, then, I guess I'd promise to wreak terrible vengeance." At the moment, she couldn't think what, but it would have to involve tying him to a bed...

"Such as?"

She batted her lashes at him. "Vengeance is most terrible when it's unex*pec*—" The sky tilted suddenly; they were falling—backward. "Mac!" Landing in a splashing pratfall, he hugged her to his chest, somehow kept her above the water, though half the puddle seemed to be raining back down on them. "Ughhh!"

"Ugh? What'd *you* mean, ugh?" he laughed, and wiped his mud-splashed face sideways against her breast. "You're not the one with a wet bottom!"

"This beats the cape maneuver any day, Sir Walter!" Chortling, she tested the water delicately with one toe tip. Miraculously, she'd kept hold of her purse, and now she tossed it up onto the road. Another five feet and they'd have been home free.

"So what color is it?"

"I'll never tell."

"I'm in a great position to make good on all threats." Turning, he held her out from his chest a few inches. "Identify this quotation: misery loves—"

"Mac—"

"What color?"

"No! You wouldn't da—"

"Company." He dropped her.

Or tried to. Her arm around his neck brought him toppling with her. Squealing, wriggling beneath him as his weight forced her into the mud, she clung like a monkey. Bracing a hand on either side of her, laughing, Mac did a push-up that lifted them both. Tey freed one hand to scoop up a handful of mud and slap it on top of his head.

The rest was free-for-all as Mac retaliated by squelching a fistful of sloppy clay above her breasts. Yelping her indignation, she shoveled a good portion of the pond onto his shoulders. But might proved right in the end. Pinning her arms to her sides with one arm, Mac drew a loving red handlebar mustache beneath her wrinkled nose. "Ick! Brute!"

"Who started this?" With a sensuous, muddy fingertip, he decorated the tip of each of her breasts with a two-ring bull's-eye.

"You did! And cut that out!" *You silly, gorgeous fool.*

The design wasn't dark enough to satisfy him. With more mud he retraced the pattern, more slowly this time. Then, as inspiration took hold, he added a vertical line between her breasts and a big goofy grin across her stomach. Still holding her prisoner, he leaned back to inspect his artwork. "Now you're too dirty to kiss," he complained.

"I wasn't exactly asking you to," she growled, but his hand curved in a gritty caress around the back of her neck and he pulled her forward. Tracing her full bottom lip with the tip of his tongue, he waited for her to grant him entry, lingered teasingly on her moist threshold until her lips slowly parted. With a soft, hungry groan, he slid inside.

So *sweet*, the taste and feel of him. Wet, prickling warmth of tongue against tongue, the arousing roughness of the mud trapped between their upper lips. Her hands slithered up around his neck. *Oh, Mac, have I ever felt like this before?* Running her fingertips up through his hair, she encountered his cap of mud, and suddenly she was laughing inside his mouth, laughing too hard to continue. Pulling back, she found he now shared her mustache, and that was funnier yet. "Look at you!"

"Me?" Catching a fistful of her curls in either hand, he pulled her close again. "Wait'll you see—" Those blue eyes widened and slewed sideways.

"What?" And then she heard it, too—the laboring growl of an unmuffled engine, coming their way.

"Lord, look at you!" Loosing her, Mac wrenched his T-shirt over his head. "Here, put this on!" He pulled it down over her head, grinning as she popped through the neck hole with a mutinous glare. Leaving her to find the arm holes, he dipped his head in the puddle and scrubbed at his hair. The car sounded very close now. It was coming from the direction in which they'd been heading.

"Up you come and think decent." Mac pulled her up beside him.

"Your face—" Standing on tiptoe, an elbow crooked around his neck, she leaned against his chest and scrubbed his mustache with the edge of his shirt. It didn't help much. He looked like a blond Comanche caught in a rainstorm—war paint smeared every which way. Giggling, she turned as the car roared around the bend.

With a grinding of gears, the car bounced to a stop; after a moment, it crept warily toward them. The man at the wheel leaned out his window to inspect them with frank disbelief.

The picture he presented was just as striking. A young man, he had the face of an African carving, high cheek-boned and glistening like some polished, exotic wood. His hairstyle had been stolen from a lion; kinky, reddish-brown dreadlocks stood out in a glorious mane.

"A rasta mon," Mac murmured at her ear.

"Stuck, mon." Directed at Mac, these uninflected words could have been question or statement.

"'Fraid so." Mac inspected the Rastafarian's vehicle with the same cool interest.

Once upon a time, it had been a Volkswagen bug. The back half of its rusty yellow body had been cut down to seat level and floored with rough boards. Wooden sides had been added to this platform; the effect was that of a tiny pickup truck.

"Ride, mon?"

"Thanks!" Mac stooped to collect Tey's bag, then took her arm.

There being no passenger's seat in the cab, they rode in back. Mac curved a protective arm around her as they bounced backward down the track. After a quarter mile or so, they came to a wide spot and the driver reversed. Talking was impossible. Pillowed on Mac's shoulder, Tey watched for glimpses of the sea. Half-hypnotized by the noise and the flicker of sunlight and leaf shadow overhead, wrapped in the warm smell of Mac's T-shirt and the safety of his arms, she had never been so happy. Mac's lips brushed her temple as his arm pulled her closer. *All I need, for this to be heaven, is to get Josh back to Lori.* Like a cloud shadow, the thought darkened her day for a moment, but more miles of sunlight and blue vistas drove the nagging worry to the back of her mind. Lord, they were ninety miles from nowhere. If this man hadn't happened along, it would have taken them forever to get out of here. All day at least. That thought seemed suddenly vital.

Mac's lips touched her ear. "Know where we are?"

Startled, she looked up from her thoughts. A lone tree leaned away from the sea; a meadow sloped up to a bare hill, then vanished as the truck rambled downhill. "Oh! Where we trapped the first day?"

"Right."

And how far was that from camp? Tey stole a glance at her watch. She would have to know that. And how fast could a man walk? Or run? Though Bo wasn't in the kind of shape that Mac was; the heat would slow him down quickly enough. Eyes on the sky, she let the idea revolve and grow.

When they passed the baobab, Mac let her go. Scrounging in his pocket, he brought forth a red pocket knife—a Swiss army knife. While she watched, he opened the rusty toolbox that was tied to one side of the platform and placed the knife inside. As he shut the box, his face wore an odd look of satisfaction that turned her heart right over.

The rasta man let them off at the camp driveway. Acknowledging their thanks with a peacefully distant nod, he headed on toward Thisted; they could hear him long after he'd vanished around the bend. Staring down the road, Mac rubbed the line of hair along his flat stomach, then glanced down at himself in absent surprise. That expression spread to a grin as his eyes switched to her. "You're a mess!" Lifting his T-shirt, he inspected his graffiti beneath it. "Delectable, but a mess. Come on." He led her toward the gate to the beach.

They were in luck; there wasn't one volunteer in sight. Doubly lucky, Tey realized exultantly, as she peered down the beach. Beneath the palms, she could make out the red blanket, then movement as Bo waved an arm from the shade. She waved back.

Squinting in the direction of her salute, Mac made no comment.

Waist-deep in crystal water, Tey stripped off Mac's T-shirt. Scrubbing at her breasts, she removed the worst of the clay stains. "Need some help?" Mac wiped the hair out of his eyes and stood.

Smiling, she shook her head. When he continued to watch, she ducked under the water and finished the job submerged.

As they waded ashore, Mac dropped an arm around her shoulders. "Let's hope Gerry's back by now. There's a tow chain in his van. I want to get her out of that puddle before someone else finds her."

It would take at least a couple of hours to rescue the van. Josh and Bo would be gone before she could return. "Mac..."

"Hmm?" he mumbled through the folds of his T-shirt.

"I'm so hot, would you mind if I stayed here?"

Pulling the shirt down over his chest, he glanced up sharply. His chin made a quarter turn toward Bo's distant blanket, and jerked back again. "If it wasn't for you, I wouldn't have chosen that route." His teeth clenched together over his protest, as if it had popped out without his expecting it. Had shamed him somehow. The muscles along his jawline were suddenly visible.

"I know. And it was lovely. But I'm not all that handy with towing and things..." Her voice trailed away lamely. By all rights, she should help him. *Mac, if there were two of me—*

"Don't you think it's time you learned, in that case?"

Dammit, what did he expect? That she'd tag along at his heels every minute of the next week? Day and night? That would wreck everything; at some point, she was going to need her privacy. If she had to account for her time and actions to Mac... "Not especially." The words came out colder than she'd meant them.

The odd and tender curve of his mouth had straightened to a line. "Okay. Fine." Turning on his heel, he left her there. He didn't look back, though she waited for one backward, forgiving glance until he vanished beyond the gate.

Her shoulders lifted in a slow shrug. Probably better, this way. Definitely better. *So why doesn't it feel that way?* Taking the purple bikini out of her shoulder bag, she trudged back into the water to change.

CHAPTER EIGHT

BEACHCOMBING HER WAY toward the red blanket, Tey took her time. It wouldn't do to seem too eager for their company. When at last she sauntered up from the water's edge, she held a collection of pink shells. Still hinged together, they looked like tiny butterflies. "Hiya, guys." She dropped beside Bo.

Looking up from the portable typewriter before him, the bodyguard blinked and then grinned. "That's what this joint needed—a little decoration!"

Smiling at the compliment, she turned to Josh, who was playing in the sand a few feet away. "Hi, Josh."

Her nephew's frown of concentration deepened a trifle, but he didn't acknowledge her. The cloth chessboard was in use again today, but the battlefield had changed. Josh had spread the cloth over a mound of sand; chessmen perched precariously on their squares like wobbly rock climbers. At the moment, a black bishop appeared to be king of the mountain.

There was no way to force the acquaintance. She glanced back to Bo with a rueful shrug and found he hadn't missed the snub.

"Some people are hard to get to know," he murmured comfortingly. "I guess it was a month before I was accepted."

Two years ago, on her last visit to L.A., Josh had been as confiding and affectionate as a six-week-old puppy. Every time she'd sat down, he had climbed into her lap.

"I brought you something from Josh's journal." As if he felt he had to compensate for his charge's aloofness, Bo seemed extra friendly today. He pulled two pages out from under a pile of typing.

"Oh, great!" Without a title, the typewritten story was triple spaced. The arrangement of the phonetically spelled words was original, to say the least, as if Josh had been taking typing lessons from e.e. cummings.

Nobody wawnted Jo. He wuz a ruf tuf tahmcat
and he dihdihnt cer.
Thu mows
dihdihnt wawnt him. I dont cer Jo sed. Il eet yoo
and he
dihd. Thu dawg
dihdihnt wawnt him. so Jo sed I dont cer and he biht
thu dawgz tal.

"At last I've met someone I can outspell!" she joked, glancing up to find Bo's eager eyes on her face.

"That's how I've been teaching him, of course. I've reprogrammed the computer he uses so each of the keys on the keyboard denotes one phonetic sound. When he needs the sound of *O* as in *dog*, he strikes the *AW* key. When he wants to make a long *O* as in *Joe*, he uses the *O* key. And so on."

"This is what your dissertation is about?" It was easy to follow, once you got used to it.

"Uh-huh. Teach kids to communicate first—and to communicate about what *they* want to talk about.

Teach 'em to read later, and to spell last. Psychologically, it makes a lot of sense."

"Yes, it does," she agreed, and returned to the story. Nobody seemed to want Jo the cat. Not the duk, or the hors, or any of the other animals he met in his ruf, tuf, angry travels. "Speaking of psychology..." She glanced to the side; Josh was still in earshot.

Bo's good-natured face had darkened. "Divorce hurts more than two people, sometimes. Especially one like this. Our friend's mother—" he mouthed that last word silently "—didn't want him, and I guess she made it pretty plain."

It took an effort to purge the fury from her voice. "Who told you that?"

"My boss. He doesn't discuss her much—guess it's pretty painful still—but from what he's hinted, she isn't wrapped too tightly. Or maybe just selfish as all blazes. She was apparently neglecting our friend pretty badly toward the end. Very cold and rejecting. Aston said the last straw was when he found out she'd been doing cocaine all day long while he was off at work. He had to take our friend away, once he discovered that."

This portrait of Lori should have been laughable, it was so far from the truth. Looking down, Tey found that, out of Bo's sight, her hand was clenched savagely on a fold of blanket. "And so custody was awarded to the father?"

"She signed it away. She wanted no part of our friend. Hard to believe, isn't it?" Bo glanced across at the child with an almost fierce protectiveness.

Now that was the first thing he'd said that could be easily disproved! To hide the flaring hope in her eyes, Tey turned to watch Josh. If she could get Bo to a phone, get him to talk to her sister, Lori could—

would—passionately deny she'd ever given Josh up. If that didn't shake his conviction in Aston's story... "Yes, that is hard to believe."

"But things got even messier." Bo's head swung around as Josh stood and trotted uphill into the palms. When the child crouched to examine a fallen palm frond, he relaxed again. "Once they got into the nitty-gritty of the property division, she began to feel cheated, as someone always does in a divorce. And apparently she hit on the idea of using Josh as leverage. If she could get him back, she could use him to blackmail Aston into giving her more money, though I understand he's been more than generous with her already."

That bastard! Aston had simply reversed the facts. It was as neat and elegant a solution as any software program he'd ever created.

"So, apparently, she's trying to have Josh kidnapped. Snatched is the word, I guess, when it's your own kid. I'd been figuring Aston was overreacting, if he wasn't downright paranoid on the subject—the globe-hopping we've been doing these past few months—till last week in Switzerland—"

"What happened?" She was careful not to look down at Bo's splinted finger.

"Um...I'm talking too much, aren't I?" Bo decided maddeningly, as he turned to check on Josh.

Josh was engrossed in thrashing the trunk of a tree with the palm frond. "No! Not at all. What happened?"

"Well...I nearly blew it. We'd biked into town, and I was reading on a bench, in a little park, while Josh played. A girl—uh, woman—asked me what I was reading, so we were chatting, when I heard Josh yell.

This sleazy-looking dude had him under one arm and was heading for a car.''

"What'd you do?'' *And why couldn't you have done it a little slower?*

"Tore across the park, popped the jerk one, grabbed poor Josh and hightailed it for home. Aston freaked, and we left the country that day. And so now it's no more field trips for us,'' Bo finished regretfully, then scanned the beach as if Herbert Kopesky might pop up from the waves in a frogman suit at any moment. "Hey, Josh! We miss your sweet shining mug. Bring it back over here!'' he called.

"Is that how you hurt your hand?''

"Yeah.'' Bo examined it ruefully. "I never hit anybody before. Guess I did it wrong.'' With a cheerful shrug, he turned to welcome Josh back. "What you got there, partner?''

Clutching the now broken-necked palm frond, Josh gave an awkward imitation of Bo's burly shrug and studied his toes.

"Let's see.'' Bo took the frond from the child's unresisting hand. "Looks like an Injun headdress to me. Betcha the chief tamale of St. Matthew wears one of these.'' Snapping the stem off, Bo struck a noble savage pose with the frond held behind his head. To Tey's mind, he looked more like a teddy bear with a fierce bout of indigestion. "Now let's see you.''

But Josh shook his head emphatically.

"Not your style, huh? Okay. Did you save that string we found this morning?''

While the pair of them searched their discarded shirts for the string, Tey finished Josh's story. The lonely adventures of Jo the tuf cat ended on a note of wary hope. He met a bear, name not given, but she could make a fair guess. Jo was teaching his friend to play gotcha as the tale closed.

"So give that to Tey," Bo directed.

"Oh, Josh, what a lovely hat!" Tey gave him her best smile as he thrust the palm frond at her. They'd added bonnet strings to it, she noticed. While she tied them beneath her chin, Josh stood before her, frowning faintly, his eyes on her face. *You almost know who I am, don't you, Joshems? You just can't quite put your finger on it, and it worries you.* "There, how do I look?"

"Like the Statue of Liberty on vacation," Bo decided.

"Thank you, Josh!" The bladelike leaves drooped over her forehead. "I brought you a present, too." Still holding his gaze, she reached for her purse. Pulling out the bag that held his mongoose, she made a production of groping inside it, as if she were trying to catch a wild and agile captive. "Aha! Got you now!" Glancing up, she found his wide eyes were fixed on the bag. "Come on out, you!" Twisting her wrist, she poked the head and shoulders of the toy out of his lair, then wiggled him slightly, as if he were peering around.

Her efforts were more than rewarded by her nephew's enchanted smile. "Do you know what this is, Josh?"

Shaking his head without looking away from the toy, Josh put forth a hand.

The mongoose slid out from his bag to sniff Josh's fingers. "Smells like a kid," he remarked in a reedy version of Tey's voice.

"It's a mongoose," she told the boy. "For you." She set the creature gently on Josh's shoulder. "I don't know his name, though. He wouldn't tell me."

While Josh introduced the mongoose to his chess-men—the mongoose was immediately crowned King of the Mountain—the adults talked in an undertone. "That was awfully kind of you," Bo told her grate-fully.

"He was just too cute not to buy. I'm glad Josh likes him."

"Yeah, you chose a winner there, I think. But it's the attention you're giving him that's even more impor-tant. I think he's been missing a woman's touch. He had a nightmare again last night."

"Oh? What about?"

"I never can get him to say. Don't like to pry too much, and I'm not sure he even remembers. I just hug him till he stops crying. You hear the words Momma and Bogie—that's his name for me—and that's about all I can make out. After a while he settles down. I give him some water, tuck him back in and wait till he falls asleep. Doesn't happen as much as it used to. We're down to about one every three weeks . . . or at least we were. Something's set him off again lately."

"Sounds like he misses his mother." She pro-nounced that last word as quietly as Bo had done.

"Far as a kid's concerned, even a worthless mother is better than none," Bo agreed.

"But I suppose his father makes up for that." She couldn't resist sticking the needle in. "He must be de-voted to Josh."

Bo looked uncomfortable. "Uh, sure. He's pretty busy though. Travels a lot. Great provider type. Any-thing I need for Josh, he gives me."

Anything but time and affection, of course. Aston had been the same back in California. "And he's away, you said."

"Uh-huh. Down in Rio. He's setting up some kind of research and development lab with government subsidies. We'll be joining him there in a week or two."

So that was what Aston was up to. A fresh start in a country where his mind would be a national asset. He could bank his share of the Haley-Astech offering, probably in Switzerland, and continue the work he loved with Brazil picking up the tab. And if he took his son down there, with the influence Aston would have, Lori would never get Josh back. Not legally.

"Do me a favor?" Bo broke into this grim reverie. "I haven't gotten a chance to do any serious swimming, with our friend here. Would you mind keeping an eye on him for five minutes or so?"

This is absurd, she thought once Bo had left them. *I should grab Josh and run.* But it wasn't that simple. They needed more of a head start than five minutes. It would be useless to dash to the airport with Bo on her heels, only to find there were no seats open on the next flight out. No, it would all have to be planned, the tickets reserved, and with some way to keep Bo away from a phone.

When Bo returned, dripping and beaming and groping for the glasses he was apparently blind without, they chatted lazily for another hour. Then Tey went for a last dip herself. The water slid like wet silk along her naked limbs; the sun was a ball of gold dropping toward the silver-blue horizon. By the time she padded up the beach again, Bo and Josh were packing up.

"Speaking of field trips," Bo murmured as they ambled toward the gate, Josh and mongoose leading the way.

Which they hadn't been. "Mmm?"

"I...uh...the housekeeper told me she could stay with Josh tonight, if I wanted to go into town. Would you like to come along? Maybe we could find a steel drum band?'' He glanced at her hurriedly, then busied himself in finding the keys to the gate.

In spite of Marty's innuendos, somehow this possibility had never crossed her mind. It was probably the easiest way to play this game, the easiest way to gain power over Bo, but her stomach rolled over at the thought. As it was, she was going to have to outwit him, probably make him lose his no doubt lucrative job. To defeat him by using and betraying his affections was more than she could bear. And there was another reason that the thought of dating this kind man left her cold. "I...that sounds like a lot of fun, Bo, but..." She'd never been good with brush-offs at the best of times.

"Maybe you're right," he agreed immediately, as he ushered them through the gate. He'd caught her note of rejection, all right. "It's probably hard to find decent music on a week night."

"It's not that..." A car was coming—the red van— and she reached down to take Josh's hand as Bo locked the gate. Surprisingly, he smiled up at her. "It's just that I broke up with someone not very long ago... I guess I'm looking for friends more than dates at the moment."

He took it very well. Shyness faded slowly to warmth and then he nodded. "I can understand that." He took Josh's other hand.

They both looked up as the red van swept past them, beeping its horn. A grinning Gerry kissed his fingers to Tey and swung the van into the camp turnoff. "Hoo— eeee!'' he yelled back over his shoulder. Presumably this was a reference to the bikini. She'd chosen to carry her muddy clothes rather than put them on again. Laughing, she and Bo crossed the road, Josh linking them in a friendly intimacy. In the distance, Mac's blue van hummed around the curve.

"Well..." Bo unlocked the main gate and nodded to the islander who sat on the stoop of the nearby guardhouse. "I guess we'll see you at the beach?"

"Tomorrow," she promised. "Bye, Josh." She gave him a special wave, was delighted to receive his solemn "Bye" in return, and turned toward the camp driveway.

The blue van rolled to a stop beside her. "Get in." Mac jerked his chin at the passenger door.

No way. Not with his mouth in that slash of a line and his jaw muscles bunching like that. This wasn't her warm, silly friend of this morning. "Thanks, but I'd rather walk, Mac." She stole a glance over her shoulder; only a little way up his hill, Bo had indeed noticed their confrontation.

That gesture seemed to be the final straw. Mac yanked the safety brake on and half opened his door.

"All *right*!" If he was going to make a scene about it. Stalking around the front of the van, she got in beside him.

TURNING HIS BACK on the pair, Bo headed uphill. A stone lay in the path ahead, and it took a real effort not to kick it. *I'd have picked her up, too, Mac.* Groping for pockets to jam his fists into, he discovered he was still in his swim trunks. Damn. He lengthened his strides, then shortened them again when Josh broke into a trot.

Did women know what they did to men, dressed like that? And if they did, why the hell did they do it, if they just wanted to be friends? "Beats me," he murmured aloud, and glanced down to find Josh looking up at him. "If you figure it out, Josh, will you tell me?"

THE VAN LURCHED into gear and lunged up the turn-off. Bracing herself with a hand on the dashboard, she turned to stare at Mac. His muscular legs were red with dried mud. He must have had to do some pushing; it looked as if he'd fallen to his knees at least once. Sweat darkened his shirt from throat to navel. Halfway up the track, he pulled the van over and cut the engine.

In contrast to that hot, wet body, the eyes that looked out of it were chips of ice. In the sudden silence, they moved slowly down the length of her, from head to toe and back up again.

Her response to this arrogant appraisal was mixed. Damp heat flushed her face, her skin, and rolled in slow waves down her legs, while beneath the cotton triangles that curved to fit her breasts, her nipples rose and hardened as if she'd been dipped in ice water.

And Mac didn't miss that reaction. His mouth jerked in what was almost a smile, then tightened again as his eyes lifted to hers.

As if he was daring her to deny it—damn him. "Well?" she asked coldly.

"You missed the orientation lecture the first day, but I would have thought you knew better. That's fine for beachwear, but you don't walk around naked on the streets down here. The Mateans don't like it."

"I am *not* naked!" And who had chosen this suit, after all?

"You're one sneeze away from it, darlin'." His hand shot out with a lazy, deceptive speed. Catching one end of the bow that tied the breast triangles together, he wound it around his finger. "You're one itty bitty tug away from an all-over tan, darlin'. The average man's got that much imagination, believe me." He pulled gently at the bow.

One of the bow loops diminished by half an inch. *Go ahead, Mac. Just go ahead, and see what happens!* Eyes flashing, she sucked in an angry breath, and found her breasts rising with it.

He tugged another taunting half inch from the bow.

It was his dishonesty more than the action that enraged her. It wasn't proper streetwear they were fighting about, it was Bo, wasn't it? Bo and perhaps some ridiculous hurt that the bikini she wouldn't show Mac had been worn for another man. But what right had he to feel that way? "Do that, and you'll be sorry," she growled.

"Oh, I don't think so." His voice was a mocking caress as he twisted the tie around his finger again.

The blood was pounding in her ears. Odd how close rage was to raging want. Mad as she was, she wanted him suddenly, wanted the hard warmth of his hands cupping and smoothing her naked flesh, molding her to fit his damp body with a hungry violence that would match her own. For she would punish him, too, would wrap her arms around him and squeeze him till he groaned for mercy, would rake her nails down his back till he writhed and pressed close and even closer—

Perhaps this vision gleamed in her eyes. The hard line of his lips softened, and with a final gentle tug, the bow came apart. Mac spread the triangles like the doors of a cabinet and stared down at her with fascinated pleasure.

Rage returned with the cool air against her bared skin. Just who did he think he was? What gave him this right—"Would you like your eyes scratched out?"

"S'too late, darlin'," he murmured huskily, without lifting his gaze. "I'd see 'em, anyway. They're engraved on my brain now."

"Tie it back," she got out between clenched teeth.

His eyes flicked up to her face, widened as they registered her anger, then flicked down again. "Yes, ma'am!"

But Mac took his time restoring the bow. The ribbons vibrated as he crossed them and pulled one against the other. Quivering lines of force, they encircled her body, tying her tight to his slow-moving hands. As his knuckles brushed the inner slopes of her breasts, a warm lover's knot tightened between her thighs. His fingers paused for a moment as she sighed, then resumed their slow work when she didn't speak. A soft, final tug made the bow. Mac lifted the two loops, studied them, then adjusted one minutely. "Satisfied?" Still holding the bow, he looked up at her, his eyes crinkling.

Satisfied? Damn him, he knew the answer to that. "Yes," she lied shakily.

"Anything to please a lady." Drawing her forward by his grip on the bow, he dipped his head to the nearest triangle. Through the sheer cloth, his lips claimed the tautly waiting peak. His wet and melting kiss mocked the protection of the fabric, brought her leaning forward in her seat to meet that thrilling touch. And, when he turned that teasing, torturing tongue to her other breast, her hands crept up into his warm and silky hair.

"Damn you, Mac," she breathed, and pulled him closer. If they went on like this, she would spend the night with him. But one night would be just a taste; it wouldn't satisfy. She'd want, he'd want, the next night and then the next. And when the time came to put her plan into action, when it was time to go, a lover reaching for her in the night, pulling her back into bed, demanding to know where she was off to and why wouldn't do. *Think of Josh.* "Mac!"

"Mmmm?" Nibbling on the bow between her breasts, Mac was in a world of his own.

"Mac, stop." *Oh, don't stop.*

That command brought his head up. "Love?"

Stop. She narrowed her eyes at him warningly, but she couldn't say it aloud again. It was a word that made logical sense and emotional nonsense.

Sliding his hand softly up her cheek, he twined his fingers into her hair and pulled her gently forward. "Tey..." he murmured shakily.

One kiss, then. That's all! Surrendering her lips to him with a grateful, hungry sigh, she found that one brushing kiss turned into the next, melted into another, and then another, each one longer, sweeter, deeper than the last. *You can't do this. You cannot do this. You made a promise to Lori.* She twisted her head aside. "Stop!" she panted.

"What's that mean?" Mac kissed the side of her throat, then lipped damp velvet kisses down to her collarbone.

"Means quit! Halt...cease and— And desist." As his teeth closed gently on her bare shoulder, she shuddered convulsively and grabbed fistfuls of his shirt-front.

"That's what it means?" Mac raised his head to give her a skeptical grin. "Maybe you better show me how," he challenged huskily.

You don't think I can stop, you conceited man? Glancing down at her hands, Tey found she was holding on to him. Willing her fingers to open, she flattened them one by one against his chest, then looked up at him despairingly. *You might be right, Mac!* But somehow she found the strength to straighten her arms and push him away.

"Possum?" His amusement was changing swiftly to bewilderment.

Against her resisting palms, he was a hot, wet deadweight. She had only to bend her elbows to take him back again. But she had herself under control now. "I want to stop, Mac."

Caressing the underside of her wrist where her pulse still hammered, Mac shook his head. "No, you don't." When she didn't answer that, didn't take him back, he shook his head again. "I don't understand you at all."

"No one's asking you to!"

Slowly he settled back and away from her. "Why, Tey?"

Because...because... There was no acceptable reason she could think to give him. She stared back at him hungrily.

"Don't clam up on me, Tey! What's wrong? Talk to me."

Mac, I just can't. Sadly, she shook her head, then swung around to peer up the hill. *What—*

The sound she'd heard came again—music. "Looks like we've got company," she murmured thankfully.

But the question was, was it from base camp or outer space? Turning fully around, Tey studied the pair limping out from under the trees. The one playing "Yankee Doodle" on the harmonica was identifiable as George, in spite of the white bandage tied around his forehead. The high-stepping one clad in swim fins, mask and snorkel and international orange swim trunks looked like Elliot, a Team One volunteer.

"Cripes, they've been hitting the rum early tonight!" Mac growled as he slid behind the steering wheel again.

On closer inspection, George's bandage proved to be a brassiere—Marty's, judging from the cup size. "And you were worried about me hurting the expedition's image?" Tey marveled.

As the pair drew up at attention outside her window, Mac leaned across her. "This had better be good, guys."

That dry tone didn't faze the Southerner. He snapped a cheerful salute. "You left the poker game too early last night, Mac."

"I ran out of pennies." One of his hands found Tey's knee and rested lightly there.

"So did we. So we started betting other things."

"And you lost," Mac concluded. His other hand joined the first, then feathered tentatively up the top of her thigh. She caught it, and his fingers curled comfortably around hers.

"Yup. We've just got to go down to the beach and soak our heads and then we're free men again." George backed away a step.

"Need some company?" Tey opened her door a crack. Mac's hand slipped to her wrist, but she slid to the ground, anyway. "I wouldn't mind one more swim before supper."

"A gen'l'man never says no to a lady. Not one in a bikini, anyways." Putting the harmonica to his mouth, George broke into a rousing rendition of "Dixie" and Elliot tried a frog-footed tap dance.

Still Mac held on to her, their linked hands hidden by the van's door. Looking over her shoulder, Tey ignored the message his eyes and his fingers were sending her. *Mac, I have to go. I just can't get involved with you. No matter how I want to....* And if she stayed, she would become involved; it was that simple. His first surprise was shading quickly to hurt. Mac's eyes flicked to George, then back to her face, and his own slowly hardened.

Oh, Mac. But she held a brisk, impersonal smile between them like a mask. As if she had this sort of encounter a dozen times a day. As if it had meant nothing to her, had been just a pleasant, meaningless interlude... His fingers loosed her slowly, and she shut the door between them.

Marching away downhill with her fellow fools, Tey stole a glance behind, then another. The van didn't move till they reached the main road.

HANDS CUPPED, Bo splashed cool water into his face, rinsing the last of the soap away. Straightening in front of the sink, he groped for the towel and scrubbed himself dry with it.

Meeting his own squinting eyes in the mirror, Bo examined his face. It was pink from the washing, and a little bit glum, but otherwise unmarked, as far as he could see.

But what did women see? He must carry a brand on his forehead, visible only to the opposite sex. Or a message written in special feminine-specific ink— *Suitable for best friend and big brother only.* Funny, he didn't feel brotherly.

Anyway, I prefer blondes, he told the mirror.

I seem to recall some story about this fox and some sour grapes...

No, really, it's true. Rummaging in his kit, he found his toothbrush.

Sour grapes. You liked her fine, till she turned you down.

I still like her fine. But there was something he'd sensed—or so it seemed to him now, anyway—even before he asked her out. Squeezing out a half inch of toothpaste, Bo capped the tube and rolled its end to take up the slack. No chemistry. All the friendliness in the world—Tey was good company, and God knows, she was good-looking enough, but somehow, the spark hadn't leaped the gap. His heart hadn't gone pitty-pat.

Right, his counterpart jeered around a mouthful of foam.

It's true. Tey was too... well, strong wasn't exactly what he meant. He wasn't a chauvinist who preferred his women helpless... was he? Too capable, that's what she was.

Chauvinist oink.

No! It was just... somehow... he wanted to feel... needed. The word dropped heavily between them; his twin met it with a silence that was more withering than any comment. Rinsing their teeth, they turned away from each other without meeting eyes again.

In his bedroom, a small rumpled heap of white was curled at the foot of his bed—Josh, whom he'd tucked in two hours ago. Asleep, Bo determined as he collected his glasses from the bureau and slipped them on. Must have come looking for one more bedtime story, or maybe fleeing the claws of some nightmare. Josh was frowning in his sleep, but his expression looked more like his fiercely thinking frown than any sort of terror.

Sliding his arms slowly under the child, he gathered him up and turned toward the door. *Out like a light,* he decided thankfully, watching that soft, pink, determined little face. Good.

You make a much better father than you do a lover. His inner voice managed just a trace of a sneer, then faded away again.

Yeah, maybe he did. Pity you couldn't be one without first being the other—he glanced down at the child sharply.

Not usually, anyway...

Don't be a fool! He couldn't stay here, couldn't take Josh with him when he went.

You should have known you couldn't pull this off. You even missed Anna's mangy tomcat when you moved out on her. How'd you think you could take on a kid and not love him? Oatmeal in place of brains, that's what he had. Easing Josh's bedroom door wide with his foot, he sidled through the doorway, careful not to bump the child's head or dangling feet against the frame.

He held his breath as he lowered Josh onto the bed; the sleeper's long lashes fluttered, then squinched, and he let out a little moan of discontent. But then he settled again.

In that bedtime story he'd made up, the true father had ransomed his son with a puppy. Stealthily, Bo pulled the sheet up to Josh's chin and the child sighed, then smiled in his sleep. What would Aston take for Josh? A computer? *Aston, I've got this used Macintosh...*

Right. He caught his breath as Josh flopped onto his stomach, but then he curled into his customary sleeping position—like a frightened doodlebug—and his breathing deepened.

And that wasn't fair, anyway, to think Aston would—People just loved in different ways; that didn't mean they didn't love. Fathers loved their sons. That was like the tides, or the sun rising. A natural law...

So forget it. Turning back in the doorway, he pulled the door nearly closed, but the lump in the bed never stirred. *You've been saying goodbye to people you love your whole life long. So what's one more?* Ears alert for any sounds behind, he padded away down the dim hallway.

"THURSDAY: JOSH'S MONGOOSE now has a name. Melvin. I suspect Bo had a hand in his christening."

A burst of laughter from the kitchen brought Tey's eyes up from her notebook. The opposing charade team—Mac's team—was out there preparing for their entrance. The members of Anne and Gerry's team slouched around her on the couches and chairs of the common room. Tey had chosen not to play this evening; she had her own charade to sustain, that of Tey Hargrove, writer. So she was working on her research notes, or at least so she hoped it appeared. In reality, she was keeping a journal. It looked writerly enough—

provided no one read her entries—and it was a good way to clarify her thoughts.

"I took a trap down to the beach today to show Josh what the expedition is doing."

Mac hadn't liked that at all. He hadn't said much when she'd asked permission to take one; he'd even helped find one free of old bait. But she'd felt his silent disapproval following her all the way down the hill from camp.

But then he'd been like that all last evening after her escape with George and Elliot, and all today during the trapping. Coolly remote. The effortless, oddly comforting rapport that had been slowly growing between them had withered back to its roots again. The easy laughter, all the warmth that she'd come to expect from Mac had been missing. And had been sorely missed by her, though he had seemed his usual self with the others. With Marty, in particular... Wrinkling her nose as she realized where that thought was leading, Tey forced her attention back to her notes.

Josh was fascinated. Poor Melvin was obliged to spring the trap over and over again, and then to spend much of the afternoon behind bars. I told Josh how we catch mongooses, how we have to hold them, and how we put tags in their ears. That especially caught his imagination; he has all the normal small boy's bloodthirsty curiosity. Tomorrow, if Mac will let me, I'm going to bring the tagging tools down to the beach, maybe tag long-suffering Melvin if Josh wants me to.

"Hey, guys, we haven't got all night!" Gerry directed this yell toward the kitchen.

Marty poked her blond head around the doorway. "Keep your shirt on!"

"Is that all?" the redhead asked hopefully, but she was gone again.

Tey didn't have all that long, either. In eight more days the trapping would be finished. So she had perhaps seven days, perhaps less, to work on Josh and through him, on Bo. For Josh was his bodyguard's weak spot, she was coming to see more and more. Bo was genuinely fond of her nephew, and whatever Josh wanted, Bo tried his best to deliver. So it was Tey's task to see that Josh wanted—most desperately—a trip outside the confines of the fenced beach. An excursion to trap mongooses up on the Scenic Road. And he had to want it soon.

A razzing cheer broke out from the volunteers around the room as Mac's team made its entrance. With a trench coat framing his bare chest, the professor swaggered ahead of the others; whatever his part was, he was playing it to the hilt. Tey's eyes lingered on the soft gold of his chest hair for a moment, then took the rest of him in. The coat he wore certainly wasn't his own. Probably David's; it was a good five inches too short for Mac. And he had a cigar clenched between his teeth; held at a rakish angle, it gave him a comically daredevil air.

Behind him, dressed—if that was the word for it—in a blue bikini with a diaphanous blue scarf at her throat, came Marty. Her arms waving and undulating in a hula sort of motion, the blonde pirouetted before her audience once, twice and sank at Mac's feet.

The group assumed their tableau. Mac faced the audience squarely, his long legs braced apart. His right hand was raised, with middle and forefinger making the sign for V. With his left, he pointed down at Marty, who, from her kneeling position, had curved herself into a voluptuous back bend. Supporting herself by clutching Mac's knee with both hands, she stared soulfully up at the cabin ceiling. The other two members of Mac's team—David and Lucy—also stared at Marty. Shielding their eyes with their left hands, as if to see better, they both pointed at the pliant blonde with their right.

Yes, she was making a bit of a spectacle of herself, wasn't she? Glancing around, Tey found every male pair of eyes in the room was on the blonde or on her admittedly remarkable breasts, which were pointing the way to heaven at the moment. Every pair including Mac's. *And why should that bother you?* a small internal voice nagged derisively. *You didn't want him, after all.* No, it was better this way, but still . . . Shrugging that green, nibbling thought aside, she dug Eric Hoffman in the ribs. This balding gentleman—a high school principal back in what they all called the Real World—gave a guilty start. "What's the topic?" she whispered as he turned.

"Classical music." His eyes drifted back to Marty.

"Beethoven's Fifth?" someone ventured doubtfully.

Grinning around his cigar, Mac shook his head.

I want him. The thought came from nowhere, fully formed. *It's not just that I can't resist him when he wants me. I want him.*

"Hurry up, you guys!" Giggling, Marty rolled her eyes at the audience. She was beginning to tremble from holding that position. Leaning back a little farther, she propped her head on the side of Mac's thigh.

Don't do that! Tey looked down to find her hand slashing an angularly hostile-looking doodle across the entry in her journal. *Just keep your hands off him, you floppy nympho!*

Gerry's team had determined by now that the first word—surprise, surprise—was victory.

So let's just finish this nonsense, can't we? Why couldn't someone come up with the answer?

Marty was making coy little squeaks of pain by now. Leaning over, Mac slipped one hand under her neck to support her. The encouraging grin he bestowed on her upturned face turned a knife in Tey's heart. She squinted, screening out the gruesome details of their intimacy with her eyelashes. *Just look at her! How blatant can a woman be?* That's what the other members of the tableau seemed to be saying in mime, as well. *Just look at her. See her.* See her. Through the sweep of her lashes, Tey could hardly see her. She looked like a human letter, bent over like that—the letter *C*. Victory... C. Victory in high C? No. Victory where, then? The attention was all on Marty. At Marty. Victory at Marty—at C. Wasn't that the name of—"Oh! Victory at Sea!" she yelped into a momentary lull in the guessing.

Oblivious to the groans of agreement and the congratulations around her, she read the answer on Mac's face as his eyes met hers at last. Unsmiling, unblinking, they faced each other across the room in a moment of total connection. No one else existed. *You. It's you I want.*

"But you're not on Gerry's team, are you?" Marty asked sweetly, and the spell was broken. Might never have been. Ignoring Gerry's protests that Tey was a belated but valued recruit, the blonde rubbed her head against Mac's thigh, and smiled up at him. "I'm stuck, Mac!" When he knelt to help her out of her back bend, she collapsed across his knees. Laughing, Mac caught her and eased her to the floor.

Fine. If that's what you go for, Mac, go for it! But I don't have to watch. Collecting her notebook, Tey sailed out of the room. But lying in the dark on her bed at the end of the sleeping porch, concentrating fiercely on the song of the tree frogs to shut out the laughter from the room beyond, Tey was a long, long time in finding sleep.

CHAPTER NINE

"Tey?" His eyes cool, Mac looked up from the caged mongoose at his feet. "Do you want this one?"

"I'll pass, thanks. I've done two already." By now Tey had learned that the little ones—like this red-eyed bouncer—were the hardest. Their necks were so tiny and fragile feeling in your hand that you didn't dare hold them as tightly as you should. Jean had already lost one like this today over on the A line. "Isn't it about your turn, Prof?" she added. Mac had been so distant, so formal again today; the temptation was growing to needle him, just to make sure he remembered she was alive.

Screeeeek! The mongoose whipped around in the trap again.

Mac's face hardened for a moment; he hadn't missed the edge in her voice. "Maybe so." Wiping his sweat-dampened hair out of his eyebrows with a bare forearm, he knelt by the trap.

Already regretting her dig, Tey accepted the hole puncher as penance; it was the one job in the trapping routine that she hated. Dropping in the high grass beside Mac, she waited for her part in the ritual.

"Four hundred grams," George intoned, as the needle on the spring scale stopped jiggling.

"Just a baby!" Marty cooed while David added this datum to the field notes.

A very frisky baby. Once inside the darkness of the handling sack, it didn't calm down as they usually did. Mac was having trouble cornering it. Moving gently, he gathered up the excess fabric; with no place else to go, the mongoose wriggled toward the neck of the sack. "That's a fella," Mac murmured soothingly. But then, within the last few inches of his freedom, the mongoose went wild. Whipping end for end like a small whirling dervish, it finally stopped from either dizziness or exhaustion; through the cloth they could see the heave of its flanks. "Spunky devil." Mac's thumb and forefinger nipped its neck precisely.

His touch galvanized the youngster to one last effort. As Mac slowly untangled the struggling animal, its paws and tail appeared. "Easy, you little runt!" Even as Mac muttered this, one flailing back paw hooked up into the fabric still hiding the mongoose's head. Kicking against that purchase, the animal twisted around as Mac snatched for its back with his free hand. "Damn!"

White teeth flashed into view, punching through the fabric. And into Mac. "Sonuva—!" Red slid out over his thumb, flowered instantly on the cotton, and Mac dropped the sack. Exploding into view, the mongoose made a mad dash at Jean's feet, spun on a dime and scuttled across Tey's lap. Her shriek came after the fact, the mongoose was gone, leaving Mac hunched over and squeezing a dripping thumb. "Mac!" Tey caught his arm, but he flinched away from her. "Are you all right?"

His lips dragged back in savage amusement. Eyes shut, he nodded a jerky yes. Blood was dripping down his good hand now. Ignoring the surrounding chorus of concern, he opened his eyes again and studied the savaged thumb as if it were a specimen he'd found in a trap.

She couldn't take this. The urge to kneel behind him, to wrap her arms around his waist and squeeze, to press her cheek to his tensed shoulder blades was overwhelming; it might not help his pain, but it would surely help hers. Well, if he wasn't going to take sympathy, he could damn well take a bandage. "I'll get the first-aid kit!"

It was a quarter mile across the sun-drenched savanna where they were trapping today to the place they'd left the van. By the time she'd thrashed her way to the dirt road through the breast-high guinea grass, Tey was wet as a blown pony and covered with grass cuts. Staggering back along the path she'd crushed, carrying the kit and a gallon jug of water, she felt suddenly cool; the brassy light seemed to have grayed, as if someone had dropped a blue lens filter over the sun. Squinting up, she was startled to find no cloud veiling its glare.

And more startled to find no one waiting at the trap site. Perhaps this wasn't the one? All sites looked alike here, just a circle of trampled grass and the orange marker hanging limply from a bush. Tey sucked in a shaking breath, and the sky seemed to dim and go bright again, as if the sun had blinked. What had the trap site number been? She couldn't—

"Tey?"

"Mac!" She spun around, scanning the wall of grass.

"Over here. By the tree."

The closest thing to a tree was a scrawny acacia a dozen yards off the trap line. Resting the injured hand across his bent knees, Mac huddled in an umbrella's worth of shade beside its narrow trunk.

It was hard to see his face, though he seemed to be looking up at her. "Where are the others?" She dropped the jug at her feet.

"Sent 'em on to finish the grid." Mac continued to stare at her as she sank to her knees beside him.

"Oh," she murmured stupidly, and groped slowly through a mind gone fuzzy for something else to say. They hadn't been alone together in a couple of days; it felt like years. If only there were enough shade for two...

"Lord, look at you." Mac's voice came from a distance. "You're dripping. You can't move like that down here, possum. You're half heat struck already." A hand closed around her upper arm, pulling her forward. "C'mon in out of the sun and put your head down."

"I'm not the patient—you are," she growled, as she crawled into the blessed scrap of shade.

"Patient, I'm not." The short braid she'd forced her hair into this morning dangled across her shoulder. Mac tugged it downward, bringing her chin toward her lap.

When she felt better she would resent this, Tey decided, as she propped her forehead on her open hands. In the meantime...

Icy wetness splattered on the back of her head—water. "Urkk!" She tried to sit up, but a hand closed on her neck, holding her in place while Mac soaked her hair and shoulders with the frigid drizzle. "Mac! Ugh!" She shook her head helplessly; it was getting in her ears. "Dammit!"

"Just lowering your temperature," he explained, setting the jug down.

"Lowering it!" Glaring at him—he was clear this time when she looked, and clearly fighting a grin—she shook her head again and wiped her eyes. "You... creep. Brute." The blood had clotted on his hand; how could it have bled so? Reaching out, she caught his wrist, felt an odd, almost physical jolt of surprise at the size and hardness of his bones within her grasp. "Does it hurt?"

"Not half as much as my pride." He made no effort to pull away this time. "Damned little thing was so small, I was afraid I'd throttle him."

"Ought to have. He did a tune on your hand." She turned his wrist gently. The mongoose had laid open the side of his thumb, right up to the edge of his thumbnail—no wonder it had hurt so. "You ought to have stitches, Mac, though it's so ragged."

"A bandage'll do."

"It'll scar." Letting him go reluctantly, she found the water jug.

"One more for the collection."

"Macho man!" she teased and poured a dribble of water onto his thumb. His hand jerked, then stilled in the air before her.

But the blood had dried too well, and there wasn't enough gauze in the little kit to spare much for cleaning. Wetting down his whole hand, Tey rubbed his skin gently, slowly rinsing the stain away as her own fingers reddened. Keeping her head down, she concentrated on the job. The blood had trickled everywhere, had pooled in the soft skin between his fingers, across the palm. He gave a little grunt as she rubbed the underside of his wrist. "That hurt?"

"Mmm," he murmured noncommittally. "You missed a bit there."

With her head bent, he couldn't see her smile. She stroked the spot even more lightly this time and watched his thighs flex beneath the taut denim of his jeans. *I'll remember that!* His breath skimmed her cheek; he was leaning almost above her now.

But lovely as this was, she had to get the wound itself clean. As her fingertips neared the savaged flesh, Mac drew away again. Switching to gauze and alcohol, she cleaned the cut, her bottom lip caught between her teeth. "You're going to need a shot, at least, aren't you?"

"For tetanus?" The last word ended in a hiss, as the gauze caught on a flap of skin. "No, I'm up to date." His free hand was braced on the ground by her shoe. As if by accident, his thumb touched her foot. When she didn't react, his hand slid casually, confidingly around her ankle. The gauze dragged again and his hand tensed, then relaxed.

"Hurt?" she murmured, and saw him nod from the corner of her eye. She could feel her own pulse pounding through the circle of his fingers, feel her blood throbbing slowly up her thighs. The consciousness of his touch seemed to rise, as well, as if those warm fingers were tracing the course of her veins heartward.

Moving slowly—to prolong his touch as much as not to hurt him—Tey dressed the bite with an antibiotic cream. His hand tightened almost painfully when she pulled the edges of the wound together with Band-Aids, and stayed tight until she finished the dressing with a protective layer of gauze. "There." She looked up at last. "That's about all I can do for it."

Those blue on blue eyes were not quite in focus, their pupils wide and pulsing. Mac nodded absently.

"Except..." As long as she was reminding him of his mother... Her mouth curved. Raising his hand to her lips, she kissed the bulbous tip of his thumb. But somehow it came out more tender than mocking. "That should make it well."

As her lashes swept up again, she found his eyes were now intensely aware of her. "That's not the only place I hurt," he observed huskily.

Oh, murder. Now she'd done it. "Where else?"

Without a hint of a smile, he tapped his blue work shirt above the heart.

"Your pocket hurts?" she asked carefully.

The line of his lips tilted. "Aches something fierce lately."

"Think this'll help?" Slowly, she leaned forward, her nostrils flaring hungrily for the scent of him.

"It's sure worth a try."

Spreading one hand on his ribs to support her, she pressed her lips to his pocket. Inhaling the warm, welcome smell of him, she kissed the cloth again. Tingling with the damp roughness of the cotton, her lips wanted something smoother, warmer—

"It's not the pocket!" Mac jerked at his shirt buttons.

He wasn't the only one hurting; she ached for him. Pushing his hands aside, Tey undid the top button. Another one. Sliding a hand into the gap to hold it open, she brushed her lips back and forth through the curly gold above his skin. *Mac...*

His good hand was twining up through her hair, his fingers light and shaky against her scalp. His bandaged hand smoothed her shoulder, her back. With just the tip of her tongue, she found the delicate nub of pink standing up in a clearing in the gold.

"God, possum..."

He tasted salty, familiar. She licked him again, a broad lick like a cat this time. He tasted exquisite. *Oh, Mac...*

"Maybe they're back at the van?"

Mac's hand tightened in her hair, pressing her forehead to his chest for a frozen moment. Then, with a growling little sigh, Tey pushed herself away. The pleasures of communal living—humbug!

"I can see the van from here." George's drawl reached them clearly. "Nobody there."

Mac was still fumbling the first button, and looking more inclined to rip it off than to fasten it. Brushing his fingers aside, she did it for him. "We're over here, guys."

On the way back to camp, Marty preempted the front seat, as usual. She insisted on helping Mac work the gearshift—as if he couldn't do it himself, injured thumb or no! Mac seemed half amused, half annoyed by her fuss, and totally cooperative. Tey clenched her teeth hard as the giggling blonde clashed the gears shifting up into third.

On the other hand, what could she do? For wanting Mac—admitting to herself finally that she wanted Mac—could make no difference in her plans. To throw herself headlong into an affair with the professor would jeopardize her chances of rescuing Josh. And if you put a fling with Mac—the delicious, silly, loving little fling that she knew they could have—on one side of the heavenly balance, and you weighed that against Josh's and Lori's happiness in the other, what did you get? *You get no contest, that's what you get.* There would always be other men, other affairs. *But I don't want another man, I want...* Her gaze returned from the middle distance to travel slowly, hungrily across Mac's shoulders, the back of his neck. Darn it, even the back of his head looked good to her! *It's you I—* Blue eyes gleamed back at her from the rearview mirror, questioning her, claiming her. Tey dropped her lashes like a curtain and turned aside.

"Watch the goat, Mac!" Marty squealed, and Mac cursed and swerved the van.

White and tall as a wedding cake, a cruise ship had docked alongside the pier in Thisted. Packs of tourists searched the shady galleries in vain for gift shops, or aimed their cameras at the lovely Victorian gingerbread on the wooden buildings along the waterfront. The van slowed to a crawl.

David brought out and passed around the instant photos he'd taken that morning as they ran the trap line.

"You two look like the before and after advertisement for some cheapo dentist," George decided, passing a photo to Tey.

She took it and laughed. It was the one where she had posed with the mongoose she'd been handling. They'd taken the cover off his eyes for the occasion, and the two of them were showing their teeth at the camera, she in laughter, and the mongoose in a gaping snarl. "I won't ask which is supposed to be which!" She passed it on to Jean, and then the thought occurred. "David, could I borrow that one?" If that didn't enthrall Josh, nothing would.

"It's yours. I took these so that we'd all have souvenirs."

What a sweetie he was! Jean was a fool if she couldn't see it. "Thank you!"

"And here's the other one of you, unless Mac wants it." David passed her another. It was a clear shot of her smiling down at the animal. Almost cheek to cheek with her, Mac leaned into the picture. He'd been struggling to close the tag in the mongoose's ear, and he must have moved as the shot was snapped. His profile was out of focus, as if he were dissolving slowly into some golden haze of fantasy. As if she'd awakened some morning to find she had only dreamed him, that the sweet memory was already fading with the sunlight . . . And someday this blurred photo would be the only evidence she'd have to prove that he'd ever existed. . . .

The van stopped again as a gaggle of tourists wandered across the road. "Let's see it," Mac requested, stretching a hand back. He and Marty studied it together, then he glanced back at David. "Can I have this one?"

"Mac, I wanted it!" The words popped out before she thought. "You're not even in focus!"

"I've got a better one of you, Mac," David volunteered, ever the peacemaker. He passed another one forward. Craning to see it over Marty's and Mac's huddled shoulders, Tey felt a pang of pure envy. It was a wonderful shot of Mac! David had caught him in a moment of laughter as he looked up from the clipboard on which he'd been making some notation.

"But it doesn't have a mongoose in it," Mac objected, and compared it with the first shot, which he still held. "I'd rather have this one, David."

"Then I'll take the other!" Marty slid the photo of Mac face down into her breast pocket. "I'll hang it next to my poster of Harrison Ford.'' She gave Mac a dazzling smile.

Murder had doubtless been done for less, Tey decided, slouching back in her seat as the van hummed out of town.

When they reached the turnoff to camp, Bo was just locking the beach gate behind him. Giving the van a cheery wave, he disappeared in the direction of the water. No doubt Josh ranged somewhere ahead of him.

Tey leaned forward. ''Mac, could you drop me off here?'' In hope of just such an encounter, she'd worn her bikini under her clothes today.

Nodding tightly, the professor braked the van without speaking. Angie, George, David and Jean climbed out ahead of Tey. As she slid the door shut, Mac turned to meet her eyes. His own were remote and blue as chips of Antarctica. ''We've got supper duty tonight, remember.''

''Yes.'' Why did he take it this way? If he wanted her, why wouldn't Mac compete for her? He couldn't really care much for her if he gave up at the first sign of rivalry. But then, Marty made an ample consolation prize for any man—so why should he bother? The blonde wasn't coming swimming, Tey noticed grimly.

''Tey, you comin'?'' George waited for her at the open gate.

''Yep.'' Turning her back on the van, she flogged her thoughts back to the real problem. How to convince Josh that he had, just had, to see a live mongoose...

''OKAY, JOSH, which ear do you think Melvin wants to wear his earring in?'' Tey squeezed the handles of the leather punch, illustrating her intentions with a suggestive snicking sound.

Looking up from his portable typewriter, Bo watched them in silent amusement. "Doesn't that depend on Melvin's...um...inclinations?" he asked finally, since Josh was still dithering.

"I expect it does, but I never could figure out which ear meant which!" She snicked the punch at the toy again. "So what do you think, Josh? Which ear shall we tag?"

Watching fascination chase worry across his charge's face, Bo had to smile. Josh wasn't at all certain he wanted to put Melvin through this, apparently.

"This one," he decided finally, lifting Melvin off his lap by the chosen ear.

"That's a great choice—the left one it is!" Sliding closer across the blanket, Tey knelt beside him. "Now it's not going to hurt him at all, Josh, but you've got to hold him very still."

Hands around the toy's throat in a stranglehold, Josh held him out for the sacrifice.

"That's fine. And why don't you take that finger—that one, Josh—and put it over his eyes? That's what we do so they won't get worried."

Josh nodded obediently, his grayish-greenish eyes about to pop out of his head. Maybe this wasn't a good idea, Bo considered. He found himself flinching as Tey slid the punch onto Melvin's leather ear.

Snick.

"Yeep!" Josh let out a nervous shriek and then an excited giggle.

"See, he didn't even squeak! Melvin's got the 'right stuff,' all right!" Tey put down the tool. "Now don't let him get away, Josh, and we'll give him his earring, just like we do with the real 'gooses.'"

Why is she being so nice to us? Bo wondered, as he followed the procedure. *Nice to Josh, you mean,* he corrected himself. An overdeveloped maternal instinct? But she didn't look the type; even in a bikini, with that braid she was wearing today, Tey looked more like a pretty teenage sister than a mother. She did seem to prefer their company to that of her trapping buddies, though. *Guess it's our scintillating wit.*

Heads nearly touching, she and Josh crimped the ear tag into place. Then Tey lifted the mongoose. "There we go! What do you think, Josh? Doesn't he look great?"

"Looks funny," Josh decided. His glance at Bo suggested the need for a masculine opinion.

"He looks like a pirate mongoose now," Bo assured him. That seemed to satisfy Josh, though come to think of it, he probably didn't know what a pirate was.

"So that's what we do, Josh, every day with lots and lots of mongooses—big ones, little ones, nice mongooses, nasty mongooses. I wish you could see them!"

Bo shifted uneasily. It wasn't likely he would see a live mongoose, since they couldn't leave the grounds. At Josh's insistence, they had scouted the tall grass at the back of the estate this morning, but no such luck. Mongooses must be wary little critters. So there was no sense in building up his expectations.

The onshore breeze that had been blowing all morning gusted just then, spattering his back with fine sand. A blank sheet of typing paper escaped its coral paperweight, eluded Bo's grab and sailed off toward the road.

"Ooh!" Hunching over, Tey put a hand to her eye.

"Are you all right?"

She nodded without looking up. "Mmm, just sand in my eye." A tear trickled down her finger.

"Want me to look?"

"Umm . . . ah . . . please!" Laughing, she rubbed her nose and nodded helplessly.

"Let's see what we got." Lifting her chin, he found his hand tingling with the softness of her skin. *She's not your type, remember?* "Can you open it, Tey?"

"Sure." She sniffed again with comic bravado.

A wide, gray-green eye stared up at him, brilliant with tears, and vanished with a sweep of dark lashes. "I see it. Just hold still now." Holding her lower lid down, he touched a forefinger delicately to the bit of pink coral sand that swam in the corner of her eye. Such a beautiful color, her iris—lichen color, slate color—where had he seen eyes like these recently? The blonde in Switzerland? No... "Got it." He leaned back from her hastily and noticed she mimicked that gesture.

"Thanks!" She brushed her nose again and laughed.

Such an unusual color . . .

They both flinched as another flurry of sand sprayed across them. But this was just Josh, returning with the fly-away paper. "Good catch, partner!" Putting beautiful eyes firmly out of his mind, Bo stood. "Anybody feel like a game of Frisbee?"

THE JEEP'S HEADLIGHTS swept across Mac's cabin as it swung up the last curve into camp. But no lights gleamed through the bushes sheltering his deck; the professor must still be in the main cabin, or off visiting at one of the other cabins. Cutting the Jeep's engine, Tey leaned back in her seat and shut her eyes for a moment.

It had been a hectic but very productive afternoon. Stretching a hand out blindly, she stroked the shoulder bag on the seat beside her. *Not long now, Lori.* For the bag contained two airplane tickets to California. Not direct flight tickets—they'd have to change planes in Puerto Rico and again in Atlanta—but those were the best connections she'd been able to arrange at this short notice.

The screen door of the main cabin banged open, and two volunteers headed uphill to one of the smaller cabins. Talking softly, they passed without seeing her. She'd racked her brain over the question of the escape route. Would it be wiser to take a roundabout way back to California, thus hoping to throw Bo or any other pursuers off the trail? Or was it best simply to lunge straight for home, hoping to stay one step ahead of the hounds? With fingers tightly crossed, she'd opted for the second tactic, reasoning that Bo was no dummy. The instant she made the snatch, he'd guess she was working for Lori, guess that California would be their destination.

But she and Josh should have a two-hour head start on Bo, at the very least. That was the other task she had completed this afternoon—measuring to the last eighth of a mile the distance from her chosen site down to the paved road, then finding the distance from that junction to Aston's estate, then from the estate to the airport. It was essential that she know how long it would take her to drive those distances, and how long it would take Bo to follow on foot, and then by car when he reached one—pray God not before he made it back to the estate!

After inhaling a deep breath, she let it out in a sigh. Bo was going to half break his big heart, trying to stop her; she knew it. If there was any other way... Dragging the purse over her shoulder, Tey stepped out of the Jeep. And Mac was not going to be all that pleased with her, either, she suspected. She had snuck out of camp this afternoon, after trapping, without telling him where she was off to, and then she'd missed supper, as well. There was no rule against either of those actions, but he was bound to be curious and annoyed all the same.

As she approached the main cabin, Tey realized the lights—or rather the electric lights—were out there also. The dim light shining through the screens was softer, yellower than the usual illumination. The cool bluesy notes of a tenor saxophone washed over her as she entered the sleeping porch; Elliot must have brought his portable radio down from his cabin. Dropping her purse off at her bed, she followed the jazz and the murmur of voices to the kitchen.

By the light of the kerosene lantern, Gerry was mixing himself a drink at the counter. "We're being romantic tonight?" A moth bound for glory fluttered around the radiant glass chimney. Tey trapped it deftly.

"There you are! Mac's been turning the camp upside down for you!"

"Has he?" Soft wings battered at her cupped palms; soft wings were brushing at her heart tonight. A second lamp threw its golden arc across the floor of the common room. The shadow of a couple, locked close and swaying to the music, swirled across this glow and vanished into darkness again.

"The power's been out for a couple of hours now." Gerry returned to the original topic. "So it's use it or lose it on the ice supply. Need a drink?"

"Love one. Be back in a minute." Eyes wide in the faint light, Tey stepped into the common room and headed for the back door. This exit gave onto a flag-stoned patio, surrounded by a garden fast reverting to jungle. Out here the frogs played the lead and the sax blew a haunting backup. She tossed the moth high into soft blackness and turned inside again, where the sounds traded dominance. Her eyes were adjusting to the dimness. There were three couples slow dancing and half a dozen spectators lounging on the couches around the room. Where was Mac?

"Here you are." Looming up beside her, Gerry pressed a cool glass into her hand. "Want to dance?"

"Dance and drink at the same time? That's got to be illegal." Smiling, she turned into his arms.

"The best things in life are." The redhead swung her out on the dance floor, then touched his ice-cold glass to her shoulder blades to bring her closer.

And where was Mac? With Gerry's height, he blocked most of her view. One cheek brushing his chest, she scanned the room to the right. David and Jean rocked gently in a reverse of her situation, though David at least made it to the level of Jean's chin. Beyond them, Tey could make out Eric Hoffman and his bird-watcher wife on one sofa, and Lucy curled in the chair next to them. Leaning away from Gerry, she took a hurried swallow of rum and Coke—more rum than Coke the way Gerry had mixed it—and looked the other way.

Facing away from her, Mac bent his head to a part-ner whom Tey couldn't see. But she could make a fair stab at who it was. There was only one woman in the camp who would dance that way, with her fingers wrapped around the back of Mac's neck. As Tey

watched, one plump hand twined up into his hair.
Damn her. Turning away, Tey took a fierce gulp of her
drink and nearly choked on an ice cube. *"Oh!"* Throat
seared from lips to gullet by the burning bubbles, eyes
stinging, she pressed her face to Gerry's chest and tried
to breathe. Damn Marty, anyway!

"You all right?" Gerry pounded her on the back
cheerfully.

"Guess so..." The music had stopped, hadn't it?
Sucking in her first full breath, she raised her head and
found Mac standing beside them.

"My turn, sport." Plucking the glass out of her
hand, he passed it to his research assistant. Gerry
flashed her a rueful grimace and backed away as Mac's
hands locked behind her waist in a grip that brooked
no argument.

So he was mad; that made two of them. The roughness of his touch had started her pulse stuttering in her
veins; the blood thumping in her ears intertwined with
the backbeat of the music. Pushing away from his wide
shoulders, she found this only brought them closer
from the waist down. Mac muttered something under
his breath and gave her an inch of freedom, then negated that illusion by the ease with which he swung her
around, spinning them both into the darkest corner of
the room.

"Where were you?" His eyes caught the lamplight
and gave it back in golden splinters. The music was
looping, closing around them in a net of purple shadows, and when Mac swung her around this time, the
whole room seemed to flow with them.

"I drove into Julianasted. I wanted to make some
notes on the town. Didn't get a chance to, the other
day."

"Don't you ever do that again!" he whispered savagely, his arms tightening as he stared down at her.

"Do what?" Beneath the heel of her right hand, she could feel his heart thudding as fast and heavily as her own. Sliding her hand down his chest an inch or so, she cupped that rhythm in her palm.

"Don't go running off like that without telling me where you're going! I thought you'd—I'm the goddamned head of this outfit and I need to know where my people are. This isn't Boston, darlin'. If you drive off a mountainside or get run down by a taxi bus, I want a goddamned hint of where to start looking for you!" As he swung them around to the music, his thigh pressed between her own, then jerked back as if it had been burned.

Drunk with the nearness of him, her body responding to his movements, following his lead with its own eager, instinctive submission, Tey tried to focus on his words. Tell him where she was going, that's what he wanted... But tomorrow, no, the next day, she would be leaving for good, and she couldn't tell him.

"Do you hear me?" Mac demanded. Spread wide on her spine, his hands slid slowly up her rib cage and back again. A blind man, a sculptor... a lover would touch that way, learning the feel of her, the precise volume that she occupied in space.

"I hear you." *With all my heart, I hear you, Mac. But I can't obey.*

He nodded tightly, satisfied—with her words, at least—and swung her around again as the cool, passionate notes ended with a long moaning slide into silence. The song of the tree frogs shimmered into the vacuum. Mac stood staring down at her, his desire gleaming in the lamplight.

Thoroughly unnerved by the mix of emotions swirling through her head, she could think of no solution but retreat. "Thanks for the dance . . . I think." Twisting out of his arms, she crossed to the couch next to Lucy. Drawing her legs up in front of her, she clasped her arms around her shins and glowered back at Mac, who still stood watching her. His mouth twisted. He turned on his heel and left the room.

Anger, guilt . . . regret—was that what she was feeling? A new tune had started, and her body throbbed and fluttered to the sound like a softly stroked drum. The shadows of the dancers reeled and drifted around her; regret and desire were two figures locked together, spinning within her brain. Desire. *Or lust. That's what they call this.* But that didn't begin to describe what she'd felt yesterday, when she'd kissed his silly thumb. *A simple, old-fashioned case of the hots!* Yet that didn't explain the way she'd reacted to the hurt she'd seen hiding behind his anger just now.

A hand waved gently before her eyes. "I'll repeat the question," George drawled, grinning down at her. "Would you care to dance?"

"Oh . . . oh, sure." Tey scrambled to her feet and followed him out onto the floor. Anything was better than sitting there going round and round with her thoughts.

The Hoffmans were dancing now, putting the younger volunteers to shame with their old smoothy routine. Jean and David still floated in a world of their own. David appeared to be doing the talking; Jean was listening with a look of startled, disbelieving pleasure. George swung her briskly around till Tey found herself facing the kitchen. And Mac, leaning in the doorway with a drink in his hand and a scowl on his face. *It's you I want!* She looked quickly away.

"Amazing what people will do for fun when they can't get to a TV, isn't it?" George murmured in her ear.

She smiled and nodded and returned to her own thoughts. *So why don't you just take him, if you want him that much?* But she shook her head quickly.

"Say something?"

"What? Oh...no." *You know why not. You can't sleep with Mac tonight, then just walk out on him tomorrow night. The man will ask questions. He'll want answers. Give him a claim on you, and he'll claim you just when you need your freedom.*

The next time she was turned Mac's way, she saw a laughing Marty dragging him out on the dance floor. Not that he was putting up much resistance. Damn. What could he see in her? *Forget it. Get back to the States and you'll get over him.*

But I don't want to forget him, she realized as the music ended and George escorted her back to the couch like a gentleman. I don't want anything serious—but to never touch him, never to know him...

Curled tightly into a corner of the sofa, she watched as Marty and Mac danced on through a short newscast and into the next song. Never to know him... *I can't stand that—I won't stand that!* And with that resolution, the hard ball of misery in her chest cracked as if she'd smashed it down on the cabin floor.

Who says I have to give him up entirely? A shining thread of excitement pulled tight around her heart. So she couldn't get involved with Mac now. There was always later. Once she'd delivered Josh to Lori, she'd still owe Mac an apology and an explanation. Why not de-

liver them in person? He'd be back in the States by
then, back in Virginia, at his university. He'd told her
last week that he'd be doing independent research there
for the rest of his sabbatical. And her job was surely
gone by now. There was no reason she couldn't stop by
and see him for a few days on her way back from California, before she started job hunting. She'd have that
fling yet!

But what makes you so sure he'd have you? a spiteful internal voice wanted to know. He didn't look exactly lovelorn at the moment, with Marty glued to his
chest, her face snuggled into the side of his neck. *Lord,
that's where I should be!*

And Mac knew that, too. That's what he'd been
trying to tell her all along. *But maybe it's too late.
You've done nothing but snub the man right from the
start.*

Taking a deep breath, Tey unclipped her barrette and
shook her hair down. Well, there was no way to know
until she tried. If she wanted Mac in her future, the
time to show some interest was now.

The music was ending, though Marty showed no
signs of noticing. It was going to be no easy trick,
peeling the blonde off Mac's chest. *What I need is a
gallon of paint stripper,* Tey decided, as she halted beside the still swaying couple. She tapped the blonde
briskly. "Mind if I cut in?"

"Uh?" As she lifted her head, the blonde's eyes reminded Tey of a sleepwalker—no one home at the
moment. "Well..." Marty glanced back at Mac, as if
hoping for support.

But Mac was supporting no one right now. He surveyed them both with a somber detachment that was
downright chilling.

It was too late to turn back now. "Thank you," Tey said pleasantly, and put a hand on Mac's free shoulder.

"Well, really..." The blonde flounced away. Side by side, they watched her intercept Gerry at the kitchen door and melt into his arms.

That seemed to be a good move. But Mac wasn't making it easy. Turning to face him, Tey rested her fingers lightly on his shoulders. "Well?"

Still he didn't smile. But his hands came up automatically to hold her in place and he started to sway.

It wasn't how she'd imagined it, but it was good all the same, Tey decided. No matter how angry Mac was, he felt so right, so warm and solid, there in her arms. Her head just fitted under his chin. Wrapping one arm around his neck, she snuggled closer and arched against him. Filling her lungs with the scent of his skin, she sighed contentedly. *You smell right, Mac. Like my lover. Someday soon, I hope you will be.*

His arms tightened so suddenly that she squeaked against the side of his throat, but he made no apologies. "What the hell do you think you're doing?" he hissed in her ear.

Just trying to show you that I do care, even if I can't follow through on it at the moment. "The samba?" she teased lightly. "I'm just following you."

He muttered something under his breath that sounded like a curse. "If you're following, then follow this." With one hand, he opened the screen door they were passing and spun her out onto the patio.

The door banged shut behind them. Out here the frog song ruled the dark. Moving slowly to the half-heard horns within, they glided along the flagstones.

This was better—this was heaven, with no one watching them. Tilting her head back, leaning back in his arms, Tey stared up at the stars. The action molded her body to Mac's from thighs to lifting breasts. With a stifled hiss, he slid his hands down her back, shaping her to him. His hands curved round her hips, not gently; she gasped a protest as he yanked her up on tiptoe. She gasped again as she felt the extent of his arousal. "Mac—" Her back bumped the side of the cabin, and Mac crowded closer, pinning her there, letting her feel every inch of him. This wasn't love or anything like it. This was—

"If there's anything I . . . hate, it's a woman who won't make up her mind." Mac's whisper in the dark above her was downright murderous.

God, what was wrong with him? This wasn't the man she knew at all! Tey bit back a cry as his hands kneaded her hips, bruising her, but there was no way he could bring her any closer with both of them clothed.

"If there's anything I won't stand, it's a woman who leaves two men dangling." His lips trailed across her face in a feverish, untender caress. "Tease one, and when that gets old, go tease the other, right?" Rocking his pelvis forward to hold her captive, he slid his hands round her hips and slowly up the front of her, exploring and rejecting her all at once. His fingers cupped her breasts and held her with a gentleness that did not match his strained voice. "I'll be damned if I'll take that again, Tey!"

"No one's asking you to take any part of me!" The tears trembled in her eyes; thank heaven it was too dark for him to see them.

"Oh, no?" His thumbs found the rigid peaks of her breasts and circled them with delicate precision. "You dance like that with everybody?"

No, only with you, and I'll never make that mistake again!

Abandoning her breasts, his hands slid higher. Curving to shape her throat, they framed her face for a moment, then plunged into her hair to pull her head back. "Damn you!" Mac whispered against her lips. "Why did you have to be so goddamned beautiful?" But he gave her no time to answer that as he claimed her mouth in a savage kiss.

She went with it as a swimmer goes with a wave— sinking beneath its silken and rushing power, then swept head over heels and praying for air. But just as the night flickered and darkened, Mac ripped his mouth away and thrust himself back from her body, though his hands still held her bruisingly.

She should have been angry—would be angry, once she could breathe again, but right now she only hurt. Why had he...? What had she...? Gathering her wits and the words to hurt him back, Tey pulled a shaking breath.

But Mac spoke first. "I don't need a woman who turns it off and on like a faucet, darlin'." His hands dropped away. "That's the last—the very last—thing I need." He backed away a step, and his low drawl seemed to be coming from a great and indifferent distance now. "So do us both a favor, will you?"

She nodded bitterly. She knew what was coming.

"Stay the hell away from me!" Turning on his heel, Mac stepped into the garden and vanished between two bushes.

Somewhere downhill a branch cracked. Then there was only the sad, silvery cry of the tree frogs, and the sound of her shivery breathing.

CHAPTER TEN

STAY AWAY FROM HIM, he'd said, and so she did. She sat in the back of the van the next day—her last day of trapping—on the way out to their grid. Setting the traps, she tagged along with George and Angie—much to their surprise, and she kept her face grimly averted from the A line, where Marty romped along behind Mac's soft-footed strides. On the way home, the back seat was full, so she sat in her usual seat behind Mac. But each time she looked forward, his eyes waited for her in the rearview mirror, so she settled for the view out the side window.

At the turnoff to camp, she climbed out with several others.

"Tey?" Mac looked over his shoulder as she caught the door.

Wide-eyed and somber, she stared back at him. *You wanted me to choose between you and Bo, Mac? Well, I'm choosing. Are you happy now?* But he looked no happier than she felt, looked as if he'd slept no more than she had the night before.

"You're cooking tonight?"

That wasn't what he wanted to know; his eyes held other questions. Ones she wouldn't, couldn't have answered even if she'd known the answers. She aimed her response somewhere over his left shoulder. "Yes— chicken. It's marinating in the fridge."

"Sounds good." His smile was too stiff to be natural.

She slid the door shut and turned away. *Think of Josh. Think of Lori. This is no time to be thinking of Mac.* For this was the payoff. If she blew the next hour, she would have lost the whole game.

But because it was so vital, she was in no hurry to make her request. She played Frisbee with Bo, Josh and Jean—or rather the three of them threw the Frisbee and Josh chased and retrieved it. When her nephew pooped out, she told Josh a mongoose story under the palm tree while Bo took a well-deserved swimming break.

It was only when Bo returned beaming and blinking to the blanket that she realized she'd been stalling. *What if he says no?* She could cancel the airline tickets, of course, but then what would she do? She'd put all her eggs into the one basket of this harebrained scheme, and it could be overturned in so many ways. Bo had only to refuse to upset the whole plan.

He won't refuse. Bo's too nice to turn me down. And if he did, all was not lost. She'd simply have to get Margie and Lori down here pronto, and they'd file for custody here. Without the home court advantage... On an island where Aston was a valued contributor to the economy and Lori was a heartsick and fragile nobody... And how long would Margie be able to stay and fight, with the rest of her practice neglected in California? And how would she stack up against the legal big guns that Aston could afford?

"I've got spinach stuck between my teeth," Bo decided.

"Huh?"

He plopped down beside her. "Or I'm going bald, and you're too kind to say? You're looking awfully strange, Tey."

"Oh... I am?" Shaking her head to sling the worries out, she grinned weakly. "I was just trying to figure out how to ask a great favor."

He settled his glasses on his short nose and regarded her with amusement. "Open your mouth and speak, that's how."

"Well, I'm in a bit of a jam." Picking up the Frisbee beside her, she tossed it across the beach. As she had hoped, Josh scrambled to his feet and lunged after it. "You know how interested our friend has become in mongooses?"

"I'll say! He wrote me a dissertation on the life and good times of Melvin Mongoose this morning. I meant to bring it to show you."

"Great... Well, I had a brainstorm, too. I decided after I saw you two yesterday that it would be fun to show Josh a live mongoose." Josh returned in a spray of sand at that moment. She waited until Bo had lofted the toy downwind before she went on. "So after I left the beach, I wangled the van from Gerry, and went out to that site I told you about up on Scenic Road—the really spectacular one where you can see all the way to St. John—and I set out four traps."

"No kidding—for us?"

"Uh-huh. I was planning to check them this afternoon. I was sure I'd get at least one 'goose—that site's teaming with 'em, and I was going to bring it back to show Josh before I set it free."

"Eeeeeeeeeeeeeeeee-rrroooom!" Waving the Frisbee before him, Josh galloped back. He brought the toy in for a wobbly landing on his bodyguard's head.

Ducking against the child's stomach, Bo tipped him over his shoulder and suspended him upside down and delightedly shrieking across his broad back. "So what happened?"

"Umm..." It wasn't easy to smile and lie at the same time. "I can't get a van. One of them's off in Thisted for the afternoon on a laundry run, and the other one—Mac thinks the brakes are going. He doesn't want me driving it till he gets it checked tomorrow afternoon." She managed a rueful little grimace. "And early tomorrow, the good van's needed for an airport trip. Anne has to get back to the States to start teaching some class..."

Thoughtfully, Bo tickled the soles of Josh's waving feet. "So you need a ride up there?"

"Would it be possible? I remembered you said you have use of a car, and I hate to wait until tomorrow afternoon. They should be okay in the trap till morning, but once they get dehydrated..."

"Bad news, huh?" Bo nodded sympathetically. "Sure, we could manage it. When do you want to do it?"

"Would early be all right? Say...six? That way I wouldn't miss the regular trapping run—I can't skip that; it's our last day."

Making a cheerful face, he lowered Josh gently headfirst to the blanket behind him. "You would! I'm no morning person."

All the better. A sleepy, unsuspecting Bo was just what she needed. "It'll be worth it. The sun will rise right out of the ocean... It'll be gorgeous."

He looked unconvinced, then preoccupied, as Josh tried a hammerlock from behind. "Ooof!"

Rising to her knees, Tey brushed the sand off her thighs. "Well, if that's settled, I'd better get going. I'm the cook tonight."

Nodding absently, Bo reached back to tickle his assailant in the ribs.

"Oh—and Bo?" In the midst of gathering up her clothes, Tey stopped as if just struck by an idea. "Why don't you bring Josh along? That way we can let the mongooses go right there. It's sort of a shame to disrupt their lives by bringing them back here."

The use of his name had caught Josh's attention. "Mongoose?" He leaned over Bo's shoulder. "Want to play mongoose? Melvin eats snakes and bananas."

"Would you like to go for a car ride tomorrow, Josh? To see some real, live mongooses? To help me catch them?"

"Uhh..." A frowning Bo was trying to catch her eye, but she focused on Josh.

"Yeah!" Then his arms tightened around Bo's neck. "Is Bogie comin'?"

"Of course. Bo's going to drive us."

"Yeahhh!" Josh breathed reverently. Releasing his captive, he started hopping in place. "Can Melvin come? Can we go now? Can I drive?" Not waiting for the answers, he tore in a widening circle around them. "Monnnnnngoose! *Eeeeeeeee*-yow!"

"Now you've done it!" Bo murmured gloomily. He yanked off his glasses and started to clean them on his T-shirt.

"You didn't mean to take him?" Tey turned a stricken face his way. "I thought if you were going—"

"I'm not supposed to take him off the estate. Remember?" Bo twisted his head to follow Josh's circuit with a reluctant, worried smile.

"Oh, Bo, I'm sorry. That was stupid—I just wasn't thinking..." *Easy...don't overdo it.* "Maybe he'll forget by tomorrow?"

"Monnnnnnnngoose!" Josh proclaimed, beginning to run out of steam. His circles were contracting around their center. "Mon-mon-monnnnnngoose. Melvin meets a mongoose!"

Bo shook his head. "Not a chance. No, I'm stuck now. He'd never forgive me if I went without him."

"I'm sorry."

"Hey—" Bo shrugged and gave her a forgiving smile "—it's okay. I guess we can bend a rule once in a while."

"If it's...kidnappers you're thinking about, Bo, I don't think you need to worry. There won't be anybody around for miles up there, but the three of us." *Oh, don't let me laugh! Please don't let me laugh.*

"Monnnnngoose." Josh collapsed between them, panting. "Gotcha, mongoose!"

Glancing down at his blissful charge, Bo looked up again and shook his head. "No, that doesn't worry me. It's not like going into town, where there are so many people to watch at once." He scratched Josh's belly, then desisted when Josh grabbed his hand. "Besides, any self-respecting...'napper will be napping at that ungodly hour. It's just the rule."

Tey stood and smiled down at him. "Well, I won't tell anyone if you don't! And I do appreciate your rescuing me this way, Bo. You're a sweetheart." She backed a step away. "So I'll meet you guys down at the front gate at six, okay?"

"We'll be the ones with bells on, and toothpicks propping up our eyelids," Bo assured her.

Glee, excitement and shame made a dreadful cocktail, Tey decided as she headed for the gate. And lying to pussycats...from the way it felt, that had to be a sin.

"STAY AWAY FROM ME," Mac had said, but cooking in the small kitchen of the main cabin, that wasn't possible. "Excuse me." Large hands closed on her waist and moved her gently aside, and Mac leaned into a cabinet. Her skin quivering from his touch, Tey moved across to the stove. Or had he forgotten that warning already? Every time she looked up, Mac's eyes were waiting for her, speaking to her, though he never smiled.

Well, if he had forgotten that bitter request, she had not. *Stay away from him.* It was good advice; she'd known that from the start. Pity she hadn't taken it. Shutting the oven door, she wiped a lock of hair off her damp forehead and looked up. And met those blue eyes again across the counter. *It's you I want.* It didn't seem to matter that he was irrationally, unreasonably jealous, that he'd hurt and humiliated her last night. Didn't seem to matter at all; her fingers itched to touch him. Spinning away, she began counting out the silverware. It was better this way, anyhow. Her original instincts had been right. She didn't need a man in her way tonight. Didn't need a man at all.

But need him or not, she had a man in her way when she tried to leave the main cabin after supper.

"I've got to talk with you."

"I don't want to talk." *It's too late, Mac. It doesn't matter anymore. I'll be gone in the morning.* "I'm late for the poker game." It would be as good a way as any to kill the last few hours till the camp settled down for the night. As good a way as any to avoid Mac, she had thought. She moved forward half a step, but he didn't budge.

"Tey..."

Footsteps shuffled behind her. "Why is it that the man with the widest shoulders always stands in the doorway?" Marty cooed.

Leaving Mac to answer that one, Tey dodged around him as he automatically stepped aside. Poker and people, and no time for regrets, no time for jealousy—that's what would get her through this night.

WHEN THE PHONE STARTED RINGING, Bo couldn't remember where it was located; downstairs, somewhere. Hurrying off the second-floor gallery where he'd been sipping a rum and cola and watching the bats swoop for their supper, he followed its ringing toward the stairs. *Probably a wrong number.* If it woke Josh, he would rip the damned thing out by its roots. Nobody but the housekeeper—Mary—ever used it, anyway.

Halfway down the stairs he remembered where it was—the library, not the living room. How many rings did that make? Someone was being awfully persistent for a wrong number.

The phone rang again as he pushed open the massive mahogany door to the library. By Murphy's law that would be its final ring, but it rang again as he got his hand on it. "Hello?" he panted.

"One moment, if you please, sir," a contralto island voice with a lilting suggestion of Paris responded. "Go ahead, sir."

"Lee?" The clipped voice in his ear sounded distant in more ways than one. "Aston speaking. Can you hear me?"

"Loud and clear." Why did he always feel he ought to add "sir"? He'd known Aston nine months now, yet he wasn't any closer to his employer than the day they'd met.

"I'm calling from Martinique. We'll arrive on St. Matthew sometime before noon tomorrow, so you'll want to pack tonight."

Damn the antsy bastard. They were just getting settled in and here he was whisking them away again! "Where are we off to?" If Aston thought he'd go along, no questions asked, he could damned well think again.

The pause at the other end of the line definitely denoted annoyance; Aston was hardly a slow thinker. "Miami," he answered finally.

Well, hurrah, at least it was the good ol' U.S. of A.! He hadn't realized how homesick he was till Aston named that destination.

"But that's a turnaround," Aston continued, coolly popping Bo's balloons. "There's some hardware I can't find in Rio. We'll pick that up and fly south the next morning."

"To Rio?"

"To Rio." The irritation was crystal clear now. "Be ready when we get there. Good night."

"Night." He hadn't even asked how his son was, Bo realized as he put the phone down. Imperious bastard, jumping them around like checkers on a checkerboard. A kid needed continuity—roots. *I need roots!*

Funny, he'd always wanted to see Rio, but now... He'd been moved around too much lately, too arbitrarily. *Well, if you don't like it, you can always get off the merry-go-round in Miami,* he reminded himself.

Right. A wave of depression washed over him. Yeah, just walk away, that would be easy to do. *I've got a dissertation to finish.* He needed at least two more months of work with Josh before he could judge results. But that wasn't the real reason—the main reason—he wouldn't walk away.

Closing the big door behind him, he scuffed his sandals across the bare tiles of the living room. The moon must have risen; the whitewashed walls glowed a milky blue. Leaving tomorrow... He shouldn't mind. He'd made only one friend here.

So you're losing only one friend. You've got so many to spare nowadays?

He'd have to find some way to meet her, to say goodbye. Couldn't just disappear on people. Tomorrow...6:00 a.m. "Oh, hell!" The promise he'd made. The blasted mongooses, trapped and waiting for someone to come rescue them. Josh, who'd gone to bed with Melvin on his pillow—he'd been hard to get down tonight, he'd been so excited about tomorrow morning. "Hell!"

But if Aston found he'd taken Josh off the estate grounds— He'd never crossed Aston before. How might the guy react? He'd keep his cool, no doubt of that, but that didn't mean he wouldn't coolly fire him.

I can't risk that. Not for some mongoose. *But what about your promise to Tey? And to Josh?* With a start, he realized he'd simply been standing there, one hand on the stairway's carved newel post. Moving softly and heavily, he started upstairs. How much risk would there be, really, if they left at six? But Aston was an early riser—didn't seem to sleep much at all, come to think of it.

And how far to the south was the island of Martinique? He knew it was several islands down the chain, but in terms of miles?

This is gonna take some thinking.

IT WAS ELEVEN when the game at the top cabin broke up. Stopping by her Jeep, Tey stood quietly and listened. A shower still ran in the cabin up the hill. Someone—Elliot?—laughed his cackling, nightbird laugh and was instantly hushed. Opening her door with infinite care, she slid inside, then shut it as carefully. There was just moon enough to read her watch face. *Give 'em fifteen minutes.*

No light gleamed between the bushes that shielded Mac's cabin. Mac... What had he wanted to talk about? She'd never know now. The realization hit her like a pain in the gut; hunching over with it, she hugged herself tightly and rested her forehead on the steering wheel. *Mac...*

Fifteen minutes later, she eased off the parking brake and shifted to neutral. Listening again, she could hear only the frogs. Eyes wide, she studied the track ahead. Without headlights, it was barely visible. Whenever a cloud crossed the moon—and there seemed to be lots of clouds tonight—it vanished into the darkness. She'd have to time this right. It would be embarrassing, to say the least, if she crashed into the bushes below Mac's cabin. As the moonlight swelled again, she eased off the foot brake, and the Jeep started rolling. *Here we go!* Gravel creaked faintly under the wheels as she glided by Mac's dark cabin. *Don't wake, Mac. Sleep on, my love.*

When she started the Jeep at the foot of the drive, the noise seemed to rip the night apart. But there was no turning back now.

Almost an hour later, the Jeep bumped off the dirt track and up into the field that sloped up to the wind-crabbed tree. Leaving the engine running, Tey climbed out and shrugged her aching shoulders. The drive up from the coast road had been more harrowing than she'd remembered. At each switchback, the drop-offs had seemed to rush at the headlights like gaping mouths. Trees lunged out of the shadows, and the brush had clawed like a vengeful animal; she'd lost the right sideview mirror, halfway up the mountain.

Taking a deep breath, she walked on up the meadow. What she had to find was the divide, where one side of the hill fell off toward the sea, and the other side sloped down to the Scenic Road. Once she'd found it, she turned the Jeep and backed slowly into position, so that it faced the road, ready for flight. Pulling the brake up to its last notch, she climbed out and turned back for a final inspection. Perfect. *Now, please, just let the brake hold all night,* she petitioned silently. *And don't let anyone find the car before morning.*

But that wasn't likely, she assured herself, as she started the long walk back. Mac had said that three cars a day up here was major traffic. Mac . . . Shoving that thought aside, she checked her watch. Now how long would it really take Bo to cover this distance? *Only one way to find out.* She lengthened her stride.

She'd thought the downhill stretch would be the easiest, but it was brutal. The third time Tey slipped on the gravel and fell, she simply lay there, eyes clenched tight against the bone-jarring pain. Lord. If she broke her neck tonight, it was all over. *Lori, I said I'd do it*

and I will. I will if it kills me! Opening her eyes, she
stared up at the sky. A fleet of ghost ships sailed the
midnight blue above. The whole Spanish Armada
scudded westward; the moonlight flickered beyond the
black clouds, edging them with silver. *Mac, if only you
could see this! If only you were here.* Bracing up on her
elbows, she rose to a sitting position, then gingerly
stood. *Seven miles to go.*

By the time she reached the coast road, the clouds
covered the sky. But even with the night darker, it was
easier going with level asphalt underfoot. Tey broke
into a sore-footed jog for a bit, then gave it up. *Six
miles.*

To her right, the black ocean sighed and rumbled up
the sand. High up in the mountains on her left, the
wind was rising. The distant trees made a whispering
hush, a stealthy rumor spreading leaf by leaf across the
dark slopes. Tey shivered and walked faster and the
wind sighed again, closer now. And somewhere up
ahead the baobab waited. It would be dancing in this
wind, the dead rats swaying below its twisted limbs.
*Mac, why did you ever tell me about that tree? And
where are you when I need you?*

The wind died away and the *cleek-cleek* of the frogs
seemed to swell in the silence, sweet and piercing,
echoing down from the heights above. The breeze rose
again and rustled slowly toward her down the slopes,
drowning out the song of the frogs as it came, as if they
were blowing out to sea before it. Leaves fluttered,
branches rattled, and a soft drumming sound marched
closer. Throwing up her head, Tey understood at last.
Rain, not wind at all—a tropical downpour stomping
down the hills after her, advancing in a silvery wall.

Not a hundred yards away now. Half laughing, half terrified, she took to her heels.

The rattling swelled to thunder and she was drenched—drowning. Cupping her hands over her nose, she staggered on, half deafened, totally blind and suddenly cold. And then she was chasing the rain; it marched away down the road before her. Thunder faded to rattling, then to a liquid mutter, then the frogs piped louder as the rain pattered away. A wind sucked after the squall, and Tey shivered and wiped her eyes. Thank God that hadn't lasted!

Far behind her, the trees whispered again. Then the next onslaught drummed slow and silvery across the mountains.

By the time she reached the turnoff to camp, Tey was as drowned as one can be above water. Shivering uncontrollably, hugging herself, she slogged mechanically up the hill through the mud. *The last hill.* Stopping just below the trees that sheltered the camp, she stared to the east. The squalls were spaced further apart now. Did that mean they'd stop soon? *It's got to stop! It's got to. I'll never get Bo out in the rain.*

Another spasm of shivering hit her, and she stumbled on. As the track passed Mac's cabin she stopped again, all her instincts crying out that here was the place of maximum comfort and warmth. Here was rest. *But not for you. Keep moving.* She flogged herself on up the hill and into the main cabin.

Numbly she squelched along the sleeping porch toward her bed. With her head bowed, she didn't even see him; warm hands caught her arms as she walked into his chest. Too tired to cry out, she tilted her head back. "Mac."

"Lord, where have you—" His hands moved up her shoulders, gathered her hair at the back of her neck. "You're soaked. What have you—"

"Car trouble." The shivers were starting once more. If he'd just pull her closer, against his chest, she'd never be cold again.

He swung her around and pointed her to the door. "A hot shower," he countered flatly.

Not at his place! If she walked through his door, she'd never find the strength to walk out again. But his arm around her wet shoulders swept her along, and he ignored her shaking head. "Rain's coming," she protested as the sound rippled down the mountain toward them, as if somehow that would stop him.

"Yep." He steered her through the screen door ahead of him and into the bedroom. Eyeing his bed, she jumped as the rain found the tin roof. Its thunder drowned out Mac's words as he pulled her into the bathroom. Numbly she watched as he adjusted the flow and temperature of the shower. He seemed irritated when he turned to find her still clothed. Frowning faintly, he moved her clumsy fingers aside.

Leaning back against the bathroom door, she watched his face as he slowly stripped her. His eyes were growing darker and his jaw muscles bunched and hardened, imposing a restraint on his features to match the deft impersonality of his hands as he peeled her out of her clinging shirt. That somber, watching stillness deepened to something that might have been anger, could have been pain, when he dragged her sodden jeans down her hips.

Balancing against his shoulders as he knelt before her, she stepped out of the icy denim. His fingers closed in the sides of her bikini underwear and she shivered violently. Her skin roughened—ached—with goose bumps as he pulled the cloth down her thighs.

As he brought the filmy bit of nylon down past her calves, his fingers reached out to encircle her ankles. Holding her captive, his hands tightened almost painfully while he stared down at her feet. "Damn!" he whispered unhappily and let her go. And stood.

He took her waist with shaking hands. Just a foot would bring her into his arms. *Yes, oh, please, yes!* she thought, staring up at him.

But Mac swung her around so abruptly that she would have fallen except for those hands. His fingers found the hooks of her brassiere; he eased her out of it and dropped it on the floor. She stood naked and waiting...

"Get in!" he muttered hoarsely.

In? Oh—the shower. Yes. Stiffly, slowly, hoping in vain to be recalled, she stepped into the stall. The sound of the curtain closing between them was like a door slamming shut. *Oh, Mac, it's you I want!*

But if she couldn't have Mac, a hot shower came a close second. Tey didn't soap for a long time, but simply turned, letting her half-frozen skin thaw and soften while the water played over her breasts, her back, her closed eyelids. As the last of the ice melted, her shoulders lifted in a sigh that welled up from her toes.

"Tey?"

So he hadn't left. His voice had come from just beyond the curtain. "Umm?" Her questioning sound was a waterlogged purr.

"You were with Bo." He made it more statement than question.

How can you possibly—ever—think that I'd want Bo over you, my darling? She smiled blindly, and shook her head. "No, Mac, I wasn't. I went for a drive—to think—and had car trouble someplace past Thisted. Had to walk home." *And someday soon, Mac, if you're still talking to me after this, I'll tell you the truth. Every last word of it.* But would he forgive her?

"Oh . . ." He was silent so long that she began to wonder if he'd gone, then the curtain slid open softly. "Need your back scrubbed?"

Oh, please! "Yes." She smiled over her shoulder, then hissed through her teeth as a warm, erotically rough palm cupped her stomach to support her. Considering the state of her knees, it was support she needed while Mac soaped her neck, her shoulder blades. Arching her back, she curved to fit his palm as he traced her spine, bone by tiny bone, down to the soft cleft between her hips. A lazy, soapy figure eight defined those curves once, twice, and once again, and then Mac turned her to rinse the soap away.

Growling contentedly, she shrugged her shoulders under the hot drizzle, and then he was drawing her out again. His arm slid around her waist, pulling her back to fit against his chest and stomach, and he pressed a kiss to the hollow between her shoulder blades.

"Mac?" She was shivering again suddenly. Hot shivers, this time.

"Hmm?" Lipping softly, deliberately, up her spine, he bit her gently on the top of her shoulder. His arm tightened as she arched spasmodically.

She got her breath again in a series of indrawn gasps. "Aren't you going to do my front, Mac?"

Laughing softly, he wrapped his other arm around her and lifted her off her feet in a bear hug. "I don't dare, possum! I'm not sure I can let you go now."

"Why should you want to do that?" she asked breathlessly. The water was growing cool; she shut it off, and was surprised to find rain still rattling on the roof.

"God!" he groaned against the nape of her neck. Setting her on her feet, he loosened his arms. His hands shaped to her ribs and slid slowly, sensuously higher until he cupped her breasts. "I've got all these apologies to make and you don't seem to want them!"

No. Only you. That's all I want. Giving herself more fully into his hands, she shook her head contentedly. "Not tonight."

"I . . ." His fingertips explored the taut and tingling buds of her breasts, tentatively at first and then with gentle greediness. "I've been trying to tell you all day. I had no right to say the things I did last night," he murmured roughly.

"No, you didn't." But her body was yielding him every right that he asked for tonight. Swaying and shivering beneath his thrilling explorations, she twisted in his arms to wrap her own around his neck.

Standing on tiptoe, she touched her nose to his and widened her wet lashes, as if she could stare through his beautiful blue eyes straight into his heart. *Oh, Mac, if you have apologies to make, then so do I!* His hands had stilled and he simply held her, heart pressed to thumping heart.

Wide-eyed, they listened to the duet for a dreamy, silent moment. Then the almost solemn line of his mouth quirked in a smile, her own lips echoed it, and they kissed.

Tongue slow-dancing with tongue, heart calling to heart, there was only one way left to come closer. Tearing their mouths apart, they stared at each other, breathing hard, savoring the silent question and the answer. "So if I can't make apologies, can I make amends?" he drawled at last.

Her face lighting with a wicked grin, she leaned out from his neck, arching her back so that her breasts teased his chest. "Amend me, Mac—please!" she petitioned huskily.

IT WAS AS GOOD as she'd known it would be. They fitted.

And celebrated that fitting, once in laughing exultance, and then a second time in silent, slow-touching wonder while the rain roared on the roof above.

As it rattled away across the forest, Mac turned them over in a gliding, weightless roll. Settling her on top, he stroked her back and hips with his fingertips. "Told you so," he murmured drowsily against her hair.

"Told me what?" she purred.

"Told you it'd be that good."

"You never—when?"

"What do you think I've been saying since the first night I met you?"

"Mmm." She smiled against his throat.

Hypnotized by his touch, she was toppling into sleep when he spoke again. "You hungry?"

"Uh-uh." She shook her head peacefully.

"Well, I am."

Waking a little, she propped her nose against his and stared down at him. His eyes were catching light from somewhere. "Too bad! I've got you pinned."

"Oh..." With a sudden roll, Mac was now grinning down at her. "I hadn't noticed." Sliding off her and then the bed, he gathered up the rumpled blanket and her within it. "Well, if you won't eat, come keep me company." Ignoring her growling, he started out of the room with her, then stopped. "Oh." He turned back to his bureau. "Open the top drawer."

"Why?" But she was opening it already. A smoothly folded rectangle of brilliant scarlet, with a turquoise hibiscus emblazoned across it, was stacked on top of his T-shirts. "Is it—" As she touched it, she knew that it was. "My java wrap! But you sent this to your sister!"

"I sent her a green one. I couldn't see anyone but you in this one."

Pulling his head down, she gave him a smacking kiss. "Let me down, Mac! I've got to put this on."

"Put it on and I'll just have to take it off you again," he warned.

"Why else would I wear it?"

In the kitchen, curled in a chair with the wrap swirling around her thighs, Tey watched in sleepy contentment. Nakedness became him. Absorbed in making an omelet, Mac moved with the unselfconscious grace of an animal. With a kind of wondering possessiveness, she traced the line of soft gold along his flat stomach when he stopped beside her. "Last chance, possum. Shall I add an egg or two?"

"Two." Her touch was arousing him, wasn't it?

But he grinned and backed away. "I thought you weren't hungry."

They ate in companionable, smiling silence. Then Mac rose to pour two mugs of coffee from the pot that had been perking on the stove. "We'll be up all night if we drink that!"

"Dreadful," he agreed smugly, and fingered the knot of cloth tied above her breasts.

Laughing, she accepted a cup. And come to think of it, it was best that she not sleep at all. Normally she woke at five-thirty, which would have given her plenty of time to meet Bo. But after a night like this, once she slept, there was no telling when she'd awaken.

"A frown?" Mac touched her eyebrow.

Oh, Mac, why can't I tell you? Forcing a smile, she shook her head.

They drank the coffee in bed with the lights out and their legs entangled. "'Bout those apologies..." Mac laid a coffee-flavored kiss on her lips.

"Mmm?"

"I'm sorry I've been so...jealous...this past week. I know I had no right. I've had no claim on you...just a lot of hopes and wishes."

She stroked the sole of her foot up his hairy, muscled calf and down again. "Do you always get so jealous, Mac?"

She felt rather than saw him shake his head. "Just the past few years..."

"Joanne?" she guessed, and after a long moment felt him nod again.

"We were trying a commuting marriage." His voice had lost its vibrant warmth, had flattened into an expressionless half whisper. "I was teaching down in Virginia, just about to make tenure—I couldn't quit that. She was partner in an up-and-comin' ad agency, in the city. No way would she quit that." He took a long swallow of coffee, then sat silent so long she feared that was all he'd say. "She met a man..."

Oh, Mac. She wanted to wrap her arms around him, squeeze the pain right out of him, but somehow she knew he wouldn't want it.

"He was the kind of guy she ought to have married in the first place. A client of hers...investment banker. A guy on the fast track. He knew all the things that mattered. The in jokes. The right people. Which places to be seen, what tailor to go to, the proper wines to order."

"All the important things in life," she agreed, her voice dripping sarcasm.

He laughed softly under his breath and nodded. "To the kind of people in that world—yes."

"So she left you?" *Bless her, the silly moron!*

But he laughed again—there was more pain than pleasure in the sound and shook his head. "Nothing so clean and easy. She couldn't decide."

"Oh, Mac." She rubbed her cheek against his arm.

"She'd been seeing him for about a year when I found out," he continued quietly. "I asked her—should have guessed sooner, but somehow you just can't let yourself see it—and she broke down and cried, said she loved us both." Setting his mug down beside the bed, he turned and buried his face against her breasts. "So that gave me a little hope. I still wanted her. I decided I could be patient."

Setting her own mug down, she rested her cheek on his head and clasped her arms around him. "So how long were you patient?"

"Six months." His sigh warmed her skin. "She was still sleeping with both of us. Wasn't any nearer to making up her mind. So one day I just packed up her things and shipped 'em back to her."

"Good for you."

"Mmm." He lipped her gently. "And I thought I'd come through it okay...with no more than the usual scars, till I met you."

"Me?" Sliding down in the bed, she pulled him with her.

"You, possum. I haven't exactly been a priest since the divorce. I've been seeing women, but I haven't felt this . . . angry . . . this rotten . . . since Joanne."

"I make you feel rotten?"

"Seeing you interested in another man makes me feel rotten. I guess you're the only one who's mattered enough to make me feel so bad."

"Then let's see if I can make you feel good." Pushing gently against his shoulder, she rolled him onto his back.

But much later, when Mac slept in her arms, and she waited for the dawn, it was Tey who felt . . . rotten, yes, that was the word for it.

Why should you feel rotten? You've been wanting this since you first met him. Now you've had your fun and it's time to get back to business. Remember what you came down here for?

Yes, but all the times she'd dreamed of making love to Mac, she'd pictured the event, not the aftermath. She'd seen Mac as a beautiful body, a heart-stopping smile, a delightful sense of humor, but she hadn't seen his pain, his uncertainty, the damage that her loving, then leaving, might cause.

I can't do that to him! Here he's trusted me enough to love me, to tell me about Joanne, and then I'm to walk out on him without an explanation? I can't do it!

But there was no way to tell him. Even if Mac saw things her way, that snatching Josh back was the only way to save him—and she wasn't at all sure an outsider would see it that way—still she couldn't tell him. For there was the chance that Bo, or Aston, would go to the police. Not much of a chance, but if it happened, there was only one way she could protect Mac. He had to be able to testify, without hesitation, without a twinge of guilt, that he hadn't known what she was up to. Hadn't even known her real name . . .

Mac twitched in his sleep—dreaming—and cuddled closer. She pressed her lips to his brow and felt him relax. *I could leave him a note—an explanation. An apology.* But the plane left at 8:30. Even if Mac slept till eight, if he woke up, read the note, then dashed straight to the airport, he might catch her before she got Josh off the island. And there was no way she could risk a last-minute confrontation at the airport, no way she could jeopardize Josh's retrieval. Not even for Mac.

So figure a way to leave a note that he won't find till we're gone. And wondering how to do that, she fell asleep.

CHAPTER ELEVEN

SHE WAS FALLING—the plane was dropping out from under her as she clutched Josh and tried to scream. Just as they smashed down, Tey awoke with a sickening jolt. Mac murmured softly, protesting in his sleep, and she loosened her death grip. Lord. Lord! What time was it? It was daylight.

Slowly twisting her wrist, she consulted her watch. *Five-fifty!* Her breasts were pressed to Mac's side; the sudden racing of her heart should have been enough to wake him, but mercifully he slept on as she untwined herself and slid across the bed.

There was no time for silent, lingering farewells. Kissing her fingers, she held them just above his lips. *Oh, Mac...* No time to write a note. No time for clothes, even; her scarlet wrap was lost beneath the blanket, so, wrapping a towel around her, she pulled the car keys from her sodden jeans, collected her shoes, and glided out the door. Five minutes later, dressed in dry T-shirt and shorts, and carrying nothing but the shoulder bag that contained the plane tickets, Tey hurried down the hill.

"I'M GLAD YOU INSISTED on driving." Smothering a yawn with one hand, Bo pulled Josh back from the open window with the other as brush whacked the fender. "It's nice to sit back and gape."

"Wait'll you see the view from the top!" Tey eased the car around a curve. As the valley opened out in a dizzying sweep below, she stole a peek at her watch. *Right on schedule.* Was Mac awake yet, or still curled in their rumpled sheets?

"There's a mongoose!" Josh proclaimed for the seventh time. He pointed down into the valley, then giggled triumphantly when they looked for it.

"Yeah, I'll mongoose you, partner!" Ruffling his hair for him, Bo pulled the child back from the window again and decided he was glad they'd come. They nearly hadn't. If there'd been any way to back out on his promise to Tey, he would have.

But a promise was a promise. Besides, Tey had set these traps for Josh. And he'd remembered her description of the mongoose who hadn't been removed from its trap in time—he couldn't leave any animal to that kind of fate.

Once that was decided, bringing the short one was inevitable. Mary didn't come in from Thisted till eight, and he didn't know her phone number. There was no way he could leave Josh alone in the house, to wake up and find him inexplicably gone. Josh had had enough important people walk out on him to last him a lifetime. If the kid couldn't depend on him, who could he depend on?

Choosing a moment when Tey was concentrating on the so-called road, he glanced down at his watch. *Plenty of time. Relax.* Aston would have to shake his surly pilot out of bed. They'd have to check the jet, the weather, receive permission to take off. They'd have to clear customs at this end, and a private jet coming up from the south would get more than a cursory inspection. *Plenty of time.* He hoped...

"Josh, look up there! See the hawk?" Tey took one hand off the steering wheel to point through the windshield.

I wish she wouldn't do that! Bo glanced out the side window, then swung his eyes determinedly forward. He still hadn't told her about their leaving today—no sense in spoiling her expedition. He'd tell her on the way back. Once they'd gotten down on the flat again.

"We've got company," Bo observed a short while later, as Tey guided the station wagon up the hill toward the Jeep that she'd positioned the night before.

"Yes. Bird-watchers, I bet, at this hour. Hope they haven't stumbled over any of my traps." She snatched a glance at Bo's face. He looked thoughtful but not alarmed. *Now, please, don't let him object to the parking site. I've got to park this just right.* To distract him, she recounted Mac's information about Columbus. *Oh, Mac...*

But, spellbound by the view as the car topped the rise, Josh's bodyguard made no objection when she parked the car a few feet past the Jeep. Just a few crucial feet beyond the divide. "Wow..."

"That's St. John to the right. The other's St. Thomas." Tey pointed out the islands as she stepped from the car. *Keep talking. Don't give him time to think about the keys.* "It's much clearer today than it was last time. Guess the rain cleared the air." The world was a plate of star sapphires strewn with diamonds. Far to the east, a tiny sailboat cast an amethyst shadow where it blocked the sun's rays. "And the view's even better from up there." She nodded to the crest of the meadow, some fifty yards away and slipped the keys in her pocket as Bo turned. "Our traps are on the other side."

"*Eeee*-yow!" Josh scampered away before them as they strolled up the field. "I saw one! I saw one!"

Tey checked her watch again. *No hurry. Take your time.* But her heart ignored that advice, and her palms were slick with sweat. *Lori, I can do this. I can.*

"Incredible," Bo said softly as they reached the top.

"I guess that's Puerto Rico." Tey nodded to the distant lilac points. Puerto Rico. A couple of hours and she and Josh would be there. It was impossible to believe. Columbus wouldn't have believed it for a minute.

But Josh had more immediate concerns than panoramas. "Gotcha mongooses! Gotcha!"

"Wait, Josh!" Bo caught up with him as he hit the taller grass, and lifted him to his shoulders. "Now I bet you'll see a mongoose." He turned to wait for Tey. "See any sign of our bird-watchers?"

Tey shook her head. "Probably down in the trees." She gestured toward the wall of green that edged the lower slopes of the headland. *Just a few more feet now. I wonder—I hope—he'll be able to hear it.* She stopped short. "Oh...darn!" Her words came out too high, and she swallowed dryly.

"What's the matter?" Bo glanced at her sharply.

"My camera. I left it in my purse. Back in the car."

"No problem." The guard swung around.

"No!" Wincing inwardly, she softened her voice. "No, I'll just get it myself, Bo. Why don't you two go on down to the traps?" She pointed to a small tree halfway down the slope. "They're set around that tree. Maybe Josh can find some of them." And maybe he couldn't, since she hadn't really set out traps. Backing away, she waited tensely for his nod.

With the sun reflecting off Bo's glasses, it was impossible to read his eyes. He seemed to hesitate forever, then nodded. With a reassuring smile—or so she hoped—Tey turned uphill.

By the time she made it to the ridge, her heart seemed to be pounding its way through the top of her skull. Her stomach swirled sickeningly. Starting down the other side, she checked her watch and broke into a run. *Ten minutes late!*

Panting, she reached the car. *The purse—don't forget the purse!* She whirled to check the hilltop—no sign of Bo, thank God—then yanking her purse out of the car, she shoved it under the driver's seat of her Jeep.

Now do it. When she returned to the station wagon, her hands were shaking so badly, she couldn't fit Bo's key into the car's ignition. *"Please!"* It went in with a click. Unlocking the ignition, she shifted to neutral. And let the parking brake off. She was breathing audibly now; the gasps seemed to echo off the windshield. *Now do it.* She took an unsteady breath. Remembered to check the crest of the hill again. Still bare. *So do it.* But her foot seemed frozen to the brake pedal. *What if it moves? What if I can't—"Do it!"* she snarled aloud. Stretching one shaking foot to the ground, she kept the other on the pedal. Holding tight to the open door, she scowled downhill. And let the brake off.

The car went smoothly, as if pulled on a string. She'd forgotten to let go; her grip pulled her in against the back door. "Uhh!" *The wheel!* Stiff-arming the sliding metal, she fell backward—away—tottered and sat. Gasping, staring downhill, she watched the car—Aston's car—bounce over a hummock and gather speed. It was racing away down a constricting black tunnel.

I'm fainting, she thought as it ripped into the trees. The black hole where the car had been an instant before was the end of the tunnel... And the end of consciousness.

"YOU'RE OKAY! *Are* you okay? Tey, what happened?" Bo shook her shoulder and she looked up slowly. He was panting and red faced. "What happened? I heard the—are you all right?"

The words had been planned long ago; they came without thought now. "It started...rolling." Her voice was a child's squeak, but that was okay. "I climbed in to reach my purse and it just started rolling." Josh galloped up to them; his eyes were enormous.

Kneeling beside her, Bo gathered him in automatically without sparing him a glance. He touched her cheek gently. "God, you—thank God you got out!"

Suddenly she wanted to cry. He was so wonderful, how could she—? But she had to. *Lori.* "But my purse. I didn't get my purse!" she half whimpered.

Bo grinned in spite of himself and ran a hand through his hair; it stayed up in stiff peaks. "We'll get it. I don't think the car reached the water. Hit a rock or a tree from the sound it made."

"Bogie, where's the car?" Josh tugged at his shirt. "Bogie?"

"It went for a drive without us, partner." Bo stood, and then his face changed, its pink healthy flush draining away as she watched. "The birders!" He glanced down at her quickly. "What if they were down—" He shook his head as if shaking that thought aside. "Tey, will you be all right if I go down and take a look?"

"Yes, Bo. I'm fine. Really. Shall I keep Josh?"

"Right." Patting Josh on the head, he started away.

"Wait, Josh!" Tey caught his T-shirt as her nephew lunged after his friend. "Stay with me."

"Wanna go!" He strained against her hold.

"Josh, I think we better help Bo." Shakily, still holding on to him, Tey stood. "Do you want to help Bo?" The receding figure had almost reached the line of the brush.

"Yeah!" Josh looked up at her expectantly.

"Good!" Tey drew the Jeep keys out of her pocket. "Let's go get help then." Bo vanished into the trees. "Hurry!"

And miraculously, Josh followed without protest as she crossed to the Jeep and opened the door. Leaning out his window as she let the brakes off, he stared back toward the trees. "Bogie?" he ventured doubtfully.

"We'll call for a tow truck," she assured him as the Jeep bumped silently down toward the road. *Why, oh why, do I have to lie to him? Will I ever feel right again? Mac and Bo and now Josh. Oh, Lori, if only you knew what I've had to do!*

Bo HAD NO TROUBLE finding the car. It had crushed a trail like that of a maddened elephant through the thickets, and the path widened to a boulevard where the car had started its sideways rolling. The trail ended abruptly at the base of a crazily leaning tree.

"Lord." Hanging on to the trunk of a shattered sapling, he stopped a few feet up the slope from the wreck. If Tey had been inside... White sunbursts of smashed glass bloomed on the windshield and the side windows were out entirely. With its wheels pointing skyward, the car looked like some big, ruined animal, giving up the ghost in cartoon fashion.

And what about the birders? Nerves prickling, he stood still a minute longer, but all he could hear was the wind picking its way through the trees and distantly, faintly, the murmur of waves on the shore below. *So what did you expect, a groan? If anybody's under that car—believe me—he's done groaning forever!*

No blood to be seen anywhere, he noted thankfully, as he slithered down to the car. They were going to be lucky all the way around; somehow he was sure of it. Some sixth sense was telling him there was no hapless bird-watcher flattened under this heap; that there was no one—dead or alive—anywhere close. Standing in this sun-splattered glade, he might have been the last person alive on St. Matthew.

But make sure no one's here. He prodded a door panel with his shoe, but the car didn't even rock. Embracing its tree, it wouldn't be going anywhere, ever again. All the same, he circled downhill of it reluctantly, half expecting it to roll down on top of him.

There was no sign of any victims on this side, either. *We've been lucky.* If you could call it luck. He put that thought firmly out of his head and concentrated on finding Tey's purse.

By some miracle, he got the back door open, but there was no trace of the blasted handbag. Maybe wedged under—which now meant above—one of the seats? Nerves screeching in protest, Bo hunched inside to crouch on what had once been the car's ceiling. His breath caught as metal groaned somewhere, but his traplike world remained stolidly, confoundingly upside down. Glass crunching underfoot, fighting down his dizziness, he searched the back seat, then the front.

No purse. Sweat dripped down his ribs, trickled down through his hair like tiny searching fingers, burned in his eyes. Pulling off his glasses, he realized he had nothing dry to wipe them with and put them back on. Enough. The purse wasn't here. Must have been flung out once the windows smashed. So there'd been a casualty, after all. Little enough to give the gods.

And maybe he'd find it on his way back.

But plodding up the slope again, his eyes combing the bruised grass, Bo wondered if a purse would be all the gods claimed.

Aston... There was no way to hide this accident from him, no way to deny that he'd disobeyed orders. *And all for some damned mongooses.* What a fool he'd been!

It wouldn't be the loss of a used car his employer would mind, it would be his breaking the rules. But how much would Aston mind, that was the question. A dressing-down, a docking of pay to cover the car—sure—those he could stand; those measures would be only reasonable.

But what if he fires me, what then? Bo slipped on the grass and cursed softly. What then? What recourse did he have?

None at all. You should have thought of that sooner, sucker. As he stopped for breath, his eyes swept the hill above, searching for a small and fidgeting figure, but Josh—and Tey—were out of sight. Apprehension and guilt swirled in his guts. He could almost believe Aston had swooped down from the sky to whisk them away.

But why would he do that? *So I blew it. So I'm human—surprise, surprise.* All the same, nobody could have cared for Josh better than he'd done these past nine months. Surely Aston realized that? Surely that counted for something with the guy? Hell, that was a'l that should count!

But he'd broken Aston's rule. And Aston saw things in black and white—that much he knew from his dealings with the man. That was how computers worked, wasn't it—only two choices? Yes—no? Off—on? With him . . . or against him?

"No," he panted and stopped again. They'd just have to thrash things out. Somehow. Searching again for a small silhouette against the dazzling sky, Bo realized at last what was wrong with the picture—the Jeep was gone. He broke into a slipping trot. *So the Jeep's gone, so what?* But it made no sense; they'd need a ride down out of these godforsaken hills. If the Jeep's driver had returned, surely Tey could have persuaded him to wait? No one would just strand them there.

Staggering over the crest of the hill, he found his answer. No one had stranded them, but someone had stranded him. Nothing moved in all that wide, sloping field—not a bird, not a mongoose, not a child. And in the knee-high grass, he could still read the darker lines made by the Jeep wheels, leading down to the trail and out of his life.

"WHERE'S BOGIE?" Josh whirled to lean out the window, and Tey swerved the Jeep out just in time to keep a bush from whacking his face. This brought them sickeningly close to the drop-off on the left.

"Josh! Joshems, please get away from the window! That bush nearly got you. Come sit down." She patted the seat beside her.

"Where's Bogie?"

"Bo's taking care of the car, Josh. You and I have to go find a phone and call a tow truck. You know what a tow truck is, don't you?"

Passing the baobab, she pointed it out to him. "Looks like a witch's tree, doesn't it?"

But Josh was in no mood for a botany lesson. Flashing a distrustful look her way, he turned back to his vigil of staring out the back window, as if he expected Bo to come jogging up behind them at any second.

"See any mongooses back there, Josh?"

He shook his head sullenly.

And now the estate—and the turnoff to camp—lay around the next bend. The roaring of the Jeep seemed to fill up her skull and push outward. *Oh, don't let Mac see us! Please don't. That would be too cruel.* Cringing inside, she studied the road ahead as the Jeep hummed into the turn. Deserted, thank God.

"Bogie!" Turning around just then, Josh recognized the estate as they reached its gates. He lunged at his door.

"Josh!" Heart in her mouth, she caught the back of his pants and hung on. "Josh, be careful!" Beyond his face, the Jeep's window framed the gate to the beach for a moment. Above the gate, Mac's fair head was frozen in a pose of startled attention. Widening blue eyes met her own for an endless split second as his hand jerked up in a detaining gesture. *Oh, Mac!* And then he was behind them. The tire sound changed as the right wheels bumped off the pavement; wrenching her eyes forward, she swerved them back onto the road just in time.

"Bogie! Le'go! I want Bogie!" Josh wailed and pushed at her hand on his belt.

"Oh, Josh, please, baby! You're going to fall out! Bo isn't back there, Joshems." *Just my heart. Oh, Mac, I couldn't stop. Please forgive me...oh, please.*

SKIDDING ON THE LOOSE GRAVEL that overlaid the mountain trail, Bo threw out his arms as he nearly went down. *Stay on your feet, damn you!* He'd done enough lying down on the job already. Just below his ribs, a hot wire was wrapped around him; it twisted tighter, burned hotter with each jarring, sliding step he took. *But how was I to know? She seemed so nice, so sane.*

All you had to do was look at her eyes, you moron. Those lovely, lying eyes—Josh's eyes. He'd seen the resemblance, recognized it on some level, and blocked it out. *Because you wanted to believe she liked you, that she wanted to be your friend as well as Josh's, you sucker.*

Steam covered the bottom half of both his lenses. Yanking the wire rims off, Bo tucked them in his shirt pocket, but the ruts and gravel patches blurred treacherously into the dusty red ahead. He put them back on without stopping.

Tey had Josh's eyes, but she couldn't be his mother; even in a year, Josh would not have forgotten his mother. But there was an aunt, the only other close relative—he'd dragged that fact from Aston soon after he was hired, when he was trying to learn all he could about Josh. Tey had to be that aunt; it was the only explanation that made sense.

So they're heading for California. They had to be. *But you've got to catch them before that. If they get him back to California, bring in their lawyers, it could be years before you get him back.*

You mean, before Aston gets Josh back, he reminded himself brutally. After this, Aston would not be keeping him on the payroll.

That hurt too much to think about; swallowing that thought, he felt like a balloon growing lighter, stretching tighter and tighter to contain the expanding pain of the stitch in his side, the ache of friendship betrayed, the loss of—*Shut up!* His loss wasn't the point; the point was Josh being dragged back to a mother who hadn't wanted him, who only wanted him now as a living trading card. *Not if I can help it!*

How much farther to the coast road—half a mile? His knees were killing him, and the sound like a punctured foot pump was his breathing, but if he stopped, he'd stiffen up. He shortened his strides and kept moving.

Maybe Aston would catch them. Trying to read his watch, Bo tripped and staggered forward, but windmilling his arms, he caught his balance again. There was just a chance Tey would run straight into Aston's arms at the airport—it was a tiny airport, with only the one runway. Thank heaven he hadn't told her about Aston.

By the time he reached the paved road, his pace was down to a hobbling walk. *I'll never catch them. Never.* But he couldn't stop; moving had become a mechanical, instinctive response. Consciousness had retreated deep inside, leaving an unseeing, whistle-breathed automaton jerking stiff-legged down the center of the deserted road.

Hypnotized by the roar of the blood in his ears, Bo didn't hear the car at first. When its unmuffled rumble finally penetrated, he swung around to find it following close behind. It stopped as he did.

He was hallucinating—that was the simple explanation. The yellow pickup truck was too tiny to be real, too rusted and battered to still be rolling. Squinting into the sunlight, Bo couldn't see a driver at all in the dark cab; maybe there wasn't one. With the thought that he might have to drive this apparition himself, he stumbled back to the driver's door.

Framed in the open window, a warrior's mask peered up at him, and for a dizzy second Bo was back in Africa, back in the Peace Corps. Then the significance of the lion's mane—the man's dreadlocks—slowly dawned. A Rastafarian.

"Go easy, mon." Spoken in the soft Matean accent, his advice sounded like a benediction.

Suppressing an idiotic urge to giggle, Bo found he was clinging to the window frame. "I need help."

"Yes, mon?"

No need to bother with details. "Someone stole my—my son."

BY THE TIME they reached the airport, Josh wore a face like a pink thundercloud, and at first he refused to leave the Jeep. "Josh, come on!" Standing in his open doorway, Tey gave him a pleading smile and held out her hand.

No such luck. Fixing her with a truly awesome scowl, her nephew stood his ground.

How much time left? Tey broke his gaze to check her watch. Twenty-five minutes till their little interisland flight took off. They had a few minutes to spare. "Don't you want to help Bogie, Josh?"

Somehow—unbelievably—his scowl intensified, showing her how stupid he found that question.

"We have to find a phone and call a tow truck, Josh. Won't you come help me?" *And you're right, Josh, I'm twelve kinds of a jerk, and I wouldn't buy a used car from me, either, but please come.*

And miraculously, after an agonizingly long moment of deliberation, he clambered down from his seat and trudged off toward the terminal. Slamming the Jeep's door, she hurried after him.

Once they passed through the tall-columned gallery and into the open air pavillion, Josh stayed by her side. Viewed from a three-foot perspective, the terminal had to be intimidating. Tourists clattered importantly across the tiled floors and smiling, uniformed porters loomed above him on all sides. "Josh?" She touched his shoulder, then sighed as he drew away. "There's a phone; come on." Leading him past their airline's counter, she checked the information board at the back of the booth. Gate Three. She glanced down at her watch again. *And hurry!*

Wide-eyed and suspicious, Josh hovered in the door of the phone booth while she dropped a coin in the pay phone and punched out a random sequence of numbers. "Hello?" she greeted the dial tone. "We've had an accident and we need a tow truck. There's a man named Bo Lee up on the Scenic Road, and he'll show you where to find the car." She paused as if to listen. "Yes, as soon as possible. Thank you very much!" It was so easy to lie to a child. Feeling like an utter heel, she hung up the phone. But if he was worrying about Bo, it was better to ease his mind than— Looking down from the phone, Tey gasped. "Josh!" Where had he— Bolting out of the booth, she glanced wildly around.

Some fifty feet away, Josh scuttled toward a news and souvenir booth. But even as she bounded after

him, he reached the counter and stopped short, his
head thrown back.

Just beyond the waiting child, a square-built man
with grizzly hair completed his purchase and turned
around.

For just that second, as he turned, Tey believed it,
too. This was Bo, down from his mountain and buying the morning news. And then he was facing their
way, and he was just another stocky, graying man,
without glasses and at least twenty years older than the
bodyguard. Walking past the stricken child with his
eyes on his newspaper, he had no idea of the blow he'd
just delivered.

"Josh." Catching his drooping shoulders, Tey knelt
beside the boy. "Josh, baby, I'm so sorry."

Tears gleamed in his eyes, and his mouth was pulling into a tiny, pugnacious knot in his effort not to cry.
They were two seconds away from a major explosion
and twelve minutes away from their flight. Desperately, Tey peered up at the counter beside them. Buy
him something? But neither a newspaper nor a straw
hat from the stack of sun hats displayed beside the papers would be an acceptable substitute for his guardian angel.

Somewhere above them, the loudspeaker blared into
life. Straining to make out the words—all she could
catch was "Puerto Rico" and "loading"—Tey turned
toward the sound, and froze. Across the terminal,
striding straight out of her worst nightmare and directly toward them, came the storklike, unmistakable
form of Jon Aston.

"Bogie!" Josh got out at last behind her. "I want
Bogie!"

Dear God, how could they have been so unlucky? And how cold-blooded could Jon Aston be—he wasn't even hurrying, didn't seem surprised, wasn't really glaring at her.

"Where's Bogie?" Shaking her shoulder, Josh yelled the words right in her ear.

He wasn't seeing them. Aston's eyes were focused on the tiles before him—he was thinking! She'd seen him act this way back in California. His body might be striding through a busy Caribbean airport, but the mind was elsewhere.

All the same, when Aston tripped over them, he was bound to notice them.

"I want—"

"A hat?" Reaching up beside her, she snatched a straw hat off the pile and plopped it down on Josh's head, hiding his tell-tale white-blond hair.

"No! I don't want a hat!" Josh stormed as he grabbed for the brim.

From the corner of her eye, Tey watched a pair of long, gray-clad legs swing into view and stop beside her. Catching Josh's hands, she held them out and away from his camouflage. "You look marvelous, baby, and it'll keep the sun off." From Aston's perspective, his son must have looked like a straw toadstool with feet. As for herself, as long as she didn't turn, she presented only the top and back of her head. There had to be hundreds, maybe thousands of dark-haired women on St. Matthew, and Aston hadn't heard her voice in two years—had never bothered to talk to her much at all.

"I'm not a baby! I'm a big boy and I want—"

"I know, I know, I know you do! And just as soon
as we buy this hat, we'll get on the plane and we'll fly
right home. I want to go home, too." *Did she ever!*

"How much?" That dry-ice, familiar voice inquired above her.

Mouth open to protest again, Josh swung around.
His wide eyes took in the legs not three feet from his
face, and slowly his mouth closed.

"Two dollars, mistuh," a soft island voice announced from the far side of the counter.

Coins clinked on the glass beside them and the pa-
per rustled as Aston pulled it off the countertop.
Holding her breath, her eyes on Josh's startled face,
Tey waited for footsteps.

All she could hear were her own heartbeats slamming in double time. God, what was Aston doing? Was
he staring down at them? Had he— There! A foot-
step. Slowly, Tey let her breath out in a shaking hiss.
She didn't dare to turn yet, but Josh was staring over
her shoulder, and his small, taut body seemed to loosen
a little bit with each retreating step. *Oh, thank you!* She
shut her eyes for a second.

"You going to buy that hat?" Leaning over the
counter, a young woman grinned down at them.

"What do you think, Josh—do you want it?" *We've
got to go, got to go! Just give Aston one more minute.*

"No!" All Josh's grievances returned in a rush.
"No, I don't want it!" Yanking the hat off, he smashed
it down on the floor and glared at her.

"I guess not," she told the woman ruefully. Brushing the hat off, Tey stood and set it on the pile. Far
down the terminal, Aston swung out through the columns toward the taxi rank. *Got to go now!* "Well, how

about a plane ride?'' she suggested, turning back to her nephew.

But Josh wasn't buying any. "I want Bogie!"

Inspiration struck. Bogart the bear—yes! She wouldn't have to lie, after all. "That's where I'm taking you, Joshems. We're going to see Bogie. Trust me!''

But Josh was past trusting. When she took his hand, he collapsed on the tiles. There was no time to reason with him, no time to explain. Hoisting the crying child to her hip—good Lord he was heavy!—she made a dash for Gate Three.

CHAPTER TWELVE

SEATED ON A SACK of something lumpy—potatoes or some kind of root, maybe—Bo could barely peer out the windshield of the converted Volkswagen. This was how Josh must see the world—looking up at everything. From this perspective, the two Matean youths lounging by the road at Thisted's one intersection with a traffic light looked like giants. It made you appreciate just how brave a child was, to face an outsize world without flinching. *Hang on there, partner. I'm coming*.

When would the damn red light change? In answer to that question, the green light switched on, and Michael—his Rastafarian savior—eased the little truck into growling motion.

As they passed under the light, a taxi bus loomed up beside them, heading the other way, and Bo found himself staring up at the cool hatchet profile of Jon Aston for a split second. "Cripes!" Spinning around, he stared out the rear of the cab, but all he could see was the diminishing back of the bus.

"Yes, mon?" Michael inquired as he nursed the VW up to third gear.

"Saw somebody I knew." But had he rescued Josh? If Josh had been sitting on the other side of Aston, there was no way he'd have been visible from this angle. Aston had looked as calm and collected as ever, though; surely he'd have looked a little...hassled, if he'd just discovered his son in the act of being snatched?

"You want to go back then?"

"No! No thanks, Michael. I've still got to get to the airport." *If Aston missed them there, then it's up to me.*

At the airport, Bo yanked his backpack from the back of the truck. They'd wasted precious minutes stopping by the estate to grab it, but it held the few things he couldn't leave behind and half a year's salary in cash—and that he might be needing soon enough. "Michael..." What to say and how to say it?

"Best you hurry, then," the Matean told him softly.

Shouldering the pack, Bo nodded. "Thanks."

"You find him." That might have been an order, might have been a prophecy.

"I will." Swinging away, he broke into a limping run.

No one remembered them at the airline counters, but at the third gate he tried, Bo crossed their trail: a young, dark woman had carried a fair, crying child onto the plane to Puerto Rico.

And when did that plane leave?

Half an hour ago. The next one would follow in two hours. Did he want a ticket?

That's not good enough! Bo thought, clenching his teeth over the image of Josh crying. *Think—use your head!* Go back and get Aston? But to find him, find the pilot, get them back here, get permission to take off— no, it would take too long. And what if Aston decided to continue the hunt without him? He was capable of that.

No, he had to get to Puerto Rico, and fast. It was the hub airport to everywhere. From there he'd have alternatives—different routes on different airlines—some way to catch up, to outflank the bitch. "I've got to get to Puerto Rico!" he muttered aloud.

The pretty gate attendant eyed him doubtfully. "Plane leaves for St. Thomas in ten minutes, from this gate."

"Can I get a flight to Puerto Rico from there?"

"Yes, sir, if you could get to St. Thomas, but this flight's sold out."

Couldn't anything go right? "I see." Hijack the damned plane, then? Stow away? So all the lucky people trailing into this waiting room were bound for St. Thomas. Taking a deep breath, Bo scanned the room fiercely. Well, one of them was about to get even luckier. Someone was going to get a chance to sell his ticket for twice what he'd paid for it—for four times what he'd paid, if he got stubborn. That kid with the guitar there—he looked in no hurry.

JOSH HOWLED all the way to Puerto Rico.

In the tiny prop plane, the seats were jammed too close together for privacy; there was no way Tey could talk to him, try to explain without being overheard, and Josh was too busy grieving to listen, anyway.

Nor would he accept physical comfort. Slapping her hands aside when she tried to stroke him, he huddled in the far corner of his seat and gave himself up to a hoarse and rhythmic keening that pulled at her heartstrings. *Oh, Joshems, if I could have brought your Bogie along, I would have!* And how would a ragged teddy bear ever make up for the loss of his devoted human mascot?

Not able to answer that, Tey huddled down in her own seat and closed her eyes. She ached all over. Ached for Josh, and ached for Mac. Mac... *Oh, Mac, the way you looked at me back there at the gate!* She would have to write him, explain everything, apologize abjectly for using him that way. And it wouldn't do a bit of good, would it? He would hate her for this. Had every right to. *Mac, I don't know what else I could have done. Oh, Mac, I'm sorry.* Tears pricked behind her closed lids, and she turned her face to the window. What a miserable world! Poor Josh wanted Bo's protective arms, she longed for Mac's, and every second of this droning flight swept them farther away.

When the plane bumped down in San Juan, Josh was still sobbing. The other passengers showered looks of disgust, and one or two of sympathy, on them as she carried him down the metal exit stairs.

''He's cutting a tooth,'' she assured the frowning flight attendant as they boarded their connecting flight to Atlanta half an hour later. That earned them a row of three seats by a window all to themselves, but neither spared a glance for the view as the island of emerald and turquoise dropped away behind them.

Finally—blessedly—somewhere off the coast of Florida, Josh's singsong lament wavered, rallied again in one last stubborn effort, then faded gradually into hiccuping silence. Heaving a sigh of gratitude, Tey turned her head cautiously to inspect him.

The eyes that stared back at her from his flushed little face could have been Lori's eyes, that last dreadful time she'd seen her at the hospital. *Oh, Joshems, don't look at me that way! Someday—someday—you'll be glad I did this!* But that someday wasn't today.

If only she could tell him where she was taking him! But so many things could still go wrong. To promise him his mother, then have to break that promise? No, she wouldn't risk that. But somehow she had to comfort him.

"Joshems..." If only he'd let her touch him! "Josh, don't you remember me?" A few times back there at the beach she'd thought maybe, just maybe, he knew who she was. "I'm your Aunt Tey. Aunt Tey from Boston, remember?"

But no light kindled in those tragic, drooping eyes. Solemn, aloof, Josh shook his head.

But he'd say no to me, no matter what I asked, right now. And at least he'd responded. "I brought you a stuffed tiger, the last time I came for a visit. Do you remember?" But how could he possibly? That had been two years ago, and her present had not impressed him. He'd had his Bogie, and that was all the toy he'd needed. She stifled a grimace. Not so much had changed.

What else could she remind him of? What might a child remember? They'd stayed close to the house, gone on no special excursions. Aston had vetoed Disneyland—much to Tey's own disappointment—but Josh wouldn't remember that. He'd fallen and cut his knee, down by the pool, but that was no memory to reassure him.

What books had she read him? Would he remember? But looking up from her memories, Tey found those sad, accusing eyes had drifted shut. Holding her breath, she waited a minute, but they stayed closed. *Good.* Leaning gently across him, she pressed the button in his armrest and slowly eased the seat back.

*That's the best solution of all, isn't it Joshems? Just
close your eyes and make it all go away.*

But that refuge worked only for the innocent. Leaning back wearily in her seat to try it herself, Tey found
a face waiting behind her eyelids. A face frozen in that
last instant before surprise turned to pain.

CARRYING JOSH through the echoing corridors of the
Atlanta airport, Tey watched for cops. If Bo had gone
to the police, it was possible they were seeking her by
now. But no one seemed interested in the bruised and
dirty young woman who lugged a feverish child.

With two hours to kill till the flight to Los Angeles,
she found a snack bar where they could sit. And it was
a long, long time since Mac's omelet the night before.
Her eyes filled again and she brushed them angrily.
Tired, that's all she was. But her mind filled with image after image of those tender, sleepless hours.

Josh refused to eat. She coaxed a glass of milk down
him and hoped that would do. Silent and withdrawn,
he sat beside her in their booth and watched the trav-
elers hustle past. As if a broad and familiar shape
would step into view at any time now. *Oh, Josh.* But
there was no way to comfort him, no way to pet him
into happiness. She would have to respect his anger and
hope that some day he would forgive her. Hope that
Lori still held enough of his heart to drive memories of
Bo away. *But will he even remember her? A year, that's
a lifetime to a child!*

Finally she stirred. It was time to call Margie. Perhaps the lawyer could even meet them at the airport.
Otherwise they were going to have to find a way up the
coast to Margie's mother's house on their own. Ex-

hausted already, she didn't relish that prospect, and it was hours away yet.

But Margie's staunch support was unavailable, a secretary explained cheerfully when Tey called: the attorney was out of town. Please try again Monday.

It figured. Her luck had been running too smoothly. Hastily dismissing that thought, Tey glanced down at her nephew. He sat on the floor at her feet, staring into space. All right, no Margie. They'd need a rental car, then. She'd better reserve one now. There would be a booth around here someplace.

That taken care of, it was time to find their departure gate. But someone must have heard her thought about luck. "Damn!" Hoisting a slipping Josh into place on her hip, Tey stared up at the schedule board. Their flight was delayed, its departure set back one hour. "Damn." She wouldn't feel truly safe till they landed in California. Not even then. Not till she put Josh in his mother's arms. "Okay, Joshems, let's go sit some more."

The ladies' room seemed to be a safe place. As Tey pictured potential pursuit it was male—FBI agents with shiny black shoes. Officers in blue. Bo in a towering rage, though it was hard to imagine what that could look like. When she found their sanctuary, it even had a couch; her luck was swinging again.

And better yet, Josh consented to doze with his head in her lap. She'd been promoted from traitor to piece of furniture. It was a step up in his world that she accepted with infinite gratitude. *Just wait till you see him, Lori!* Stroking one finger lightly across his silvery hair, she considered calling her sister—Margie had given her Mrs. Davis's phone number along with the address— and rejected that impulse immediately. So many things could still go wrong: the plane could fall from the sky—she shivered as the dream of that morning came back; the FBI could swoop down on them. Lori didn't need another disappointment. That letter from Herbert Kopesky—"Hell, I picked him up! I was that close!"—had nearly killed her. It was safer to leave her in peaceful ignorance for a few more hours.

Josh whimpered in his sleep, and Tey smoothed his hair again. The same reasoning had kept her from mentioning Lori to Josh these past few hours. Perhaps the idea would have consoled him, but if she promised, then couldn't deliver?

And just what do you think Mac is thinking about now? Didn't you promise something there and then snatch it away? But she drove that thought from her mind. *Don't think about him! You'll be happier that way.* She shook her head miserably. *You were the woman who was going to stay happy by not falling in love,* she mocked herself bitterly. *You sure look happy today. What happened?* Shutting her eyes, she fought back the tears. *Mac happened! How was I to predict that?* How to guard against it? And didn't he just prove her whole theory? Open yourself to love and misery follows; she'd never felt bluer than this. She touched Josh's hair again. *Oh, Josh, I'm so sorry!*

Their flight was delayed another hour. Engine trouble, the airline representative explained when she finally asked. The company was substituting another plane; it would be arriving in half an hour. All passengers should report to the gate of departure.

Standing in line to receive their boarding pass, Tey shut her eyes and hitched Josh into place again. He still wouldn't walk, would only sit crying when she put him down, and her arms were breaking. *Please, just let us on the plane. Then I can relax.*

Josh's weight lifted, then swung out of her arms. "Wha—?" Tey whirled to find herself meeting the steely eyes of Bo Lee above Josh's tow head as her nephew burrowed his face against the man's shoulder.

"Hello again . . . friend."

Her mind echoed the word blankly. Then its savage irony sliced into her. *Lord, is there anyone I haven't hurt? Bo, you were my friend, weren't you? A good friend—the best.*

Her silence seemed to provoke him. He started to speak again, then bit down on his words. Shaking his head with a grimace of contemptuous loathing, Bo turned and walked away.

"Bo!" Shame swung instantly to rage. *Who was he to—* That was Lori's son—Lori's happiness—he was taking away, as if he had some claim to him! "Bo!" Ignoring the startled stares of the passersby, she darted after him.

But she couldn't take hold of Josh; there was no way she'd subject him to a tug of war. Clamping her hands around Bo's elbow, she dug in her heels. "Stop right there, Bo, or I'll scream for the police!"

"Police!" He dragged her a foot, then turned. "Don't make me laugh, Tey. They'd probably throw you in jail!"

"For what? Taking my nephew back to his—" She stopped. Josh had twisted in Bo's arms and now watched her with wide, tearful eyes. She took a deep breath. *Calm down!* "Bo, your boss does *not* have legal custody. He's lied to you about that, and he's lied about everything else, as well. You're on the wrong side, Bo, believe me!"

"Under these circumstances, of course you'd say that." But his look of revulsion wavered. He looked like an indignant and exhausted Pooh.

At least he was listening. "My sister never gave him up, Bo. Never. Aston snatched him. Would *you* give him up?"

The logic of that seemed to strike him. After a moment, he shook his head slowly, his chin brushing the child's hair.

"She's been sick with worry this past year. She's spent every nickel she had, every penny she could beg or borrow, trying to get him back." If she could just convince him!

Silently, Bo studied her face. "Maybe we'd better sit," he said finally, and nodded at the departure lounge behind her.

Breathing a sigh of gratitude, she followed his sturdy back, which bore a lumpy backpack she'd never seen before. A jet was whining into position outside the boarding tunnel. Their plane . . . Why couldn't it have come on time? And how soon would it leave? Twenty minutes?

She had time to stop shaking, to gather her thoughts, while Bo settled Josh. Heads close together, they talked for a few minutes. From what she could hear, Bo's smiling, casual questions were reshaping Josh's day, easing the child's perception of the events from nightmare toward adventure. After a few more comments, the child curled into his lap and relaxed in sleep.

Perhaps fifteen minutes till boarding. How to convince him? Licking dry lips, Tey met the bodyguard's eyes squarely as he looked up from his charge. "She's not a drug addict, Bo. And she's not a money grubber—she doesn't want him back for leverage. That's

Aston's game. Lori wants Josh back because she loves him.''

Frowning, he considered that for a moment, then pulled off his glasses. "Can you prove that?" he asked wryly, as he cleaned the lenses on Josh's shirttail.

"Prove it? In the middle of the Atlanta airport?" She clenched her hands together. "If I could just show you Lori! You'd know in a minute. I know you would!" Lori, who could no more hide her emotions than Josh... Wait! Tey almost laughed with relief. The picture she'd taken two years ago, on her last visit to California!

"Good evening, ladies and gentlemen. We're pleased to announce the arrival of Flight 336 out of..."

Tey glanced toward the desk wildly. *Oh, no!* With shaking fingers, she jerked open her purse, found her wallet. "Here!" She shoved the picture at him. Let him believe this woman was a negligent, unloving mother!

His lips softened as he blinked down at the photograph, and even seeing it upside down, Tey found her eyes blurring. Crouching at the edge of the Aston's swimming pool, Tey had snapped the shot at near water level. Lori breaststroked toward the camera, with Josh clinging to her back, his small arms clamped around her neck. Josh was shrieking with laughter, and Lori glowed with such pride and joy that—that Tey couldn't see the photograph anymore. She wiped her eyes, then wiped them again. When she looked up, Bo was watching her. That flash of tenderness had faded to a measuring look again. But he didn't return the photograph.

"Ladies and Gentlemen, in just a few minutes we'll begin boarding Eastern flight 336 Whisperjet nonstop service to Los..."

The first few passengers got to their feet, and she spoke again desperately. "That's the kind of mother you're keeping him from, Bo. And what kind of father are you taking him back to? Tell me what a devoted father Jon Aston has been this past year! Have you ever—once—seen him read Josh a bedtime story? Have you ever seen him hug Josh? Make time to be with him? That's the kind of father you want for Josh?"

"At this time we'd like to board passengers holding boarding passes for rows one through . . ."

"He's been busy this past year," Bo muttered, not meeting her eyes now. "He's a businessman. He's trying to recover from the property settlement—to make a new life for himself and his son."

"Bo, there hasn't *been* a property settlement yet, and there won't be, while Aston has Josh. He's been using Josh to blackmail Lori. And besides, that's not the point. The point is that if you love someone, you *make* time for him. Maybe you don't have enough time to give, but what time you've got, you give gladly. What the hell has Aston given Josh gladly?"

"Okay!" Shutting his eyes for a second, Bo shook his head as if it ached. "So he isn't the ideal father—I know it! But that doesn't prove the mother—what's her name—Lori—is any better, just because she photographs like an angel. You've proven nothing." His hands moved blindly, restlessly, across his charge's small back.

"Passengers holding boarding passes for rows eleven through twenty may now . . ."

Stay calm, oh, stay calm. Tey drew a shaking breath. "Is that what you want to believe then, Bo? That there's nobody in the world who cares for Josh?"

He shook his head in frustration. "There's me, dammit!"

"But what good will that do Josh," she asked softly, "when you're gone? You've got that dissertation to finish, and then you'll move on. You can't stay a tutor all your life—you've got plans. You told me you want to start a private school someday. What happens to Josh then, Bo? Who'll take care of him next, and will he care like you do?"

Blinking fiercely, as if he faced windblown gravel instead of her torrent of words, Bo shook his head again, then ducked his face to Josh's hair.

"At this time passengers with boarding passes for rows twenty-one through thirty-one may..."

Taking a deep breath, he sat up again, then looked down at the photograph for a long, frowning moment.

"If Josh and I come with you...that doesn't mean I've decided anything—you understand?" He eyed her narrowly. "Josh is still my responsibility. You agree to that?"

A smile was threatening to break like the rising sun. Desperately, she fought it back, fought down the urge to hug him. "I understand." She glanced toward the departure desk. "Let's see if they'll sell you a ticket!"

SHIELDING HER EYES against the morning sunshine, Tey read the address on the mailbox. "Fourteen hundred. It'll be on the other side. Not far now." And thank heaven. Though they'd stopped to sleep late last night in a roadside motel—sharing a room with two double beds since neither would trust the other with Josh—they were all three still exhausted this morning.

Josh had been drowsing in Bo's lap for the past fifty miles or so.

Mrs. Davis's unpaved driveway left them unprepared for the vision at the top of her windswept hill. A weathered Victorian cottage crowned the rise. Its white picket fence supported a riot of red roses, which seemed to be holding the fort against the besieging meadow grass.

As they approached the gate to the front walk, Bo carrying his silent charge, a woman turned the corner from the backyard and stopped short.

With the sun in her eyes, sun setting her hair ablaze around her shoulders, Lori squinted at them uncertainly. Her hands were full of roses. Her lips shaped some word noiselessly.

"Lori." They should have called—prepared her, but Bo had insisted on seeing this first reaction.

"Tey?" She got it out this time, breathless and squeaking, as the roses fell to her feet. "Is it—" Gliding forward, her eyes fixed on her son, she looked dazed, emotionless, not daring to— "Josh!" Comprehension hit and her face fractured like a smashed mirror, reflecting shards of grief, and gleaming, *blazing* rapture as she broke into a run, her arms outstretched. "Josh!"

Lord, she would terrify the child; she looked like a crazed angel! But eyes diamond bright, half blinded with tears, she stopped—must have realized—some ten feet away. "Josh?" she cried softly, then walked forward.

And shooting a glance at her nephew, Tey saw the moment of recognition. "Mommy!" He leaned forward from Bo's arms, reaching for her, then changed his mind at the last possible instant. One small hand retreated to clutch Bo's collar as laughing, crying, Lori scooped him out of his bodyguard's arms. Hooking his other arm firmly around her neck, Josh wouldn't let go of either for several minutes.

And blinking fiercely against his tears, Bo didn't seem to mind at all.

CHAPTER THIRTEEN

THROUGH THE OPEN FRENCH DOORS at the end of Mrs. Davis's wonderful kitchen, Bo could see the two of them. Curled together in a big redwood chair out on the deck that overlooked the backyard, Lori and Josh were still talking. Hadn't stopped talking since they'd been reunited nearly an hour ago. *Well, a year's a long time to catch up on.* Laughing at something Josh said, Lori threw her arms around the child just then and gave him a bear hug. With her chin resting on top of Josh's head, her incredible hair merged with his lighter thatch and curled down over his shoulders. Her face, what Bo could see of it, was radiant.

You're a sunshine lady, that's what you are. I'll always remember you the way I first saw you, with the sun shining through your hair.

"Bo?"

Josh was wriggling free now, and Bo smiled to himself. A hug or two or twelve was all very well, but a man had to save a little dignity. *Josh, you old ugly mug, why didn't you tell me you had a mom like that?*

"Bo?" There was a hint of laughter in Nancy Davis's voice this time. "How about another glass of lemonade?"

"Huh . . . ?" Twisting around in his chair, he found the older woman was standing at the refrigerator now;

he hadn't noticed her getting up from the table. "Oh ... yeah. Please." He grinned sheepishly.

Beside him, Tey lifted her glass. "Could I have some too, Nancy?" As she set the glass down, she stole a glance at her watch.

"Certainly." The tall, white-haired woman strode back to the table with a flower-glazed pitcher. "This is the warmest autumn we've had in years—I've never had roses this late before," she said, continuing their conversation. "And Lori's been such a help with the gardening. I can't tell you how much I've enjoyed having her here, Tey. I'd just as soon keep her forever, and I absolutely insist she and Josh stay on here until Margie's fixed her skunk-of-a-husband's wagon for him."

"That's awfully kind of you!"

"Kind?" Nancy snorted. "That's just plain selfish! I don't get nearly enough company up here to suit me. Margie and her husband never stay for long—don't know how I raised a workaholic, but I guess I sure did. No, I like company—the more the better. You're going to stay for a while, aren't you?"

Hesitating for a long moment, Tey shook her head. "I'd love to, Nancy, but there's ... something I've got to take care of.... Could I have a rain check?"

So Tey, his one link with these two women, wasn't staying. *Where does that leave me?* Out in the sunlight, Lori was unfolding her long, coltish legs, finally getting up. No—she was just stretching, with a loose-limbed, joyous grace that tightened something deep inside him. *So where does that leave me, if Tey goes? Lori doesn't know me from Adam. I bet she didn't even catch my name when Tey introduced us. All she could see was Josh.*

"And what will you do, Bo?"

The question was so close to his own thoughts that it took him a second to realize the words had been spoken aloud. Jerking around, he met Nancy Davis's knowing eyes. *I wish to God I knew!* Beside him, Tey rose from the table.

She looks so good! Tey rejoiced as she stepped out through the back doors. *Better than I've seen her in years!* Two weeks of Nancy's cheerful good sense, two weeks of these wondrous roses and clean, country air had worked a miracle. And getting Josh back hadn't hurt her, of course.

Seeing her coming, Lori eased Josh from her lap and stood, her hands on his shoulders. But Josh wasn't as pleased to see her. Ducking out from under Lori's hands, he made a wide detour around his aunt, then dashed at Bo, who'd stepped out on the deck behind her. "Gotcha, Bogie!" he announced, as he wrapped his arms around Bo's leg and leaned back to grin up at him.

As she turned back to Lori, Tey found her sister's eyes were fixed on her son and his erstwhile guardian. Her smile wavered for a moment, then rallied as Tey came to meet her.

Grey-green eyes smiled into grey-green eyes for a moment, then Lori enveloped her in an exuberant hug. "You miracle worker!"

"The ribs! Watch the ribs!" her sister squeaked, laughing. When Lori let her breathe again, Tey twined an arm around her waist and tugged her toward the steps to the lawn. "Come show me the roses."

"Josh—"

"He'll be fine with his Bogie for a minute."

Lori slanted another bemused look over her shoulder, to where Josh was showing his friend a ragged teddy bear, then nodded reluctantly.

Arms curved around each other's waist, they paced slowly across the clipped green grass toward the rose-embroidered back fence. As always, Tey was amused and a little surprised to find that her head came to Lori's ear—no higher. It was odd to feel so protective, so much stronger, and then to find yourself the runt. "You'll be all right now, Lori?"

"All right!" Lori laughed, a breathless little hum of joy. "With Josh... With what you and Nancy and Margie have done for me!"

"And don't forget Bo, Lori. It took real courage to set his job aside, to go against his employer and his instructions like that."

"Yes... I'm... very grateful to him," Lori murmured flatly.

They'd reached the fence by now. "Why I asked is—" letting her sister go, Tey cupped a rose in her hands and buried her nose in it "—is that I've done about all I can..."

"You've done everything!"

Laughing, Tey shook her head. "But the rest is up to Margie now, Lor. And after talking with her that last time I saw her, I think she can work something out, now that Jon can't blackmail you."

"I hope... She's got to."

"She will. But in the meantime, you're safe here. I've done all I can, so... I've got to go."

"To go? Now? But you just got here, Tey!"

Nodding, Tey picked a half-open bud—Nancy could spare one—and twirled it nervously between the fingers of one hand. "I know, but I've got to. There's someone..." *Oh, Mac, I've been gone nearly a day and a half now!*

"Back on St. Matthew?" Lori prompted gently.

"Yes..." Her mind was suddenly filled with his image, that last glimpse of his face as surprise changed to—

"Someone special?" Hooking an arm through her elbow, Lori steered her back toward the house.

"Someone I...owe an apology to."

"I see." They walked in silence for a moment. "I thought maybe you and Bo—"

That startled a little laugh out of Tey and she shook her head quickly. "Bo is the sweetest, gentlest man I've ever met, Lori, but no...he's...he's...not the one."

"Then get a move on, Sis," Lori said lightly, "and get back to the one who is."

"I...yes." Not that it would do a bit of good, but all the same...

On the deck, Bo slouched in a chair while her nephew played around his feet. Josh hadn't strayed out of grabbing distance of either Lori or Bo since he'd arrived, Tey noted wearily; it might take him a while to get over yesterday's snatching. *Wonder if he'll ever forgive me?* Bo looked rather rumpled and down at heart, as well.

"Bo?" She stopped by his chair. "I've got to get back to Los Angeles this afternoon. Do you need a ride anywhere?"

"Guess not." His mild brown eyes stayed on her face for a second, then dropped down to Lori, who was kneeling beside Josh. "Nancy's invited me to stay for a few days, till I figure what comes next. Guess I'll take her up on it."

Out of the corner of her eye, Tey saw Lori's head bob up, then down again as quickly. "That's great, Bo," she said sincerely. *Poor Bo. I've torn apart his life to patch up Lori's. I wonder what he'll do now?* Rising gracefully beside her, Lori strode off into the kitchen. Tey held out her hand. "Forgive me, Bo?"

His smile was wryly bittersweet as he took it. "There's nothing to forgive, friend," he assured her quietly. "I'd have done the same."

Friend. Tey nodded slowly. Yes, she'd hold him to that. He was a friend worth having. Dropping beside her nephew, she waited until he met her eyes. "Josh-ems?" Smiling under his solemn inspection, hiding her anxiety, she offered him the rosebud. "Forgive me?"

After an endless moment, Josh took the rose and held it to the buttonless nose of his teddy bear. He didn't look up again.

"Guess I'll have to settle for that," she decided ruefully as she stood.

"Short ones have short memories," Bo reminded her. "It'll be fine next time."

"I hope so." *And I hope things will be fine for you, too, my friend.* Touching his shoulder, she went on into the house.

Leaving the farewells to the women, Bo gave an absentminded support to Josh's explorations of the backyard. Wandering moodily behind him, he commented dutifully on the bees Josh discovered in the flowers, then cheered him on as he chased a monarch butterfly. *He needs a nap.* When he got this hyper, it meant he was tired. The next stage would be crankiness. *But it's not your job anymore—remember?* Twenty-four hours ago he'd had a job, an exciting dissertation, someone to care for. Now what did he have?

Well, easy come, easy go. And what was the alternative? Josh had received more love in the past hour than he'd gotten from Aston in the last year. *Not that I could take him back if I wanted to! Lori would be biting my ankle every step of the way. But that's okay. She can bite my ankle anytime she feels like it.*

A screech from Josh snapped his head around. Over by the roses, Josh whipped a hand to his mouth, then yanked it back out to bellow again. He plopped down abruptly and burst into tears.

A thorn or a bee. Bee sting, Bo bet; it took serious pain to make Josh cry like that. "What's the problem, big boy?" Careful not to hurry, he got there quickly all the same. Crouching down by the weeping child, he collected the hand that Josh was alternately flapping and sucking. "Let's have a look here."

Roaring and hiccuping, Josh tried to pull his hand away, but Bo held on to it. Yep, there it was—on the palm. A red, rising lump with a tiny, brown splinter in its middle—the stinger. "Looks like you caught yourself a bee, partner."

Too busy sobbing to speak, Josh nodded frenzied agreement.

It had to hurt badly, but it was exhaustion on top of it that was making him cry so. Steadying his tiny paw in one hand, Bo picked the stinger out on the second try. "Looks like the bee caught you, too, fella. Bees tend to do that."

"Josh!" Lori swooped down on the both of them. "Baby, what is it?" Her hair slashed across Bo's face as she gathered Josh into her arms and hugged him frantically. "What is it, darling?"

Josh's laments doubled in volume and shrillness. Bo touched her shoulder. "Take it easy, Lori," he said quietly. "You're just scaring him that way. You'll convince him it hurts more than it does."

"Well, of course it hurts!" She threw him a stormy, indignant glance and bent above her son again. "There, I know it hurts, baby! I know it does..." Cheek to his hair, she rocked him fiercely.

Josh's howls were even louder now. With that kind of encouragement, why shouldn't they be? "Lori, stop it."

"You—" Her head snapped up again. With those eyes and that wonderful mane, she looked like a cornered lioness. "Why don't you just mind your own business!"

A blow in the face would have hurt less. *Right, Lee—mind your own goddamned business!* Eyes stinging, Bo found he was on his feet, backing away.

And with no place to retreat to, he realized bitterly. Tey had taken the car. Nancy would see his face if he fled to the house. Retreating across the lawn, he ended up against an impassable hedge of roses. *Don't turn around,* he told himself, and turned, anyway.

Lori still cradled Josh while she crooned her passionate sympathy. His crying was beginning to subside now.

He needs a bed and some aspirin. And Bo ached to supply them. Tiredly, he sank on his heels in a band of shadow by the fence. *You may not understand this, lady, but that's my child, too.* Her hair covered Josh like a curtain of silk.

I'm the father of your child. Yeah, that would go over big, wouldn't it? The silk rippled as she soothed him; she was rubbing her cheek softly back and forth across the top of Josh's burrowing head.

I'm the father of your child.... I wish I were.... For a moment he simply breathed, his lungs expanding with the sun-bright air while that thought nestled into his mind like a diamond dropping into its proper and final setting. *I wish I were....* He could see her pregnant. She'd glow like a peach... like an Italian madonna.

As if she were fleeing his thoughts, Lori rose to her feet, Josh held tightly in her arms. Without one glance in his direction, she turned on her heel and glided off toward the house.

As she and Josh vanished into the shadowy kitchen, the day seemed to darken a little. Bo watched the doorway for a while, but they didn't come back. When he looked down at last, all the colors were back to normal, not glowing anymore. Maybe the sun was behind a cloud; he didn't bother to look. Slowly, he sank back on his elbows, then all the way down to the grass. Clasping his hands behind his head, Bo shut his eyes. *So you wish—so where does that get you? A woman like that... and you?* Every inch of his mind and body had been filled with sunlight; now he just hurt all over. *It's that downhill marathon yesterday; you'll be sore for a week.* But it was more than that. Willing his mind to blankness, he shut it all out. *A woman like that... and you?*

The touch on his elbow was so light that he missed it. How late was it? Ought to open his eyes and check his watch. Must have been sleeping.

The cat's-paw touch came again. "Bo?"

Opening his eyes, he found her sitting beside him. With the sun at her back, Lori was a dim shape crowned with an aureole of gold. *My sunshine lady.* Too dazzled to move, he squinted up at her.

"Bo, please, I'm so sorry! I had no right to say that."

That? Oh... "Sure you did. You're his mother." Blinking, he pushed up on one elbow. That brought their faces too close. They both leaned apart as he sat upright.

"And you love him," she countered softly. "You're the one who's taken such wonderful care of him this past year. Anyone can see that. And all he talks about is Bogie this and Bogie that." She managed a rueful, self-mocking little grimace.

She was making him stupid, being this near to him. Or he just wasn't awake yet, maybe. "Where is he?"

"I put him to bed. He was so tired. Nancy will hear him if he wakes."

"Good." His eyes followed her arm as she reached to pull a pink wildflower out of the garden's border. She had long arms, so slender, brushed with the lightest gold. Peach fuzz... She'd be so soft.

"Anyway, I wanted to apologize... It's just been so long since I've had him. Held him..." She looked down at her flower.

"I can understand that—believe me, Lori." He tried to hold her eyes, but found them slipping away again, back to her flower. Almost as if she were shy. But as lovely as she was, that wasn't possible.

"You see... it's not just getting him back after so long..." Lifting the flower to her nose, she sniffed it, but apparently it had no smell. Twirling it absently, she brought it down again. "It's that I've never had to share Josh with anyone before, Bo. He was all mine. Jon wanted no part of him. So it's twice as hard for me, now."

She darted a pleading look up at him, and he had to smile. Josh peeked out of her eyes, and her nose was bright yellow with pollen. He ached to kiss it away. "You don't have to share him, Lori. Josh is yours. I know that."

"But I—we—owe you so much! Tey says you could have stopped her, there at the airport, and you didn't. I owe you so much more than that!" Bending over her flower, she plucked a petal off it, rolled it gently between her fingers and dropped it between them.

She loves me, he supplied wistfully. "Josh gave me as much as I gave him, Lori. There's no debt." *She is shy, isn't she? How strange.*

"No?" She slanted him a warmly skeptical glance and dodged down again as she plucked another petal.

She loves me not.

"But even so, Bo, I wouldn't want—I don't want to come between you and Josh." She stroked the next petal almost tenderly with a fingertip. "Love's so...rare...in a lifetime. *Nobody* ever gets enough love...." Pulling the petal, she lifted it to her lips and tested its softness. "Loving Josh as I do, I couldn't— I'd never deprive him of any love that came his way...." The petal fluttered down between them.

But who deprived you, my darling? How could someone like her not be wrapped in love, offered it wherever she turned? But he knew who'd deprived her, and for just a moment, all Bo could feel was a dreadful pity. *You had everything, Aston. It was all in your hand, and you couldn't grasp it.*

Another petal drifted down beside his foot. That one meant...*she loves me not*, Bo calculated quickly. But that was hardly surprising. He was no flash in the pan. He grew on people slowly, when he grew at all. *I need time. Please give me time.* And suddenly, it came to him. "In that case...if you really mean that...how would you feel if I hung around for a while? I don't know if Tey told you, but I need Josh to finish my dissertation." He needed two months. But he could stretch it to three, easy.

"No...I...she didn't mention it." Frowning at her denuded flower, Lori pulled the final petal and set it carefully by its mates.

She loves me!

"I wouldn't mind, Bo—truly, I wouldn't—but I can't speak for Nancy. It's her house."

And Nancy loved company; Nancy liked him already, and—standing, Bo glanced back at the house critically—Nancy had a house that needed painting. No problem. "Well, let's just see how it goes, then." *Take it slow, fella, take it slow. Remember how Josh was the first month?*

He held a hand down to her. "In the meantime, I've got something to show you." Thank heaven he'd made time to go back to the estate and collect it all! All but the computer itself, but he ought to be able to rent one, back in town.

"What?" She hesitated a minute, then gave him her hand.

She was so light, so soft and warm, that he could barely let her go again. And thank goodness, he was the taller, if only by a couple of inches. "Josh's journal."

"He *writes* now?" Her face flickered like a torch, with regret following delight as she realized she'd missed a stage.

"I taught him . . . and I've saved every scrap he ever wrote. I have it all in order." If she wanted her missing year back, he could almost give it to her.

"Where is it?" she demanded.

"Up in my pack." He caught her elbow as she spun around, then stared down at his own hand, astounded by his daring. "Wait a minute."

"What?"

And now he had to follow through. He rubbed a gentle finger across the tip of her nose. "You had a bit of pollen there."

And she smiled.

CHAPTER FOURTEEN

THE HILLSIDE LAY IN DARKNESS, but the sky over the muted silver sea glowed a fiery, fading magenta. A conga line of purple clouds bumped its way after the sun, which winked and vanished as she looked. Tey parked the Jeep at the foot of the turnoff and walked. Somehow she couldn't drive into camp as if she still belonged there. How many days had she been away? It seemed like a lifetime. Three? No, two nights—one spent in the motel north of Los Angeles, then last night in the airport motel in Miami. So that made today the third day that Mac had had no word from her.

But would he even want word by now?

Let's go find out, she told herself firmly, but each step came slower than the last until she stopped again. Automatically, Tey turned back to face the sea. Silver had changed to blue-gray velvet; the water seemed to be sucking in the last of the light rather than giving it back. She was such a fool for coming back—hadn't meant to come back. Mac was not likely to forgive her. Not when she'd taken all the love he had to give and run.

And that's why you had to come back, she reminded herself.

Mac had given all his heart to a woman once before, and she'd thrown it back in his face. The more Tey had thought about it, the more she'd realized that she couldn't leave Mac thinking that his love had been rejected again. *I can't—I won't let him think that I left because he wasn't lovable, because of some lacking on his part.* Smiling at this absurdity, she turned uphill again. No, somewhere in that long flight west she had realized she owed Mac an apology and an explanation in person. And then, once he'd had it, if he wanted to reject her—as he probably would—that gesture was a luxury she owed him.

Under the trees, the frog symphony was tuning up. A clear, tiny voice called through the dark and another answered from almost underfoot. Did they ever seek and find each other, she wondered, or did they just cry forever in the dark? Waiting for her eyes to adjust, Tey could hear no sounds from the cabins above. No lights pierced the gloom.

Most of them would be gone by now, she realized with a pang. For the trapping had ended three days ago. Mac and Gerry would be closing down the expedition, readying the traps and data and specimens for shipment back to the States. And most of the volunteers would have flown home, back to their jobs and families waiting for them in the Real World. She'd never know if David succeeded in wooing Jean, never tease George about his accent again. *Perhaps never see Mac again after this night.* Shivering, hugging herself as that thought sliced into her, Tey stared upward into the velvet-black canopy of leaves, waiting for the pain to fade.

When it did, she moved, finding her way to the little boardwalk that led up to Mac's cabin. *He won't be here. Probably in town drinking with Gerry. I don't see a light.*

But as she pushed the last branch aside and stepped out on his deck, Tey could see a dim glow coming from the kitchen. *Oh, Mac.* Crossing the boards silently, she paused outside his screen porch.

Mac. He sat at his kitchen table, with a kerosene lamp casting its light across the papers before him. A glow as warm and golden as that light was welling up within her at the sight of him. *Oh, Mac, I didn't come back just to apologize, did I?*

He was working at a calculator, consulting the papers before him and punching numbers into the machine. The result didn't please him. Scowling down at it for a moment, he jotted a figure, reshuffled his papers and started over.

She'd forgotten how beautiful his mouth was; it twisted into a grimace as he pushed the calculator aside and cursed softly. Ruffling one hand absently through his hair, he stared at the papers and sighed. And looked up, seeming to meet her eyes where she stood in the darkness. His own eyes narrowed. "Somebody out there?" he called quietly.

Kenyon women were unlucky in love. Did she need to prove that once again? If she stood quietly, Mac need never know she'd returned. When he looked down again, she could fade back into the night.

But he didn't look down. He sat there waiting, his chin raised slightly as if in challenge, and finally she took it. "Mac." Her knees were trembling as she stepped forward and opened the screen door.

His chair scraped back and then stopped. Silent and unsmiling, Mac watched her advance. And he didn't offer her a seat, merely tipped his own back a bit so he could see her face better. "Well?" he said finally.

"I've a confession to make." *I love you.* It was funny—no, not funny at all—how you never knew how much you wanted something—someone—till you'd lost him.

"What makes you think I give a damn?"

"I don't expect you do," she agreed bleakly. *I didn't want to take you seriously, Mac. How can I blame you if you won't take me at all?*

"Bo didn't live up to your expectations?" Rocking his chair back to the floor, Mac wrenched himself out of it and retreated across the kitchen. Coming up against the counter, he swung back to face her. "Is that why you're back?"

"Bo?" Is that what he'd thought, not just that she'd run, but that she'd run with Bo?

"He disappeared, too, didn't he? Some poker-faced son of a bitch came asking for him and the boy, the morning you left m—" He bit off the last word and wheeled to face the cabinets.

Left you...I should never have left you— Oh, Mac. Rigid back still turned to her, he was rearranging an aimless collection of artifacts on the counter before him—a spoon, an empty test tube, a comb, a ring of keys. She ached to walk up behind him, to throw her arms around his waist and hug the pain right out of him, but Tey knew better than to try; she'd thrown away that right. "That son of a bitch was my brother-in-law, Mac. And I didn't go anywhere with Bo. Bo chased me and Josh all the way to California."

"What?" His head swung around, then slowly, the rest of him followed. "What are you talking about?"

So she told him—all of it—while she leaned back against the window screen with her hands in her pockets and her eyes moving from his face to the flame of the lamp and back again.

Prowling the kitchen as she talked, he swept her with firelit eyes each time he turned. Finally, he sat again on the edge of the counter.

"And so Bo stayed out there with Josh and Lori. And I came back here...."

"Why?"

You know why, Mac—surely you know. Lord, if you'd just let me touch you. Hands could sometimes heal, when words failed. But then, she hadn't the courage to say the words he needed. *Because I love you.* "Because I owed you an apology."

He drew a deep sighing breath and nodded, his eyes on the lamp flame. "I wish you'd told me," he murmured bitterly. "You could have trusted me."

"By the time I knew that, Mac, I was up to my chin in lies. I had a plan I thought would work; I was afraid you might disapprove—might even try to stop me.... I didn't want to involve you or the expedition if I got into trouble with the law." Pushing away from the wall, she came toward him. "I just don't know what else I could have done! Don't you see, Mac? I was trapped."

"Trapped?" he repeated dully.

She wanted to touch him—had to touch him. Gripping his knees, she leaned forward between his legs. Just a foot between his mouth and hers. *So say it! Tell him.* "I was trapped between wanting you with all my heart and having to rescue Josh. Trapped like a silly mongoose." A heart trap, that's what she'd blundered into. Her heart was still trapped, was trying to bash its way out of her breast this very minute.

But he couldn't—wouldn't—hear it. Though she was crowding him, he slid off the counter to stand staring down at her, almost touching her. Then he caught her arms and moved her aside. "Down there on the road, Tey, when you looked at me and drove on by... If you'd just stopped..." Shaking his head, he started for the door.

Oh, Mac, please! Tears clogged her throat, but somehow she forced the words through them. "I had my nephew in the car! We had to catch a plane!"

With the lamplight gilding his face, he turned slowly back to look at her as he shouldered the screen door wide.

Oh, please stay! Oh, please. "Mac, I couldn't stop. If I'd stopped, would you have let me go again?"

He might have stood on the far side of the black and echoing universe, the words took so long to reach him, and then his answer to return. But finally he spoke. "No, I wouldn't have let you go... not that morning." The door creaked, then banged softly shut behind him.

Not that morning. That morning he'd have held her fast, safe where she wanted to be. Not that morning. But now that morning was two days gone, was receding every second further into the irretrievable past. She felt as if she were falling down a bottomless well of blackness, staring back at that bright morning. If only she'd—

She couldn't cry here in his kitchen—she wasn't supposed to cry at all. She'd always been the strong one. *Outside, then. Out—* Sleepwalking to the door, she groped through it, then shuffled across his deck. The path was over there someplace.

"Tey..."

So he wasn't gone. Didn't matter anymore. It was his place to stay—she had to be the one to go. But like the fool she was, she turned back for one last look.

Across the deck, Mac was a dark shape against the darker jungle. "Where are you going?"

That was a good question. "I—" And suddenly she remembered. "I—I'm out of money, Mac." There'd been just enough credit left on the charge card to buy her ticket back. "Could I...could I stay up at the main cabin? Tomorrow I'll..." Tomorrow loomed too black and empty to contemplate.

"Yeah... Sure... Go ahead..."

Humiliation on top of heartache. Somehow she found her way up the path to her cabin, where the power was out, as well. Didn't matter. Her bunk was still there, though the sheets had been stripped from it. But it didn't matter. Nothing did. Falling facedown upon it, she gave herself up to the blackness. *Don't cry. You never cry, remember?* But then she'd never felt like this before.

After the tears came a numbed sort of peace. Hollow as a bleached-out shell on the beach, she lay there listening to the sweet cry of the frogs, watching purple, contracting smoke rings chase each other into the soft, black distance on the inside screen of her eyelids.

That black, starless backdrop lightened slowly, grew gradually redder, as if somewhere beyond the invisible horizon the sun was climbing to meet her. Light dawned with a soft thump on the table across the porch, though she didn't open her eyes. How could Mac move like that? For the dawn glowing through her eyelids was the light of the kerosene lantern he'd just set down.

Her mattress sagged as he sat beside her. *I don't want to feel anymore, Mac. Please don't make me feel.* But the dull, peaceful rhythm of her heart was broken already; it thumped in a painful, irregular effort to establish some new syncopation. *Don't make me feel.*

Warm and hesitant, a big hand curved to fit her cheek. Turning her face into it, she kissed his palm, inhaled the scent of him, and then the tears welled.

"Oh, Tey..." Mac brushed them off her lashes with shaky fingertips, but more took their place. "Oh, darlin', don't..." An arm slid under her shoulders, lifting her to meet him as he moved farther onto the bed. "Don't..." he soothed, and gathered her onto his lap.

Oh, Mac! Throwing an arm around his neck, she buried her face against him and gave in, letting the sobs rack her silently while he rocked her against his chest and crooned nonsense words into her hair. *Mac...*

After a long while, the worst of it was past. Face nestled against his wet neck, she lay there in exhausted contentment, trying to pick out one heartbeat from the other.

His lip brushed her brow. "I came up to see if you'd had supper," he told her ruefully.

With their bodies plastered together, she could feel his silent laughter as he could surely feel hers. She shook her head against his throat. "Not hungry, Mac." *Not for food.*

"Me neither." He kissed the top of her ear. "Was just an excuse, anyway...."

She nodded and hugged him closer, then shifted slightly to get more comfortable.

Touching her leg that was folded between them, he guided it gently to his other side so that she was now sitting astride him, her legs dangling off the edge of the bed.

Sweetly aware of each other's arousal, not at all yet ready to do anything about it, they sat like that for a long time, their arms locked tightly around each other. Finally she sighed, and his lips moved restlessly against her hair. "It's just that I . . . I can't take lies, Tey," he murmured softly. "I just can't."

Pulling him even closer, she nodded against his shoulder. *Of course not, not after Joanne.* "I know, Mac, and I'm so sorry, I—" She shook her head against him. "There's no excuse for it. It's just . . . Guess I've always had to manage things by myself . . . I'm not used to asking for help . . ." She rubbed her nose across his bristly cheek.

Rocking urgently forward against her, he caught a handful of her hair and tilted her head back till he could see her eyes. "That's got to change," he said sternly. "And I don't want you ever, *ever* lying to me again." His lips brushed her mouth, then lifted away again. "I don't care if it's for my own good or not! I need the truth from you, possum. I've got to have that."

"Ever?" Were they really going to have an ever? "That sounds like a long time."

"Not ever!" Releasing her hair, he smoothed his hands slowly, hungrily, down her back, then curved them to fit her hips. "Not for the next fifty years— you've used up your quota. It's truth I want."

Eyes glittering with tears, she nodded.

Mac rubbed his nose gently along hers, but his hands slowly tightened and she felt his body tense. "So tell the truth, then," he commanded huskily. "Do you love me . . . just a bit, anyway?"

In the circle of his arms, she couldn't spread her own to show him how much. "Yes!" Laughing shakily, she sniffed and laughed again.

"That's good." Mac kissed a tear off the tip of her nose. "'Cause I sure love you, Tey Hargrove."

"Oh!" she cried as he found her lips again. "I forgot to tell you—that's not my real name."

With a snort of disgusted laughter, Mac caught her arms and tipped her back where he could see her face. "What the hell is it, then?"

"Kenyon!" Held as she was, she was unable to touch his chest; she settled for caressing his hard forearms instead.

"Kenyon..." Those crinkling blue eyes considered her for a moment. "Well, as names go, it beats uh-Hargrove by a mile." Pulling her back tight against him, he set his mouth on hers. "But I know a better one," he drawled against her lips.

"What?" she whispered, and wrapped her arms around his lean waist.

"Mine."

EPILOGUE

PUTTING DOWN HER WRITING PAD, Tey tilted her head. Yes, that was his key in the door downstairs.

She leaned across the bed to put the pad on the night table, but looked down on it critically for a second. It was good copy, she had to admit. This advertising brochure she was working up for a new computer data network was going to knock their eyes out. It would also make a good piece for her portfolio, the next time she went looking for clients. Sighing contentedly, she leaned back against her propped pillows. Virginia was proving fertile ground for a free-lance technical writer. *Just don't get too busy,* she warned herself. When Mac went bat collecting in Mexico for all of June, she meant to be with him.

Down in the kitchen, the refrigerator thunked softly shut. Smiling to herself, she started slowly unbuttoning her blouse. They were establishing their own little rituals, after three months together. She glanced down at the bedside phone. Ought to unplug it, but Lori hadn't called yet, and today was supposed to be the day. Maybe Aston's lawyers had put it off again.

She draped her blouse over one of the pineapple posts on the mahogany headboard, then hung her brassiere on top of it. Wasn't four o'clock yet; she might want it again, but on the other hand, it was Friday. Electing to leave her jeans on, she sat Indian fashion on the bed, her face vividly alert as she waited for his tread on the stairs. The third step creaked and she grinned. Thank heavens for that step!

The phone rang.

"Don't answer it!" Mac commanded from the landing, but flopping onto her stomach, she scooped it up, anyway.

"Hello?" Glancing back over her shoulder, she gave him a wicked grin. "Lori? How'd it go?"

With a glass of lemonade in each hand and his squash racket tucked under one elbow, Mac paused in the doorway. His hair was still wet and curly from the aftergame shower he'd caught at the college gym—she loved it that way.

His scowl faded as his eyes moved across her. "Hang it up, Mrs. McAllister."

"Ms Kenyon-McAllister," she corrected, covering the mouthpiece. "It's Lori. You did?" She turned her attention back to her sister's long distance exulting. "Oh, Lori! I knew Margie could do it!"

"Too many syllables," Mac complained, sticking to his original topic as he put their drinks down on the table and smacked her bottom lightly with the squash racket.

"Kenyon-McAll?" she suggested—this was an old joke—and went back to the phone. The bed bounced as her husband joined her. "That's wonderful, Lori!"

"Nope." Taking hold of her barrette, Mac found its catch and unclipped it gently. It landed with a clink on the squash racket in the far corner. "How'd they do?" He ran his hands through her hair, fluffing it out across her bare shoulders.

"Aston's lawyer signed everything! They've got total custody!" she murmured hurriedly, then shuddered as he lipped a line of slow kisses up her spine.

"Great!" he growled and nipped the top of her shoulder. "So tell her to call back after prime time."

Shivering again, she shook her head and covered her free ear as Mac tried to stick his tongue into it. "Wait, Lori. What did you say?"

A warm hand closed on her waist and rolled her gently over. Tangled in the phone cord, she smiled up at him and fluttered her eyelashes. Then her eyes widened. "You mean— Oh, Lori!"

"Interesting," Mac decided, rearranging the cord between her breasts. He fingertipped her once—a butterfly stroke, and his eyes darkened when she arched to follow his retreating hand.

"Ahh...yes. Yes, that's wonderful! When? Fantastic! Of course we'll come."

Mac studied her beaming face curiously for a moment, then transferred his interest to her jeans. Unzipping them part way, he found her navel and bent to greet it with a hot, supple tongue.

"Mac?"

"Hmm?" Engrossed in his explorations, he didn't look up at first.

She raised herself halfway on one elbow. "Mac... Hang on, Lori."

Turning his head sideways against her stomach, he met her gaze inquiringly. The contrast of his cold hair to his previous lava kisses sent her muscles into a delicious contraction, and Mac gave her a satisfied smile.

"Can we go to California for Easter?" she hissed when she caught her breath again.

"Promise her anything, but hang up that phone!" He started one hand walking purposefully up her stomach toward the receiver, but hanging on to it, Tey arched away from him. She lost track of the conversation, anyhow, when he turned his mischief instead to her breasts, fingering first the very tip of one taut peak and then the other.

"Uh-huh," she mumbled into the phone, not quite sure what she was agreeing to now. "Mmm? Uh... ahh...what?"

Releasing her, Mac sat up abruptly, then swung a leg over her body to kneel astride her waist. "Give," he demanded.

"Lori, Mac wants to talk to you," she babbled as the phone lifted out of her grasp.

"Lori?" Mac smiled against the mouthpiece, his eyes softening as he heard her lilting voice. "I presume you're making an honest man of him? Congratulations!" His free hand smoothed up Tey's ribs to her breast again. Cupping it gently, he fanned his thumb lazily back and forth across its tip. "I think you've got a good 'un there."

Darn him! How could he sound so...so collected? Wriggling between his gold-fuzzed thighs, she glanced at his blue gym shorts. Well, perhaps he wasn't quite so collected, after all.

"Yeah, that's terrific. Is he there? Sure, put him on." Flexing his thighs, he glanced down at her and gave her a wink. "Bo? Congratulations, fella!"

Fascinated by the subtle hardening of his voice when he talked male to male, she watched his beloved face for a moment, then set herself to wreaking havoc along the inside muscles of his legs. If she was going to feel

like this, she was bound and determined to have some
company feeling it!

"That's great," Mac murmured as he captured her
marauding hand. "Yeah... Bo, can I ask you some-
thin', man to man?"

Whatever Bo's retort was, it made him laugh.

"Yeah, well, what would *you* do if you had this hot
date with a foxy little brunette, and she wouldn't get off
the damn telephone?" He laughed again and lifted the
phone higher as Tey made an indignant snatch for it.

"Mac!"

"You would, huh? Yeah, me too... Nope...no
problem at all, we wanted to hear. Okay...so drink
some champagne for us, too, and we'll see you at Easter. Bye." Looking more than a little smug, he settled
his weight more firmly upon her, then unclipped the
cord where it attached to the phone. He tossed the receiver gently into the corner along with the racket.
"There. Was that so hard?"

"That's how it's done?" She stroked her palms
slowly up his hair-roughened thighs and down again.

"That's one of the ways it's done," he told her huskily. "Want me to show you another?"

She pretended to consider that, while her teasing
smile slowly widened. "I'm game!" she whispered finally.

"You're the best game of all," he agreed roughly,
and leaned forward to take a kiss.

Much, much later, when the moon found their windows, Mac stretched and brushed his lips across her
ear. "Am I squashing you?" he murmured sleepily.

"Uh-huh." Her arm tightened around his waist as he
started to shift. "I like it. Don't go 'way."

"Mmm." Taking some of his weight on his elbows, he nuzzled the side of her jaw. "So what was the rest of the deal? If Lori got Josh, what did Aston get?"

"'Bout everything else. There's some sort of trust for Josh, for college. That's about it." With one hand, she traced his spine, bone by tiny bone down to his warm, lean hips.

"Bastard..." he mumbled and kissed the point of her chin.

"I don't know... Guess everybody got what they wanted most. If they'd fought it, he could have contested forever." She sighed contentedly. "Lori and Bo will do all right."

"More than all right," Mac agreed, and kissed her eyelids. "Easter... Desert should be bloomin' in Arizona 'bout then. If we're goin' out there, anyway..."

And things would be blooming here soon, as well, she thought drowsily. Mac said you hadn't lived till you'd seen a Virginia spring.... Was going to be the most beautiful spring of her life.... Her hand wandered slowly up to bury itself in his silky hair. Going to be the most beautiful *year* of her life. *Life* of her life... She smiled as he smoothed a curl off her forehead. And the love of her life would be hungry soon, if she knew her man; he was getting restless already. The steak in the fridge would take care of that. Ruffling his hair, she swung her head lazily. Their room was so beautiful by moonlight.... His squash racket cast nets of shadow in one corner.

"Hey, who won?" she murmured, turning back to smile up into his moonlit eyes.

"I did." Bending his head, he took her lips in an endless, dark and dreamy kiss.

"I meant the squash game," she told him when she could breathe at last.

"Huh...oh, that?" Mac followed the curve of her smile with one fingertip. "Oh, I won that, too...."

Harlequin Superromance

COMING NEXT MONTH

#238 TEMPTING FATE • Risa Kirk
Reya Merrill thought that handling public relations
for the controversial Geneticon account would cinch
her promotion. But when Colin Hughes, owner of
the genetic research laboratories, defies her every
move, she loses her job...and her heart.

#239 A DISTANT PROMISE • Debbie Bedford
Advertising copywriter Emily Lattrell seemed to have
it all until she met handsome real-estate magnate
Philip Manning. Almost overnight she quit her job,
moved to a northern Texan farm and became
adopted mom to Philip's nephew and two nieces.
Now she'd truly have it all...if she could learn to
accept Philip's love.

#240 SEASON OF MIRACLES • Emilie Richards
Schoolteacher Elise Ramsey had chosen duty over
love once. Then, in the middle of her life, she was
offered another opportunity to find joy in the strong
arms of Sloane Tyson. Her first lover. The boy was
gone forever, replaced by a man impossible to deny.

#241 GYPSY FIRE • Sara Orwig
After star witnesses Jake and Molly escape the
watchful eye of the Detriot police, they find
themselves holed up together in the Ozarks. Molly
can't bear Jake's workaholic lists and thirst for
success. But Jake discovers he can't bear to take his
eyes off Molly....